T0147143

TALES OF
ARCANE

A Journey Into Fate

A TRILOGY

MICHAEL R. ESTEE

authorHOUSE®

AuthorHouse™
1663 Liberty Drive
Bloomington, IN 47403
www.authorhouse.com
Phone: 833-262-8899

Published by AuthorHouse 10/13/2022

ISBN: 978-1-6655-7372-6 (sc)
ISBN: 978-1-6655-7370-2 (hc)
ISBN: 978-1-6655-7371-9 (e)

Library of Congress Control Number: 2022919096

Print information available on the last page.

PROLOGUE

He could feel the footsteps behind him, drawing closer and closer. It wouldn't be long now until they found him. Still, he set upon completing his task, knowing nothing else was more important. Not even his life.

Almost there, only a few more minutes, he thought. He knew this day would come, but even knowing about it didn't make the preparation any easier. He had spent many decades of searching and protecting. Nurturing and creating. Learning and teaching. It all led to this, as he'd known it would eventually. But now, every moment became more precious to him than the last.

The wind rustled his gray hair and blew back the hood on his dark brown cloak. Wrapping it tightly around him, he could feel the air rustle through the rips, the cloak having been battered and tested against time. A bow wrapped around his back, armed with a quiver full of arrows. He slowly went to a knee and pressed the side of his head to the ground, the hilt of his tattered leather sheath scraping the stones that had loosened beneath his steps. The slight rumble deep within his ear told him he had gained some time—not much but hopefully enough. He stood up, leaning heavily on his staff, and pressed his midnight-black boots into the gravel and continued his advancement upward, drawing himself closer and closer to the gloomy sky.

The ridges and pathways became more difficult with each passing step. Most couldn't make it this far if they didn't know where to look. And even if they did know where to look, traveling along it was another thing altogether. This trip still took a toll, but he knew what must come next. It wouldn't be the first time he'd tried it but never to this extent, never this far. But he couldn't let that affect him now, not anymore. It brought him some solace when he bent down and listened again. Even more distance had grown between him and his pursuers. *They don't know the path*, he thought. He laughed out loud and began to quicken his pace, climbing higher and higher up the mountain.

Finally, after another half day's climb, marking the fifth day he'd been climbing, he broke the final ridge. Standing at the top of the world, he looked down toward the summit. The ground began to slope inward on itself, creating a bowl at its peak, with an inner circle surrounded by sleek-looking black rocks that were at least double his height. Inside lay the place where he had been born, where his entire family had been born. It was also the place where he watched his father die, turning to ash in front of him, right before his sister brought about the darkness.

The Topless Mountains sat almost in the middle of the land that his father had created, and his home was at the highest point. You couldn't get to the top unless you knew how to get there, and you would only know how if you had been brought there before. This had once been a place for the five of them to gather, he with his two brothers and sister alongside their father. His family. Now, nothing stood on these slopes for miles around. You couldn't farm up top the slopes, nor could you for miles around. The only thing that this mountain held was this forgotten place on its peak—no villages, no caves. Animals didn't even make their homes here, and birds had no place to nest. This mountain was made for one reason, and that reason now was gone. Lost in a moment and turned to ash. Today, though, he needed the power that lingered here. He needed them to know. Once up here, he knew he could channel enough energy to get his message to all who needed to hear it. There was still enough power here left—he hoped, at least.

Running along the edge of the ridge, he found the staircase, untouched by time, and he hastily began climbing down, skipping every other step. Once he reached the bottom, he crossed the loose-stone pathway leading up to a small outer ridge; the encircling black rocks seemed like walls protecting the room inside. He stepped around the first large obsidian stone jutting up from the ground, and that place he had been searching for opened before his eyes onto a path.

He was surrounded by the tall, jagged black rocks on all sides, but the inside of them held scripture where his father had written the first rules for them to follow and to break. He traced his fingers along the carvings in the cold stone. He knew this place almost better than anything in existence and could recall every detail without setting his eyes upon it. In the middle of the enclosed circle, a stone table lay cracked in two pieces, an encryption ran along the side. He knew what it said without reading it: *The Will of All Is the Will of One.* The air swirled around him, but not a single wind gust touched him. The sun's rays started slicing through the white clouds that hovered close, shining down upon the obsidian stone that soaked in the sunlight.

The memories were all too familiar to him, and he would relive them day after day. The argument, the building tension, veiled threats, and those eyes. Those eyes haunted him every time he closed his own, and he feared to look into them ever again. He helped banish them once, and he knew that one day, they would return. It's what made this journey important and his message even more so. If only he had known what was coming that day; if only he had seen it in the conversations he'd had with her. *How could I have known? My will was not my own then.* These thoughts did nothing to lessen the burden he felt. He'd wanted to end it all, back when he could have, but he couldn't bring himself to follow through with it. It wasn't for him to decide her fate, but the one who could decide was gone by then. Once he realized how to bring him back, it was already too late. He needed her to return first; then he could start moving his pieces across the board. Then he could finally put an end to all this.

The staff and the sword already, then the pen, the hammer, and the necklace, he repeated in his mind, over and over again until the thought became an unwanted buzz in his head. *Then it'll be done. The staff and sword already, then the pen, the hammer, and the necklace.*

He placed his staff across and lay his calloused hand upon the broken stone table and quietly hummed. He could feel the energy rising from within him, traveling through his fragile arm and out through his outstretched wrinkled fingers. The mountaintop all around him began to vibrate—slightly at first but with each passing second, he could hear it getting louder and louder, until all he could hear was a buzzing sound filling the air.

It was at that moment that a dozen, maybe more, Wood Elves finally peeked over the last ridge of the mountain. He could hear their footsteps, even from inside the rock wall, even over the noise he made. *How did they find me?* He'd thought no one knew how to get here except his family. It didn't matter now. They'd found him, and the reason could be figured out later. He had to deal with this now, but how? All they had to do was walk down the carved-out stairs, down into the inner bowl on the peak, and there they'd find an old creature humming to the birds and plants—and they could end everything right then. Hopefully, they wouldn't know or quite honestly understand the importance of his sound and wouldn't kill him on the spot. But the birds knew. They could hear his words so perfectly.

Prisoner of the Dark Elves must be set free before it is too late. Come, my old friend. Time is running out …

And they would sing those words to each other. From the *Topless Mountains*, down to the *Golden Plains*, and across the cities of men. Through the rivers and over the *Greenhills* and into the *Blaonir Forest*. Through the treetops, the nightingales would sing. And in the rivers, when the robins stopped to drink. On and on the message went, all through the land. The eagles of the mountains and the bluebirds of the wetlands. Birds who lived on top of trees or even inside them heard the message too, and they sought out anything they could find to keep his words moving. The beasts that roamed the hills, munching on the grass. The critters that made their home on the coastlines. Animals on four legs, two legs, no legs—it didn't matter; they all knew that their master, their friend, their guide was in trouble. They all spread the word as far as they could, yet he knew it would still take weeks for the news to reach Mellom Elvene. But that was fine, if it got there; he knew he could not. Soon, the dozen elves turned into nearly fifty, and he knew he wouldn't be able to overpower them, but he wasn't going to go down without a fight.

In seconds, his hands went from glowing and vibrating to shooting arrows at his attackers. The first arrow pierced an eye, and the second caught a throat. Already he could taste the blood that was seeping into the ground. *They're still my people,* he thought with a touch of sadness. *Even if their minds are poisoned by her.* He notched and loosened three, four, five arrows before they were even within distance to strike at him. A few steps back and a couple more arrows, and three more Dark Elves fell. Grabbing his last arrow, he notched it tight, pulled back as hard as he could, took aim at the first fools through the rock opening, and let loose.

The arrow struck the first wood elf through his lower forehead and almost split his head in two. His bleached white face was covered in red blood before his mouth could open in shock. The eyes rolled loose from their sockets and plopped to the ground. The arrow had continued its flight after the first elf died and lodged itself through the mouth of the elf behind it, with its tip sticking out the back of its throat, dripping in blood. They fell in one motion along the side of the rocks, leaving a bloody trail on the way down, lumped over on top of each other. Three more elves had already made their way past them before the bodies touched the ground. The first advancer was too clumsy, though.

He easily sidestepped the elf and, in the same motion, whipped a hidden dagger from his sleeve, slicing it across the throat of the clumsy elf. The elf's pale face looked shocked, as if he didn't expect to fail and die so quickly. *Has Nathrak trained his soldiers that poorly?* He was never the king that his father was; still, he'd thought Nathrak was at least a little competent, since he did kill his own father. *Hard to criticize the king when he's got you cornered on top of this mountain, old man*, he thought.

More elves poured in through the opening. He dropped his bow and unsheathed his sword, ready for whatever they threw at him. He knew the sword in his hands had been there on the day it was made. The Sword of Will, it had been called, and he had been trained against it. His first memories were sparing against it—never beating it, of course, for its wielder was its creator, his father. But his father was gone now, since the day he surrendered the Will, and *she* had come. She had come to take the sword, but none other than its master could wield it, so instead, she hid it, unable to bend anyone to its Will.

But she had other things to use, and the shadow had crept forward and almost enveloped the land long ago. It had led to these vile elves, who made their home a long way from their origin, deep under the roots of the Dark Woods, an atrocity to what he had created, a twisted version of the image he himself had spent centuries on. A twinge of jealousy had never ceased in her, for man could never amount to the perfection he had gotten with his elves in Mellom Elvene. So she *stole* some and corrupted their minds, until what followed were the generations of these abominations. A pitiful image of what he had shaped with his own hands. If he could, he would eradicate all of them from this land, but he knew not all were corrupted these days. Too many generations had passed for them to remember the beginning, but still, the shadow grew deep inside them, and where shadows grew, she could still influence.

Finally, there were too many of them. He would cut down one, and two more would step up. A dozen would fall, and they would already be replaced before their cold, white faces could touch the ground. Throats sliced and limbs hacked, but still they advanced, merely stepping over their fallen comrades. Scream after scream, gurgling and choking on their own blood, the sounds of death could be heard in between each clang of swords clashing together. His feet danced their way around the fallen, and his body moved like branches in the wind, but soon the dead piled at his feet as he was driven closer and closer to the rock wall. Yet still the elves pressed on, trying to reach him, climbing and trampling their dead or dying. You could hear the bones crunching or flesh squishing with every step they took. The screams didn't stop as they finally cornered him against the wall and the dead.

The blood was beginning to collect too, and it made moving difficult. Each step was like trying to walk through mud; his feet sank in the ground as his back brushed the stone. Two Dark Elves jumped at him, and he easily blocked the first strike, but the second caught him across the back, tearing into his flesh. He could feel the warmth of blood run down his back, but he didn't worry. Bleeding out wasn't a way for him to die. Stumbling forward a step or two, he quickly twisted back around and blocked the next swing, ducked under another, and drove his sword through the rib cage of the elf who had cut him, lodged it against his spine, and ripped the blade out his back. The other elf had recovered from his block and was trying to swing again, but before his arm could come for the downswing, it was cleaved right off his body. Dropping straight to the ground, the elf began squirming and squealing. That moment, though, three more elves jumped in the fight, then two more. Finally, they were able to disarm him and brought him to his knees. Fists connected against his face, blood spattered with each hit, and soon his eye became swollen shut, both lips grew fatter, and his nose became a twisted piece of cartilage attached to his face.

"All right then!" he screamed, pulling on the arms of his captors. "Come out, Nathrak, and let's get this over with." He growled toward no one in particular, but his words were heard, and soon the commotion ceased. The Wood Elves all stopped moving, all eyes looking back out from the enclosed circle. The wind had suddenly stopped blowing, and silence gripped all who stood there.

This can't be; it can't be her. His hand trembled in thought, but he knew it to be true. Everything made sense now. How he was found in the first place, and how he was even followed up here. It was her all along. He had done all he could with the time that was given; now he just hoped it was enough. War was coming, and darkness would precede it.

Stepping out from behind the surrounding elves, she strolled toward him, raven hair flowing down past her shoulders to the arch of her back, skin so pale she looked almost like a ghost strolling through the land, violet eyes that could send a shiver down anyone's spine yet leave you entranced if you stared into them for too long. Her strapless black dress flowed with the wind on the mountaintop, moving back and forth with every step she took towards him, almost gliding along the rocks behind her. With a slit down the middle of her skin-tight dress, her elegant legs appeared with every step she took, and overlapping again around her hips, but splitting up toward her neck, leaving the middle of her lustrous figure exposed from the waist up. The lace on her sleeves stretched from just below her shoulders to down across her hands and covered the skin between her thumb and forefinger, exposing only her long, skeleton-like fingers, which seem to be ripped and worn, yet elegant, as if they had been knitted this morning. A silver necklace hung just above her chest, so bright it caught the sunlight with every bounce it took. Her blue lips parted in the slightest smile, and tiny dimples appeared at the corners of her mouth. She knew she had won.

She approached him, her hand outstretched, lifting him off slippery rocks, careful to not get any blood on her or her dress. When she spoke, everything became quiet, as if the land was terrified of missing a single word. "I'm afraid it's me you'll have to deal with, dear. I know I'm earlier than you expected, but to be fair, you have had a long time to prepare." She looked off into the distance before snapping her head back to him and locking her violaceous eyes with his. For a moment his conviction fell, but only for a moment before he made himself return her stare. There was beauty behind the darkness; it had been there before it came. "I do hope you've used the time wisely."

After a brief laugh, she entwined her arm in his. "Come now, Jord. We have a lot of work to do." She laughed again. She started to lead him toward the top ridge to head back down the mountainside, a hint of grace in each of her steps. The screams of the dying faded in the background. "You know, you could have avoided all this nonsense in the first place if you would just have listened to me," she said, sighing, letting her shoulders drop. "It could have been us, you know. We could have ruled this land, but that is not the choice anymore. For either of us." And with that, she turned to lead him downward.

"It never could have been us," he growled at her. She had tried this the last time too, and it had no effect on him then either. "There is only one who should rule, and it is neither of us."

"And do you see him anywhere?" She swung her head around with her arm motioning out to the air. "*He* does not exist anymore. You witnessed that. I have taken up the mantle, and even if I have to wipe the slate clean, I will rule this land."

"The others won't allow you to go that far," he said, hoping she'd see how foolish she had become. "Vatn and Magni won't just let you wipe away their subjects too. And what of your own? Would you sacrifice the very ones you are supposed to watch over, just to get what you want?"

She sounded a blood-curdling laugh; her skin was so white that it reflected the light with each bounce of her laughter. "Shows what little you know these days, huh, Jord?" Her vicious smile returned as she bent down to pick up his sword. *Now it's only the staff.* "Vatn is in hiding and has been since I did what I did all those years ago, and, well, Magni—let's just say he'll do whatever *I* ask of him. It was all too easy with those puppy dog eyes of his. He needs someone to follow, and why should he care if it was our father or me? He thinks it's probably better for him to follow me, that someday I just might fall in love with him. As if a queen loves the servant." She sneered the last sentence out with a hint of disgust. "Still, he has his uses. Love is easier to keep at bay than fear, and as long as I let him believe, he'll never disobey."

"You're pathetic!" He flung the words as hard as he could at her, hoping that they would stick. Somehow, he knew they would not.

She continued on as if he had never spoken them. "As for my subjects, as you like to remind me, well, they were the ones who abandoned me first, and most, if not all, have even forgotten of my existence." She once again resumed their walk down the mountain, with his sword against her hip.

The staff already, then the pen, the hammer, the necklace, and now the sword. "No, I will not suffer myself for those who stand against me. They have chosen their side, whether they know it or not. And now, all must be reborn with the shadow."

"You know you won't get away with this. My subjects will come looking once they realize what has happened," Jord spat, trying to fight her grip on his arm. "You may have the upper hand now, Fensalir, but it won't last forever. Life will win out—that you have my promise on." He knew that would stick.

"Life? What? Like this life here?" She motioned to a few flowers that had survived the harsh mountainside and were springing up through the gravel. She reached down and pulled them out, down to the roots, and held them in front of his face. "This is what I will do to your precious life, you fool." Her hands began to glow brightly for a second, and when the light faded, the flowers had turned to dust in her hands.

CHAPTER 1

THE SUN WAS dipping below the treetops to the west, bathing the forest floor in a red tint. Dusk would soon follow, and any hope Baelath had of catching his prey would vanish. It was at that moment, just as he was about to give up and climb down, that he spotted it—a large black bear slightly crouched below the tall brush that wrapped across the forest. It was trying to hide itself behind a bushel of small trees, still young in their lifespan, while looking for a way out. Although the beast knew it was in danger, it didn't know the hunt was already over. Soon, it was in Baelath's trap, and all he had to do was spring it. He lunged from the branch on which he was lightly perched and toward the branch in front of him and grabbed it. He swung his tall frame forward and leaped upward. He used the branches like a ladder, quickly bringing himself to a great height, with his dirt-covered hands reached out like arrows striking their target. From up there, he saw what looked like an endless forest and heard the great river rushing down south of him. He had rarely ventured this far below Mellom Elvene or this close to the Zoe, but the hunt had led him here. He'd never given up on a hunt before and wasn't going to start now, not when his prey might be his biggest yet.

Its mangled black fur made it easy to see while it stalked between the small trees. Baelath could hear its claws scraping the ground, tearing at the brush that stood in its way. Even from this distance, he saw its snout dripping in bubbling snot and its long fangs bared from the back of its mouth while it growled. He could tell it was becoming more and more restless and would soon blindly attack.

1

Just another minute, he thought. *I don't see her yet.* Suddenly, Evelyn burst out of a tree, a blurry image, just to the east of him and the beast. She moved so fast and eloquently that it looked like she was running through the air, using the branches as mere steps. He had never seen an elf move that quickly.

Her black hair whisked in the air with every step, and her green cloak whipped with every movement. She closed the distance between her and the bear to almost nothing, as it realized someone was approaching it. Startled, it quickly ran away from her—and directly toward him. It broke through the brush and knocked the saplings into the larger trees that had stood for hundreds of years. The saplings shook the older trees, not being big or strong enough to knock them over. One tree contained what looked like hundreds of birds; they had been sleeping or purposely staying out of sight because he had not seen them until now. They rose from the branches and scattered in every direction. Dozens of birds flew directly at him, and each one made a different noise, a single, incoherent cry that would make a newborn's ears bleed. He had to go before the birds blocked his sight or knocked him out of the tree altogether. He placed his heels on the end of the branch and spread his arms out as wide as he could. Taking one last breath, he closed his eyes and fell forward.

The rush of air pulled his mind from everything. The feeling of free-falling grabbed his gut and pumped his heart faster. His dirt-colored hair whipped in the rushing wind and his tattered tan cloak flapped rapidly behind him. He heard the birds rush by above, narrowly missing him. Opening his eyes, Baelath saw his prey rumbling in his direction, its attention on the threat behind and not the one above. He hoped he hadn't fallen too early. A moment off and he'd crash into the ground, crippling him if he survived. He unsheathed his curved daggers, tucked his long legs toward his body, and began to somersault through the air. At the last second, he straightened his lanky body, his head facing the ground and his arms stretched out. He crashed onto the top of the bear's head, driving both daggers through the soft part of its skull. It let out a ferocious roar and reared its entire body into the air, towering over ten feet. The daggers stayed lodged into the beast's skull, and its reaction sent Baelath flying into the air, landing about twenty yards away. The air rushed out of him as he smashed into the ground, and the rough forest floor cut his body as he rolled to a stop.

Hurrying to his feet, he turned and planted his dark-brown leather boots on the ground, ready to strike. But the bear saw him first and began to charge him. Defenseless and knowing there was nowhere to run, Baelath braced for impact. He had hunted these beasts many times, and every time his plan had worked. Two daggers to the head and he would have the kill, yet here he was, facing certain death. And then, from the corner of his half-shut eyes, he saw a streak of black flash by. Seemingly out of thin air, Evelyn came flying into the clearing high above him and his oncoming death, long-sword held high above her, her cloak rippling in the breeze. She came down upon the beast and drove the weapon straight into its back. She dragged her sword along the bear's body as she continued through the air. The bear's momentum carried it right to Baelath's feet, leaving a splintered, bloody carcass slumped in front of him. His polished, stone-hilted daggers still were stuck in the top of its head.

Stepping around the dead creature and wearing the biggest smile across her soft brown-tinted face, Evelyn returned her long-sword to its holder. She tossed her charcoal-colored hair back behind her slender shoulders, revealing her pointed ears. The right one was slightly bent sideways, rather than both pointing straight, as with most Wood Elves. She hated that ear, but for some unknown reason, it was Baelath's favorite thing about her.

"Looks like I saved your life yet again, Baelath." She chuckled at him. "How many times is that now? Four? Five?"

"Honestly, Evelyn, I've lost count. But this one should have died from the drop," he said. The blood had finally stopped pouring out from the creature, and its twitching had ceased. "What in Arcane doesn't die from two daggers plunged into its head from hundreds of feet in the air?" He was still in disbelief while he walked over to the creature and reached down with his skeleton-like arms to remove his daggers.

"This bad boy, apparently." Evelyn laughed and removed her leaf-colored cloak. "Now, come. We have a lot of work ahead of us if we hope to get this back before it spoils. We still have to find our campsite and the tools, and the sun looks like it won't be up for much longer."

With that, they tied the beast to the sled, which they had hidden among the brush earlier, and began to transport it back.

3

Dusk had come and gone, and now the moon was climbing into the night sky. Transporting their hunt was not as easy as they'd thought. The damage the sword strike had done now made the carcass slip and slide off the sled. Even with both of them pulling, it still seemed to be going at a snail's pace. They had to stop every couple of minutes to fix the beast's position. Sweat poured from Baelath's forehead, blinding him, as he tried to lump the lifeless bear on top of itself, which drenched his hands in blood. *The camp can't be much farther now*, he grumbled inside his head. *We've been traveling for half the night.* Just to make sure, he glanced up at the moon to see how much it had crossed the night sky.

Just then, Evelyn stopped and looked around. She fiddled with the rings she wore, one on each finger and each with a different color and meaning that she'd once explained. Her lanky figure swayed as she shifted around, wrapping her green cloak tighter around her. She wrapped her hair over her crooked ear as a nervous look set upon her face. "I believe we're lost," she said, almost as if she were questioning herself. "None of this looks familiar to me, but we did come much farther south than we usually do." She peered into the darkness, as if searching for a landmark or something that would put them in the right direction.

"I could climb up and see if we are at least heading toward camp or if we strayed too far," Baelath said, tightening the rope on the sled. "Shouldn't take me long to get to the top of one of these old trees."

"OK, then; hurry up, though," she said, her emerald eyes still peering off in the darkness. "I don't like the feeling I'm getting."

"Don't worry." He smiled at her before turning to look up at the tree next to them. "These *are* technically my woods."

He walked up to one of the tallest trees in the area, one of the Great Trees in Blaonir. The trunk was about the width of his outstretched arms, the branches as thick as his body, and the leaves bigger than his head. He reached up to grab one of its branches and easily swung up. Using his momentum, he pushed off the branch the second his boots touched it and then swung to the next. He saw the other trees around him beginning to end and soon came above the forest roof. He could see in every direction for miles. The moonlight had no obstacles blocking its path, and it illuminated Baelath and the tree in a white glow. He even saw the stars, hundreds of them, sparkling in the sky, like diamonds along a black cloth.

He couldn't hear the river anymore, so he knew they had not gone south—or west, for that matter. That left north or east, but as with Evelyn, none of this looked familiar to him. They must have strayed eastward on their trip back, which could become a slight problem. Most of his hunting grounds were westward below Mellom Elvene. He hadn't been this far east since he was a child, and the memories seem to escape him at the moment.

Just then, he saw something in the distance, but when he turned to fully look at it, it disappeared. Not moving his eyes for what seemed like forever, he finally saw it again. Smoke. *Where there's smoke, there's fire. And where there's fire, there are others.* Hopefully, they would tell them the correct direction, or better yet, let them camp for the night. Unless it was a night hunt, then no one would be there when they'd arrive.

Climbing down was harder than climbing up. He kept snagging his cloak on twigs and loose bark. Normally, he would have jumped from tree to tree, descending a level with each jump, but now, he was stuck using this Elder Tree, which made his climb take a little longer than he was used to. Once he reached the forest roof, though, he began rapidly lowering himself toward the ground.

"Up there long enough?" Evelyn asked him once he finally touched the ground; her hands were squarely on her hips. "I was just about to climb up after you. I feel strange, as if we're somewhere we're not supposed to be." Her eyes still were fixated on the surrounding darkness.

"Why shouldn't we be here? My father is king, after all. I think we're allowed to go anywhere in the forest," he boasted. "Besides, I think I saw smoke to the east. It must be a small camp, or it might be another hunting party, but either way, they could help us."

"How far?" asked Evelyn, still peering outward, as if she was staring down darkness itself.

"Not too far. A ten- to fifteen-minute run, I suppose," said Baelath, shrugging his shoulders and throwing their gear onto his back. "But we should probably hurry. They may not linger there long if it's a night hunt, as it seems."

They tied the sled to a tree and covered it in small brush and branches, hoping that anything that might want to eat it would already be asleep for the night. After they were satisfied with the knot, they ran eastward toward the rising smoke. Baelath was a fast runner but not as fast as Evelyn. She tore through the night, ducking under low-hanging branches and jumping over fallen trees or moss-covered logs. She gracefully sidestepped trees that blocked her path, never once letting anything slow her down.

Baelath liked climbing a lot better. Up in the treetops and walking on branches as wide as him—that was his home. He could climb any tree and disappear, only to reappear fifty yards away in an instant. They passed by more Great Trees, though none as big as the one he had climbed, but they seemed to grow in quantity the farther east they ran. Soon, even Evelyn had to slow down to make her way between the trees. He hadn't noticed it while they were hunting, when the trees weren't as congested, but now that they stood an arm's length from each other, he could see that these trees were a slightly different color than the other ones in the forest. These trees were slightly browner, and almost no gray existed in them; then, soon, he could swear that they were almost red. But he didn't have time to think about any of that now because they had arrived at the source of the smoke. And they stopped dead in their tracks.

The trees opened to a clearing, almost perfectly circular, with the greenest grass he had ever seen. In the center stood a gigantic tree, wider even than the Great Tree of Mellom Elvene. It didn't expand upward like most trees but more sideways and outwards, its gigantic branches extending into the surrounding woods. He thought it must be hollow in the middle, like a huge log, because now he could see smoke pouring out from the center, reaching its way into the night sky. At the bottom of its trunk was an opening, and a yellow glow emanated from within, with shadows dancing their way across the inner walls.

He had never seen this place in his travels with Jord. He used to travel all across Blaonir when he was younger, yet somehow, all this had eluded him. He turned to look at Evelyn, and her expression told him she was thinking the same thing. *What's going on inside it?* He didn't know, but he was going to find out, one way or another. Crouching low, he began to slowly move into the clearing, his eyes darting back and forth, looking for any sign of movement around him. But nothing moved or made a sound during his entire advance, and soon he found himself against the trunk of this Great Tree, his back scraping up against the fossilized bark. He heard Evelyn move behind him once he approached the opening.

"Do you think this is a good idea?" she asked. "I'm not sure we're supposed to be here. And what is this place? It doesn't feel right, Baelath. Let's just go back."

"I agree this place is strange," he said, placing a hand on her shoulder, trying to relax her somewhat. "What could possibly harm us when my father is king of Blaonir? It is only what lies beyond that is dangerous." He turned around and peered through the opening inside the tree. "Besides," he said, lowering his voice to barely above a whisper. "I need to know what this place is. I can't explain why. I just know I should go inside. It's as if it's our fate that we're here, that we found this place. Something important is happening inside—I know it—and I intend to find out what that is." And with the charming smile that he always gave her, he slid inside and pressed his back to the inside wall.

The tree had been hollowed out and sanded down to a fine finish. A polished glow bounced the light from the fire across the floor, making waves of shadows with any movement. Baelath looked up and saw an opening at the top; the moonlight was hidden behind the firelight. Looking around, he saw that the branches that extended outward were hollow inside too, serving as small tunnels. He could see other River Elves climbing down from them, filling out the hollow tree. Already, dozens of elves were gathered, and more kept piling in from the tunnels. Some, Baelath recognized, like Rayha Dolmont and Nector Ghuld, the other leaders of the smaller cities in Blaonir. But most of them, he did not know, though they looked just as important as those he did. They began surrounding the fire that was crackling upward to the sky, and although sparks of embers seemed to whisk their way onto the tree, it did not ignite. Black smoke rose from the center of the tree and into the night, like it was being pulled and not just dissipating into the sky. In the middle of the group, hovering close to the fire, was an elf who towered over the rest. He faced the flames, his head lowered slightly, but Baelath knew exactly who it was—his father, King Daelon.

Not only did the king surpass all other elves in height, but his hair had more silver in it than all the other elder River Elves. His eyes were wrought both with gold and green, his ears perked higher than others.

His appearance was that of the older generation, the savior's generation, the ones who had fought the evils of this land, who were alive during the many wars of the elves.

Long ago, two elven brothers waged war upon war on each other, vying for the throne, leaving nothing but destruction and peril in the land. The wars brought doom and chaos to all other races and almost to their own. That was many years ago, though, and most elves now had not been around during those days. Baelath himself wasn't even born when his father became king.

King Daelon was barely grown himself when his father, Baelath's grandfather, was killed by the so-called king of these Dark Elves, or Wood Elves, as they liked to call themselves. The elves who hadn't betrayed their king, Daelon's father, were branded River Elves, as the Zoe River flowed through the middle of their forest. King Daelon was able to defend the forest not only from the traitors and evil invaders—for not just Dark Elves had waged war on them—but from the hideous goblins who had come down from the Eastern Mountains and burned the northern part of the forest. Scars from those days still lingered in parts up north, but life had returned there now, he'd heard, and the trees had grown strong since those days. Daelon had defended them and then returned the favor, beating back those who had dared to attack them to their own borders and threatening to attack their lands, as they had done to his home.

That was centuries ago now, and Daelon's rule had grown strong since then. After a while, the world had gone back to normal; the cities of men had begun to grow again and expanded along the Zoe River, leading to an alliance, and trade with them began to flourish. The entire forest then was protected from any invaders—from the northern woods, just below the Eastern Mountains, and throughout the southern parts of the forest, where the Zoe River peacefully flowed, down to the wetlands, where many villages formed, with both elves and men living together. The elves at last controlled the forest and could drive out attackers and traitors alike. The king had become the greatest elf who had ever lived, even greater than Fayaden, first King of the Elves. His rule had known nothing but peace since he had ended the goblin raiders, along with the Third Elven War. The race of men had risen back to great heights with King Daelon's help, and the dwarfs were able to make new kingdoms with his help, for the threat of the Dark Elves had all but dissipated with their defeat.

The king now turned to face the crowd, silver hair swaying side to side. His face looked hardened, more so than ever before. His twilight-black eyebrows were sternly bent inward. His bright green-and-gold eyes looked troubled, as if something great was weighing on his mind. His skin seemed less flushed than Baelath remembered; his lips closed without even the slightest twitch rippling across his smooth cheeks. His forehead was furrowed, as if he was deep in thought, and on his head rested a golden crown that came to three points in the front. The tip of each point held a jewel of a different color—one blue, another red, and the middle one was white, but not just any white. This white was purer than any other color, and nothing else could replicate the aura that beamed from the middle gem of the elven crown.

King Daelon's broad shoulders were covered by his luxurious cape. Made of a metallic black cloth, it had been one of the many gifts from the dwarfs, as thanks for the king's helping them establish their new kingdom. The cape couldn't be ripped or torn apart, penetrated or sliced, yet it weighed almost nothing and reflected all light instead of trapping it. His golden armor extended from the bottom of his neck down to his feet. He raised his head, looking outward, and Baelath quickly turned his sight toward the ground and slipped in among the crowd. The murmur of the others stopped, and all held their gazes on their king, waiting for him to speak.

"We have gathered here, for by now, we all have heard the news," the king began. "News comes from the Topless Mountains, crossing the Golden Plains and the land of men to tell us what has happened." The king stepped toward the others and away from the fire. "I have gathered you all here tonight, the leaders of our forest, to decide how we want to proceed."

After a moment of silence, a loud commotion erupted; the other elves all tried to speak at once, voicing their opinions. The murmur grew loud, bouncing off the walls of this hollow tree and deafening the entire room so that Baelath couldn't make out his own thoughts, let alone anyone's words. He looked over to Evelyn, who had retreated into the shadows of the room, almost completely out of sight.

"We need to get closer; I can't hear what anyone is saying," he whispered over to her.

"This isn't close enough?" she hissed at him. "We risk being seen if we move in any closer."

"My father gathered everyone here. I'm sure this must be important, but you are right in that we shouldn't be seen. Not yet, at least. We just need to be careful." He made his way toward the crowd, stepping up behind the last row of onlookers. He saw that Evelyn had done the same and stood next to him.

The king raised his hand, and the murmur quieted again. "This is a great travesty, and I have never stood quietly by when travesty has come to our borders." His voice grew stronger, and the others muttered in support of their king. "But this action did not occur in our lands. I have given my word that I would take no action upon others if our lands were left untouched, and so they have." Some nodded in agreement, others let out a sound of disdain, but most sat in silence. "Jord was a friend of my grandfather's and my father. I have known him since I can remember, and he has taught me everything I know. I've counseled with him, and I've listened to his words many times. But he is now a prisoner of our enemies, and if he is not gone now, he soon will be. Even if that was not certain, he lies deep within the Dark Forest, in the cells of Morketrekk."

As the king looked down upon the crowd, a fire began burning in his eyes. "But there is hope. For what I see before me is a new generation of elves, ones not stained with betrayal or deceit. I see a generation of pure blood, ones who will endure all that the darkness has to offer. For thousands of years, we have been guided. Guided to war, to death, and almost to extinction itself." Now the crowd was yelling in a frenzy, supporting the words the king spoke. "I say it is time the elves guide themselves!" King Daelon roared, raising his hands high into the air.

All the crowd was on its feet now.

Did I hear my father correctly? Baelath wondered. Did the king really plan to leave Jord, guide to the elves, locked away to face uncertain doom? The same man who had raised him, his father, his grandfather, and walked alongside his great-grandfather? Most of the things that Baelath knew were taught by Jord, as his father always had been away during his childhood years, if you could even call it a childhood. He'd spent months spent traveling with Jord, learning the ins and outs of the land, how to hunt, how to fish, how to become unseen to the untrained eye. He still couldn't believe it, and now an anger rose in him; his fists clenched into a ball.

He took a step forward, but a hand grabbed him by the shoulder and pulled him back. "Don't do it. It won't do any good. They will just laugh at you, and the king will become angry," Evelyn whispered, her emerald-green eyes pleading with him, her lips frowning, her warm brown hands holding his. "Not now, but later, you could talk to him, reason with him."

"It has to be now. I won't let them *all* abandon him," Baelath argued, his words forced through clenched teeth. "Jord was like a mentor to me, a father, even. I have to say something; later, it'll be too late." And he pulled his hands away and turned his back to her. He could hear her retreat, and she slipped out of the tree and away from the gathering.

He made his way through the crowd toward the front. It was a more difficult task than one might have imagined, as the crowd was filled with fervor now. Pushing aside those who blocked him, he finally reached the front and stood before King Daelon. Once the others saw him come forward, their voices quieted, and they shuffled back a few steps.

The king met Baelath's gaze as he approached, and for a fleeting second, Baelath could have sworn he saw a smile twitch in the corner of the king's mouth, but it passed as quickly as it came, and the king's face wrinkled with anger.

"Baelath!" bellowed the king, for he refused to call him *son* in front of a crowd. "You have no business here and have not yet been invited to this sacred land. Leave at *once!*" Glaring at his son, his eyes a fiery gold, he pointed to the way Baelath had come in.

"My king," replied Baelath—he also refused to acknowledge him as *Father* in front of the others; only Evelyn has heard him say it. "I knew not of the land I walk upon, for I became lost after a hunt, and I strayed farther than I believed. When it ended, I found myself in a part of the forest that was unfamiliar. I climbed a Great Tree, and from my vantage point, I saw smoke. So I followed it, and that is how I came here, uninvited, as you said."

Baelath slightly bowed his head but still did not break his gaze with his father. "But once inside, I heard a terrible thing, something that I cannot stand idly by and allow to happen. You have condemned to certain death not only your friend but a member of my family as well," Baelath whispered. He had to make his father understand that this was a betrayal. "How would you act if an elf had been captured instead? An elf of your blood, perhaps?" Baelath's voice grew louder now. "How many elves would have to die outside of your so-called borders before you acted?" He turned to address the crowd. "If you were in the hands of the enemy, would you not want your king to come for you? Or would you rather die alone, away from all you hold dear?"

"Enough!" barked the king. "I will not stand here and allow my actions to be questioned. Much less by a *boy.*" The king's cheeks quivered. "You have never walked outside these lands, let alone with the aura of battle. All you know of are trees, but you have not walked the plains where the dead used to pile to your knees." He stepped toward Baelath, growing in stature the closer he came. "You spend your days hunting, yet you have never been hunted. You haven't spent the night peering into the darkness, waiting for it to swallow you. You do not know these things because I have prevented them. The sacrifices made for all that lies before you are incomprehensible to you. I will not allow the darkness to return to Blaonir, and I am willing to sacrifice much more for it than what you say I am."

With those words, the king and his son both understood what he meant. Nothing was too much for him—and no one. Baelath had heard of stories when he was younger of how the Dark Elves would slaughter their enemies, leaving them hanging from trees. They would hang for days before they were found, missing limbs or eyes, heads sometimes; some were strung up by their hair with everything else torn off. He thought that these were just stories to scare the children, but he knew it now to be true. It still didn't change the fact that he couldn't leave Jord out there to die alone, in enemy hands. He had to say something, but before he could, his father turned and walked back to the fire.

"This gathering is over, and my decision is final." A hint of sadness escaped the king. "I will not hear another word on the matter, for it will be a waste of time for all involved. Now, return home as you must to let the other villages know." And in a great whooshing sound, the fire went out, leaving nothing but a cloud of black smoke that consumed Baelath's vision. "And for those who don't belong here, return the way you came and leave this area alone until it calls upon you, or the consequences will be grave." The king's eyes peered through the smoke at Baelath.

Slowly, the crowd dissipated, and many elves climbed their way back through the branch tunnels until only Baelath stood alone in the empty hollow tree. He made his way back outside into the empty clearing, shuffling his feet with every step. Strolling through the open meadow, he reached the tree line and made his way back through the forest. The moon hung low in the sky now, with the night almost over, and the forest was beginning to come back to life. Critters scurried around the leaves, and here or there, an unsuspecting elk pounced away when Baelath came too close. But to him, everything else was background noise humming in the distance compared to the raging fire in his mind. His anger rose inside him with each step, but he just kept walking. He walked past his tied-up sled, past the hunting grounds from earlier in the day. He kept walking and walking, even when his legs ached. Somehow, through all his walking, he had come all the way back to Mellom Elvene, and he stepped out from the edge of the forest and into a large clearing. Dawn had risen, with the sun breaking through the treetops; a light mist lingered in the air.

The city along the forest floor slowly bustled with activity, from doors banging as the shops opened, to the whoosh of the blacksmith's fires heating up, and the grumbles of the guards coming off the night shift and the ones taking over. Most of the earlier risers were too busy to bother Baelath. The forest ground of Mellom Elvene mostly consisted of two things. The first part were the blacksmiths and their shops. Some shops were just for weaponry and armory; while others were for trinkets and some self-endowed items. A few random shops existed here too, but most of the shops were up above. The second part of the ground level was the Watchguard.

The Watchguard were the protectors of Mellom Elvene, and they were the best-trained warriors of the Blaonir Forest. They never tired, they could see farther than the others, and they moved the fastest. They also were masters of bow and sword. Their camp was stationed behind the Elder Tree of Mellom Elvene, and close to a thousand elves guarded the city at any time. They were captained by Rhys, the best-known warrior of Blaonir, someone Baelath had grown up with and was forced to spar with too many times. Rhys had never been one to step down from him and had always shown off in front of the king, or Evelyn, or his own group of friends. Baelath was never too fond of him and even less so when his father made Rhys the captain of the Watchguard. "Rhys, the son the king never had" was whispered when others thought Baelath wasn't listening, but he heard it all.

The Elder Tree stood in the middle of the clearing, surrounded by many other Great Trees, though none of them even half the size of the Elder Tree. The Elder Tree was at least a hundred paces wide and at least half that in depth. Its deep roots sprawled along the base where children climbed and played. Its rich brown trunk reached higher in the sky than any tree in the forest, maybe even in all the land. Ladders hung from all around it, with a few large ramps on each side where large carts could make their way up. There were two small baskets where a pulley system could get you to the higher levels without going through the mess that was the market. About fifty feet up sat three platforms, almost as wide as the clearing itself, the lowest harboring the market, where you could get all kinds of elven foods—from the berry bushes that grew on the north side of the forest, to the meats of elk, boar, rabbit, and bears that roamed the woods. You could find elven bread from the wheat that grew along the east coast and the fruits that grew in the wetlands down south. When they got visitors from the cities of men, mostly from the city of Nox, you could even find food that grew in the Greenhills and the Golden Plains. Those were more like treats, though, and they sold out quickly, for the race of men rarely ventured into Mellom Elvene, though many River Elves traveled to Nox every now and then. Baelath had heard it said that sometimes even Dark Elves made it all the way to Nox, though those stories were used mostly to scare the children from running off to the city.

The second level, a little smaller than the first, consisted of little shops that sold items in which the elves were knowledgeable. Medicine shops, herb shops, and craft shops all littered the platform with no organization to any of it, leading to clusters of shoppers forming along the platform and choking the walkways, making it hard to pass through. Elders stalked the crowd, trying to talk to anyone who stopped for a second about the days "before your time." Little children ran unattended, causing chaos to those trying to sell their goods, crashing into unsuspecting patrons, and knocking over tables. Baelath usually skipped that platform altogether, for some vendors always tried to sell him something, and he was not in a mood to be bothered. Not after the night he'd just had.

Hurrying past the shops, he reached the final platform. The top level was a juncture, with the bridges from the surrounding trees connecting to the main one. The bridges went out to homes, for most elves lived in tops of Great Trees that they'd hollowed out. Dozens of bridges went out, each to a different Great Tree that surrounded the Elder Tree, which then had three to five more bridges built out from them to another smaller tree, each leading to an elf's home. The bridges themselves were strongly hung from branches, but it did lead to lots of rope crossing and hanging over.

Back when he was younger, Baelath would swing on some of the low-hanging ones, using them instead of the bridges to travel from tree to tree. Most of the young ones did this, as no one paid attention to it—that is, until one of the children didn't hold on tightly enough when swinging, and he fell the entire way, crashing through the platform below and onto the ground. He died instantly, and since then, only a few daring ones still swung on the ropes.

Baelath strolled onto one of the bridges that was brisk with travelers and then another one that was again quite lively with elves this early in the morning. He followed down a third one now, this one leading to his home, to the king's home. Pausing for a moment, he let out a sigh before walking into the opening. It wasn't a lavish place, as a king would have, but it had a feel to it, as if you weren't allowed to move or touch anything. The king hadn't been one to enrich himself with decorations and had lived a simple life since the death of his wife, Baelath's mother. He had concerned himself more with the kingdom than with whatever he placed in his own home, his only son included. King Daelon hardly gave Baelath the time of day, let alone teach him the things that fathers taught their sons. No, those duties fell to Jord, and he had taken the responsibility to heart, being there whenever Baelath needed it and sometimes even when Baelath thought he didn't need it. Jord had been there since he could remember.

The main room consisted of only a desk, a clock hanging along the bark walls, and a chair. The desk was covered in loose scrolls stacked in piles, some even surrounding it on the floor. The chair was an old, tattered-looking thing, almost as if a mild gust of wind would rip it to pieces. The cloth covering the back was torn or missing chunks altogether.

The next room was smaller than the first, but it was a more glamorous room, compared to the first. This room held the history and relics of all the elven wars—or just the victories, Baelath presumed. Fayaden's sword was in a case along the wall, with a heavy layer of dust settling on top of it. The first crown of the elves, worn by Raska, was placed beside it—a small silver crown with a point in the middle that held a bright green gemstone. Gifts from the first empire of men. Jewels from the dwarfs, and other treasure that was buried in the mountains. Ancient scrolls from the dawn of time, before any talk of the darkness coming. There was even the first goblin king's war hammer. But in the middle of the room lay the most prized possession of elves: the Stone of Life.

The Stone of Life was originally just a tale told since the beginning of time, about how life could be controlled with this stone, how the holder could create anything living. But soon, the tale grew large, and many elves went to seek the stone. Some said it lived in the Eastern Mountains, deep in goblin territory. Some believed it to be in the Topless Mountains or the lost kingdom of men and the ruins of Memarch. No one had ever found it, and most never came back. But one day, Baelath's father returned to the city, and with him, the stone, and everyone crowned him the greatest king to ever have lived. Since then, though, it had been in this case, in the middle of his home, and everyone was left wondering if it was real.

The next area was an open area with a couple of chairs and a small cot stuffed with leaves in the corner. This was where Baelath spent his time when he came here. Mostly, he would roam the woods instead of wasting his time here, but on the few days when he made his way back home, this was the room where he would be, lying in its emptiness. And it was here that he found Evelyn waiting for him, her green cloak contrasting against her rust-colored skin but matching perfectly with her eyes.

"He's just going to leave him there," said Baelath, leaning up against the doorway. "After all Jord's done for him, for all the elves, for me, and they're just going to let him die."

"I know," she said, standing up from one of the chairs along the back wall. "I overheard a group of elders talking the other day, saying they kept receiving messages—something about birds showing up every day and how the king wanted nothing to do with any of it." Sighing, she strolled over to him and placed her hand on his shoulder. "I figured what it must have been when I saw the king in that tree."

"I can't just leave him there, not after all he's done for me." Baelath couldn't understand how they all had resigned themselves to Jord's fate like that. Like it didn't matter. He could feel his jaw tighten, and his chin looked more defined, like it was chiseled from a tree trunk. Evelyn said it always did that whenever he grew angry. "I have to do something."

"I understand," she said, looking into his eyes. "So what are we going to do about it?"

"We?" he asked, stunned. "What makes you think this is a *we* thing? I feel as if this is something I must do. Besides, you are the one who left that meeting, rather than standing up for him then. *Now* you want to help?"

"I left because doing something there would do no good," Evelyn replied. "Besides, this became a *we* thing the minute you decided what you were going to do. Who else is going to save you from trouble? Those blue eyes of yours?"

For a few seconds they stared at each other, both determined not to back down from their arguments. But then Baelath burst out laughing. "I suppose you're right. I may need someone to save me."

"Again," she said, smiling.

They packed all that they thought they needed and maybe even more some; they did not want to risk running out of supplies. They brought food, clothing, shelter, weapons, and some coin, most of it already prepared by Evelyn.

Does she really know me this well?

Each of them carried two packs slung across their backs and a satchel on their hips. Evelyn tucked her arrows away and sheathed her sword, while Baelath hid his daggers and hung a couple from his leg and hips. His sword whisked behind him with each step he took, and he offered to carry some of Evelyn's arrows on his back as well. Elves wouldn't carry this much to battle, let alone on a rogue rescue attempt, but here they stood, strapped head to toe. He knew they looked odd, and if anyone spotted them, they'd surely have some curious questions. He'd have to make sure they weren't spotted while leaving; he didn't want to raise suspicion, not to the civilians, or those who gathered at the meeting last night, or even the Watchguard. He thought about leaving a note for his father but decided against it, yet after gathering up all that they could, they were about to proceed outside when the King stepped inside the home. He stared at them for a moment. None of them said anything, and then, finally, the king stepped off to the side and motioned them to the door.

"Hurry, and be quick. After your show at the gathering, I sent orders to the Watchguard to bar anyone from leaving now." The king's eyes stirred in anger, yet a hint of pride loomed behind it all. "You'll have to slip through without being seen at first; then I'll have to set the entire guard out, chasing you down. It's what would be called for given your … standing."

"Why do you have to set the guard off at all?" asked Evelyn, not afraid of the king one bit.

Daelon shifted his burning gaze toward her, and she unconsciously withered slightly. Everyone always did; there was no helping it. But she always hid her ear whenever she felt insignificant or embarrassed. "Because *my son's* actions last night has other elders worried that there will be a … commotion if I let him freely roam. So you must go now, or don't go at all."

"I still don't understand why you wouldn't want Jord back here, why you wouldn't want the one other person who's helped the elves, more than most elves help themselves, freed from imprisonment," Baelath said, his voice sharp enough to make Evelyn shift uncomfortably.

"Enough," the king said, cutting him off. "Now leave before I change my mind."

Baelath looked at his father's face, the harshness washing over everything, but when the king finished talking, Baelath saw sadness flicker across it. But it was just for a moment, and once again, he motioned for them to leave. Baelath looked at Evelyn, who nodded in reply, and just like that, they whisked out of the tree, onto the bridges, and down the ladders. No long goodbyes or words of encouragement. Just sadness.

Why did he so easily let us go? Baelath wondered, his mind still on his father's stepping aside from the doorway. There had to be another reason, one Baelath couldn't imagine, that the king would be so against sending any one of his subjects, so against sending Rhys who could easily accomplish a rescue mission. He wasn't willing to send Rhys, his Watchguard captain, his greatest warrior, but he was OK with his only son going, an elf who wouldn't be that remarkable at all if you removed *Prince* from his name.

As they moved through the crowd on the second platform, a group of patrons almost got knocked down as they ran past. They stopped at a few stores, picking up a few supplies they didn't have: bandages for cuts, ointment for burns, bread for the journey to Nox, and fire-making tools. He made sure he didn't linger too long at any place, trying to avoid attention. Hopefully, most would assume they were stocking up for a hunt.

An elder went to talk to Baelath. They always enjoyed the prince, and normally, he loved to converse with them. But they were in a rush this morning; they needed to be on their way long ago if they wanted to make it out of Blaonir by the next morning. Or before his father raised the alarm.

Baelath ran to the edge of the platform and grabbed hold of the rope. He looked back toward Evelyn and nodded for her to follow him, and he jumped off, hooking one arm to the rope, swinging to another, and grabbing that with his free hand. He swung his way around the whole tree, rope to rope, slowly lowering himself down, until he could drop to the ground and roll to his feet. Seconds later, Evelyn rolled up behind him, brushing the dirt off her knees.

"Let's not do that again anytime soon," she said with a laugh, her slim shoulders bouncing in the rising sunlight. "I would hate to waste all our energy this early."

They continued on, quickly walking past the Watchguard camp. No one yet stirred or eyed them with suspicion. They were walking briskly through the blacksmith shops when Baelath began to wonder why Evelyn was so eager to help him on this mission. Sure, she had always been there with him, even when they were little, when no one wanted to be his friend. No one wanted to be friends with the king's son. They'd act nice and friendly toward you, and let you win at everything (unless it was Rhys), but not Evelyn. She always had tried to best him in anything, from the little games they'd played as young ones, to training with swords and shooting with bows. Even in hunting, she tried to outdo him, though he usually got the last laugh there. But when she did beat him, it wasn't to gloat or to showoff to someone else; it was just for her. She never made him feel bad or small for not winning; in fact, just the opposite. She made him better in every way.

Now, a new game had begun for her, it seemed, one that she prided herself on more than any, he supposed. How many times could she save his life? What scared him the most was that this was no regular hunt, and they were not children anymore. This would be unlike any undertaking either of them had ever experienced. He knew that, but he didn't know what it would cost them. He feared it would be their lives, but it was for his friend, his family, and that was worth life itself.

A small wind whipped their cloaks as they reached the western edge of the city and looked around. No one paid any attention to them, and they knew they could easily slip off into the forest. "You know where to go, right? In case we get split up later?" he whispered to her. "Head southeast to where our secret hunting grounds are."

"Yes, I've been there before, Baelath. *We've* been there before, many times, or have you forgotten so quickly?" she snapped. "Besides, no one seems to notice us, and sneaking away has never been a problem of mine." And just like that, she dipped into the forest like a ghost into the light, without a sound.

Laughing to himself, Baelath walked on a little farther, trying not to attract anyone, especially since Evelyn had just gone in. After a few more seconds, he found a nice break in the woods. Just as he was about to duck in, he heard a voice call from behind him, freezing him in his tracks.

"*Oy!* Can I help you, my prince?"

Baelath whipped around to see Rhys standing there, a look of curiosity across his perfectly sculpted face. The elf stood in full Watchguard gear—a hard leather tunic wrapped around his torso and a mossy helmet that was placed up, revealing his amber eyes. A green cloak hung from his broad shoulders, and a long-sword swung from his straight hips.

Baelath was a tall elf, yet Rhys stood almost a head taller, and he always used it to his advantage, looking down on Baelath as much as possible. Baelath didn't know what to say at that moment; his mind drew nothing but blanks. *Why did my father have to give that order?* he thought in anger. *And of course, it would be the golden one catching me.* He could never get one over on Rhys or sneak by him, even when they were younger. Rhys always made sure that the elders never saw when he got hold of Baelath or what punishment he doled out when he caught him.

"Just back from a hunt," he quickly said to the captain, his eyes shifting in the lie.

"Where's the beast? Or did you let another one get away?" Rhys said, laughing, his dimples breaking out perfectly in the corners of his mouth.

Baelath's face turned red with embarrassment and his fists clenched in anger; even his ears pointed forward a little. He was about to answer Rhys, but before he could open his mouth, the bell for the Watchguard rang out. His father had shut down the city and was preparing to send the Watchguard out after them, and here he was, stuck in a conversation with their captain.

He turned back to look at Evelyn in the trees, watching him as her fingers twirled in her hair around her right ear, and then to Rhys, who looked more confused than before as his long brown hair swayed in the breeze. Not knowing what to say or do and without thinking it through, Baelath turned and ran straight into the forest. He could hear Rhys call out to him again, but he knew that Rhys would soon round up more of the Watchguard to chase after him. H sprinted as fast as he could, whipping along the trees, hoping to put as much distance from the Watchguard as he could before they set out.

Evelyn ran up beside him. "So what's the plan now, oh, great prince?" she said, laughing.

"The plan is to run—and run fast," he exclaimed.

"Run where? We're not separated, so the original plan is useless." Evelyn huffed at him, growing annoyed by his calm demeanor. "Where are we going to run?

"To Nox," he replied, smiling at her.

At first, Evelyn groaned, but then, turning back to him, she smiled too. The two of them set off on their mission together, side by side.

CHAPTER 2

THEY HAD BEEN running for a couple of hours, and their pace was beginning to slow. They had made their way west of Mellom Elvene and were trying to stay close to the trail between the cities of men and elves. At first, the trees were thick around them, but the ground was clear, except for a few fallen trees or small creeks. Now, the land was changing, slowly at first. The dense trees became scarcer and in their place were wild clumps of brush. Thorn bushes with vines wrapping them were between the oaks, and small berry bushes kept impeding their advancement; all the bags they carried eventually made sprinting impossible. Baelath knew they soon would need to stop, or they wouldn't be able to continue at all.

Stopping at the bank of a small creek, he called to Evelyn to stop. He took the bags off his shoulder with a heavy sigh. Evelyn too was panting. "We must rest for a minute or so. If not, our feet will drip red long before we leave the forest altogether."

Still breathing heavily, Evelyn made her way to a large rock in the middle of the creek bed and threw herself upon it. "We must not rest for too long, or they will catch up," she said, looking back in the direction where they had been running, in the direction from which they were being chased. "The Watchguard are not ones to take lightly, especially Rhys; he is endless in his pursuit, and he can last much longer than both of us."

The sun had dropped lower in the sky, coming directly at their faces, hampering their vision. As much as that was a deterrent for them, Baelath figured it would be much worse for the Watchguard. Baelath has been training his eyes for his hunts for years now. You never knew when you'd have to stare toward the sun while a beast charged you. That would at least put them on a level playing field, although they were still much faster on foot and knew these parts of the forest better. Still, he thought if they could make it until nightfall, then they might have a chance to get away from their chasers.

Putting the bags back on his shoulder, which somehow felt heavier than they had before, they both climbed out of the creek bank with a groan and started off again. After a while of hurried walking, they came upon a wide clearing basked in golden sunlight. In the middle stood a Great Tree, probably the last one in this direction. It stood like a lonely tower with a fair-haired maiden trapped inside, branches drooping, as if they were reaching down to enclose you. The leaves were a rustic color, not green and vibrant like the ones back home but rather dirty. Even the tree itself looked sad, like it had been hurt and was weary of any travelers that approached it. Baelath wondered what could have happened to it as he stopped next to the tree and placed his hand upon its trunk, almost trying to feel its pain. *It must have countless memories from the thousands of years it has stood here*, he thought, *while everything around it faded out of existence.*

Just as he removed his hand from the tree, two figures broke out of the clearing to the east, from where they had come. Baelath spotted them first, drawing Evelyn to follow his gaze. Gasping, she grabbed the bags she'd placed on the ground and began to run. Baelath just stood and watched her, rooted like a tree to this spot. A horn blew behind them, and he knew that they had signaled to the rest. Looking back at the edge of the clearing, he saw that two had become six, and they were now making their way to him. He ripped his feet from the ground, like a statue coming to life, and ran in Evelyn's direction, but he couldn't see where she had gone. Her speed had become a problem for him again; he had no idea where she had gone. He just continued to run west, hoping she would eventually find him.

Racing out of the clearing and back into the woods, he pressed on, faster than before. He couldn't be caught, not this close to the city. He would be made a fool, with everyone laughing behind his back. The king's son flees home, only to be brought back later that day. Or at all, really. Not only would it be an embarrassment from everyone else, but his father had let him pass. He didn't stop Baelath, as he had been advised. The king had *wanted* him to do this. He couldn't fail now.

He pushed his body to go even faster, moving swifter than he would on a hunt. He felt like he was flying through the air, jumping and ducking the foliage. He slid on a mossy log that had fallen over a creek bed to make some sort of bridge. But he knew this was foolish, for eventually he would tire, and the Watchguard would catch up. He had to lose them, throw them off the trail. But how? Without Evelyn, it would be impossible. She was the tracker and knew how to hunt, while he was the one to set up the final trap, the kill. But now, they were hunted, and he could see the trap forming around him.

And like that, he had it. He would head north, toward the northern part of the forest, close to the Nord River. He could head that way for a day or two, then circle down to Nox once he was clear of the Watchguard. The only problem was Evelyn. She didn't know about his newfound plan, and their meeting point was useless now, as its destination was south, and his path went north. Hopefully, she could make her way back to the city without being seen, and in a few days, the rumblings might stop, and she could avoid trouble. But if she was caught, he would have to get to Nox as quickly as possible, for she knew that was where he was headed. He knew she wouldn't give him up just like that, but if pressured by the elders, her only choice would be the truth. Either way, he needed to avoid detection, and he had no choice but to turn north.

He had been running for hours, and the sun hung barely above the horizon, off to his left, illuminating the land with a red tint, as if it were bleeding into the sky. The forest had grown thick with trees again, as life seemed more ample the closer he got to the Nord. Even flowers sprung from the ground in patches. White and red lilies, purple lilacs, yellow marigolds, and pink tulips surrounded the forest floor, covering everything in its peaceful sunder.

Soon, he came to the hills of Blaonir. While they weren't grand, it was hillier than the rest of the forest, which was mostly flat. This was where he'd hide for the night, in between the hills. If he looked in the right places here, he could find a few good crevasses. The light would easily give him away, though, so he had to make sure he departed before dawn. Tomorrow, he could make his way to the western edge, just below the Eastern Mountains. No elves would venture there, not unless they wished to view the hallowed grounds of old, where the first three elven wars had taken place and where the land was still rife with devastation. They said the souls of the fallen still walked that land. Maybe his mother's soul still lingered there.

After walking among the hills for another hour or so, he found the spot. It wasn't much, just on the leeward side of a random hill, and it formed a rather nice shelter for him to lie comfortably and build a small fire. He ate some rations and let his fire reach more of a dim glow of the embers than an actual fire, just enough for warmth. He stretched out and gazed upon the stars from his little divot on the small cliff, remembering the stories Jord had told him when he was younger. He thought of the great battles the elves had fought throughout time, facing the darkness itself, the betrayal of their kind, and the three wars that preceded them, and the goblin raids too. He thought of the fallen kingdom of men, and the dwarfen exile. He thought of his favorite warriors—Fayaden, of course, was one, but there were others, including the son of the first king of men, Naro, who founded his own city and fortress, defending against the endless goblin attacks for decades, his sword shining in the rays of the sun, blinding his enemies. Naro had fought off dozens of goblins at once while completely surrounded. His demise was rather a sad tale, though; it had brought the destruction of the Memarch kingdom. He had been in an epic battle with not only goblins but Dark Elves as well. But men were winning and driving back the enemy's forces. And then, it was said a flash of bright light erupted over the land, and soon, darkness swallowed them, and men were plunged into the abyss. The tale ended the next morning, when nothing but ash was left. Everyone was lost, and the city was laid to waste the following day. Soon after, Memarch followed, and the kingdom of men failed and withered away. It took them thousands of years to build another city, and a few hundred after that before more were built.

Baelath knew the elves were blessed. They were able to defend most of their home and saved themselves from the darkness. Men and dwarfs both had been driven from their homes, and they scoured the land for anything to call their own. It took thousands of years, but both races had now settled in new lands and had rebuilt their kingdoms and were prospering more than before.

The night became morning, and soon dawn would break. When he stood, the dew still clung to the leaves, like children to their mother's skirt.

He snuffed out the coals, packed his belongings, and headed west just as the first ray of sunlight burst through the trees. He hoped, with any luck, that he would reach the edge of the forest by nightfall. He wasn't sure of the distance; he had never traveled this far. His father would never mention it and would snap at Baelath if he tried bringing it up.

The sun continued to rise higher the farther west he went, off the foothills now and back onto level land. He slowed his pace to a brisk walk to save his energy, each footstep designed for silence. He needed to be careful and stay hidden, but unfortunately, Baelath gasped in awe as the entire forest roof opened on him, and he stepped out into a bright open meadow.

The meadow consisted of all flowers known to him and many others he had never seen. The land was alive with color. Reds and blues streaked the clearing; green and yellow patches could be seen in every direction. Long purple flowers sprang up all around him, and with every step, he could see more underneath the top layer. Little sky-blue flowers and green vines wrapped the stems of everything underneath, trying to catch some light themselves but forever trapped below. The land was open far beyond his vision, save for a few small bundles of trees popping up here and there. He made his way to the middle of the clearing, taking longer than it had seemed, each step feeling like he was walking on uneven ground. One step was on level ground; the next was higher or lower and slightly crooked. He swore that one time the ground even moved on him as he walked through the growth.

He ended up finding a nice bushel of trees where he could hide out and set up for the night, with only him and an odd crow, who seemed curious about him. He turned his eyes from the bird and peered at his surroundings. He wasn't as close as he would have liked to have been, but the journey through these lands was harder than he'd thought, and he figured no one would venture out this way anyway. After making a small fire and cooking some rations, he lay on the ground and looked up at the faint stars that hung in the sky. The light hadn't yet disappeared, especially in the clearing. He was thinking of the stories that Jord had told him or others he could remember when suddenly he heard a rustle. Sitting up, he listened intently all around him but couldn't hear any more disturbances. *Likely the wind,* he thought and began to lie down again when this time he heard a crunch, like someone stepping on leaves and sticks. He jumped up and quickly doused the embers; only a small hiss escaped into the air. Scanning the dark, Baelath watched, but nothing moved, just the trees swaying in the wind. He kept his eyes peeled into the black, hoping to see something, anything, to let him know that he wasn't crazy. His hand tightly gripped his sword hilt, ready to defend himself, if necessary. A rustle of leaves and a snap of a twig breaking occurred suddenly and swiftly behind him. He spun around as fast as he could, releasing his sword from its sheath, ready to strike whoever approached him.

His arm stopped dead in mid-swing. He stood face-to-face with Evelyn, a smile stretched from one uneven pointed ear to the other, her dark green eyes sparkling with joy.

"Did you think you could get rid of me that easily?" she said, laughing. "Did you forget who the tracker was in this little group of ours? I've been on your trail for the better part of a day, once I realized you had headed north and not west. Or south, like we had *planned*," she sniped.

"I didn't know what else to do. I had to throw them off the trail, and they had the south covered, and if they didn't, they soon would have. The only chance I had was north," he said. "I figured no one would look up here, but if they did, I would be long gone by then. I hoped you'd be able to sneak back into the city once they lost your trail."

"Well, I'm not going anywhere, and nothing you can do will make me leave," Evelyn said.

"Promise?" Baelath asked as he looked up into her eyes.

"Promise." Her fingers quickly brushed her hair over her right ear, as if Baelath did not know of its appearance, or that somehow hiding it would make him forget.

They relit the fire and talked around the flames until the moon began its descent. Soon, though, they began to tire, and Baelath was just thinking of lying out and stretching his legs when Evelyn fell completely asleep, and her head dropped onto his shoulder. Knowing she had been hunting him for over a full day, he let her sleep, and he continued staring off into the night, until he too closed his eyes and drifted off.

The next morning came suddenly to Baelath, and the bright morning sun blinded him for a moment. He was lying down, looking up toward the sky, remembering the events of the past few days: the secret meeting and the confrontation with his father; running from the Watchguard and getting separated from Evelyn; running north and walking on the hallowed grounds of old; and last night, when Evelyn found him. All in just three nights. Three nights of a lifetime ago.

Sitting up, he saw he was by himself. The coals of the fire were almost out, and he wondered where Evelyn had gone. The sun was climbing higher, and he knew it soon would be midday, and they must be on their way before anyone figured out where they had gone. With a good pace and no obstacles, they could reach Nox by sometime early tomorrow. Standing, he could see out of the grove of trees where they were hiding, and he saw Evelyn walking back from the east, toward him. The hood of her cloak was down, and her black hair swayed in the wind. He realized how much she had grown since he'd met her when they were just little children. He thought that was how she would have always looked to him, that sweet innocent child who beat him in everything, but that thought was gone. He wondered if she thought of him like that still, or if her thoughts had shifted too.

"I went back and covered our tracks here. It took a little longer since we each took a different path to get here, but I believe we should be OK for a day or two," Evelyn said. "We can make our way west and south for the better part of a day, and then, by cover of night, we can leave the forest and travel along the plains."

"Well, sounds as if everything is taken care of," he said, laughing. "Shall we leave then? I feel we shouldn't linger in these lands for too long. Something here just feels off, but I'm not sure exactly what."

And so they quickly packed up their camp and headed out to the clearing, making their way to the tree line due southwest.

They had been walking for hours, and the sun was bearing down on them with all its heat. Baelath could feel the sweat pouring from the top of his head, running down his face and into his eyes, burning them with each droplet. Soon the sleeves from his shirt were soaked from wiping his forehead. Their pace began to slow; they hadn't eaten all day. He was just starting to think of saying something to Evelyn when she stopped and turned to him.

"Here's a good place to rest for a while," she said and began to unpack some rations from her bag. "We should probably eat something too. After that, we can head west toward the edge of the forest. If we hurry, we might make it there before nightfall. I think we've traveled far enough south. We don't want to risk getting seen again, but I think a small fire would go unnoticed here."

Wondering exactly where they were, he scouted the area quickly, hoping to find a Great Tree, but none seemed to grow this far north. He did find a decent-size one, taller than the rest, and decided he could climb it to get his bearings. He made quick work of the climb. From the top, he could see in all directions, yet south was just trees that grew larger than this one; a few Great Trees even sprang up through the canopy, and same to the east too, but looking west, he could see the trees growing smaller. Squinting, he could make out the edge of the forest and the beginning of the Greenhills slowly rising against the horizon. Once he climbed back down, he gave his report.

"Well, then, let's be on our way," Evelyn said, smiling at him. "Do you think you can keep up the pace, or do I need to slow it down for you?" And after a quiet giggle, revealing both dimples by the sides of her mouth, she doused the fire and shouldered the bags, always ready to set off.

Night had fallen, and the ground was illuminated by moonlight. Even though it had become dark, their pace hadn't lessened due to the scarcity of the trees around them as they traveled west. The air had cooled too, a nice break after the damp heat from that morning, and soon, they reached the edge of the Blaonir Forest. The moon had not yet reached its highest point, so they figured they could travel a little farther south to save time tomorrow, maybe even reach Nox by the end of the day. At some point, though, they decided to stop for the night and rest.

She can keep up a pace; that's for sure, Baelath thought as he rested against a small tree. They got a small fire going and sat around it, talking about old hunts and listening to the world around them. Silence had surrounded them completely for a long time, and Evelyn's head again rested on Baelath's shoulders when, suddenly, there came roar.

Awhoooo, awhoooo, awhoooo! The horn's sounds pierced the quiet night in every direction. Springing to their feet, they frantically peered into the darkness.

Rhys appeared in the firelight, stepping out from the darkness and unsheathing his sword. "It's over, Baelath," Rhys said softly. "Come home, and maybe your father won't be as angry."

"I can't go back, not now," Baelath replied, feeling braver than he had when the horn rang out.

"Then I'll bring you back, tied up and bloodied." Rhys smiled. He always enjoyed a good beating of Baelath, especially if Evelyn was around.

"There's two of us and only one of you," boasted Evelyn, returning a snide smile.

Rhys whistled, and two other Watchguard Elves stepped from behind the trees, half encircling them. They were trapped and outnumbered.

Evelyn moved first, lunging for her bow, but that was what they were waiting for. Before she could even grab the string, the other two were on her. Rhys made a beeline for Baelath, who barely had enough time to unsheathe the sword, let alone throw up a block, and the first strike from Rhys sent him stumbling backward. Regaining his feet, Baelath moved into a more defensive stance, readying for the second strike. Still, it was a jarring blow, and Baelath barely had recovered from it when he spotted another one coming at him. He ducked just in time and threw his body into Rhys, and both the elves tumbled to the ground.

It was Rhys who fell near the swords as they clanged to the ground, while Baelath rolled by their campfire. Rhys had seen both weapons on the ground, with him in between them and Baelath. Hurrying to his feet, he grabbed one of them and raised his arm above his head. In a moment, he would swing down, ending whatever conflict the two elves had.

But Baelath got to his feet and removed a log from the fire. Still aflame, he swung it across his body the moment the captain turned to face him, and Baelath could hear the skin sizzle as the blazing timber shattered across Rhys's face. Yelling out in agony, Rhys dropped to the ground.

He turned back to the others and found Evelyn pinned to the ground by one of the Watchguard, while the other kept kicking her midsection. He felt the anger rise through him, his blood boiling higher as each blow landed. He picked up the sword Rhys had dropped, and in five quick paces, he was there. Before either saw him approach, Baelath jammed the blade through the back of the one kicking her, and with one quick shove, he pushed it out the dying elf's chest. Ripping it out violently, he let the dead Watchguard slump to the ground while he turned and locked eyes with the one pinning Evelyn to the ground. The Watchguard loosened his grip and reached for his sword, but Baelath was ready for it, and in one swooping motion, he cleaved the head clean off the shoulders. Blood sprayed both Evelyn and him, and she scurried to her feet, a look of horror and disbelief across her face.

"You'll pay for this," a voice whispered from behind them, and Baelath spun around to see Rhys climbing to his feet, his face bloodied and charred, sword in hand. "I'll make sure of that."

He was about to charge Evelyn and Baelath, but Baelath was too adroit for him at this point.

Baelath's mind worked faster than it ever had before, as if time slowed for him in this moment. He picked up Evelyn's bow, arrow already between his fingers. A sudden thump echoed in the night, and the arrow flew its short distance and landed in the good eye remaining on Rhys's face. Rhys stopped dead in his tracks and fell onto his knees, head bowed toward the ground but breathing still.

Baelath calmly walked over to his longtime rival, relieved that they finally would have some sort of a conclusion. He twirled the sword in his hand as he walked behind Rhys and held the blade to his throat, the anger still churning within him. He looked over at the other two elves he had killed, and he looked to Evelyn. He could still see the marks they left upon her, and like that, he ripped his sword across Rhys's neck and let the blood pour from it, making sure he was finally dead before he let his body drop to the ground. Silence filled the night again, and the ground glowed as the moonlight shimmered off the pools of blood at Baelath's feet.

"We must leave here," he muttered to Evelyn, who had not yet moved an inch, an expression of disbelief etched across her face. "Others will have heard the horns and will be here soon. We must not be." He grabbed the packs he was carrying and slowly walked into the night, away from the slaughter. A few moments later, he heard Evelyn grabbing her packs and shuffling behind him.

Following the tree line, they walked for a few hours. The moon was beginning to drop low in the sky, and soon the pitch-black sky gave way to gray as the night dissipated into morning. His thoughts kept going back to the night. He remembered the fear that overtook him at the sounds of the horns from the darkness. He remembered the anger that swelled within him and the horror of what he had done. No elf blood had been spilled since the goblin raiders were beaten back to their mountains. Mellom Elvene—and probably the entire forest itself—surely would hear about his killing not just an elf but a Watchguard. Getting out of the forest was supposed to be the easy part, but somehow, this was going horribly wrong, and he shuddered to think what lay ahead.

Finally, Evelyn walked up beside him; she'd spent the entire night walking a few paces behind. "Why did you do that?" she asked him.

"I had no other choice. They were going to bring us back, and every day we spend on the run makes it more difficult to go back. We've come this far and lasted this long. Every delay dims any hope I have for Jord, and getting caught destroys it all together." His gaze pointed straight ahead. "I won't let anyone stand in our way. I won't let anyone hurt *us*."

"If you thought we were being hunted and tracked before, it will only get worse now," she said, now beginning to pick up the pace. "They will be out in force and won't stop until we are caught. Day or night, it doesn't matter."

"It didn't matter before, or did you forget they attacked us at night already?"

She spun around to glare at him, her forehead showing slight creases— not a wrinkle, but it definitely furrowed at him. Her black eyebrows buried his fleeting humor and left him feeling disappointed. He knew she was angry, but he couldn't see any other choice.

They continued walking. They had left the tree line and began moving through the open lands between Nox and the forest, staying away from the road that bridged the two places. They stuck to the meadows and fields that littered this part, and soon, they heard the rush of water and came upon a river. It was wider than he had ever seen, and he had swum in the Midten River in the heart of the Blaonir Forest. This river, though, had steep banks jutting down the sides, and the water moved with such force that a constant whooshing sound echoed all around. It was not the peaceful scene he had been expecting when he thought of the rivers outside the forest. He had heard of the Zoe River and how it peacefully slithered through the land, a place where children could play and swim, a place to relax and sit around fishing.

Great cities had sprung up on those banks, yet here, rocks and dirt littered the ground. A huge rock was in the middle of the river, and water sprayed everywhere when it crashed upon its surface, bringing a slight mist over them. He figured they could walk along the bottom of the banks, staying out of sight and giving them some cover until they could reach Nox.

And it seemed like a good idea at the time; even Evelyn agreed that it was the best course for them to take. Yet it was much more treacherous than they realized at first glance. The rocks weren't buried in the earth but just on top of the ground, so every step they took, they were either slipping on wet rocks or just stumbling around if they caught a patch of rocks that rolled away when stepped on. The earth itself was soggy, making every step that wasn't on the rocks harder to maneuver. After an hour or so, they decided to climb out of the banks and follow along on solid ground above them, although it would leave them exposed.

They walked for a few more hours after that, until the sun hung directly above, with no trees for cover, no shade to rest in. He remembered how hot it was yesterday, but that was nothing compared to this day. Everything felt hot to the touch—his skin, the packs he was carrying, even the ground itself felt like fire with every step. He was thinking about stopping and diving into the river that lay fifty feet to his right when he spotted a tiny speck off in the distance. It had to be Nox. He pointed it out to Evelyn, and they quickened their pace.

After another hour or so of traveling, they came upon the city of Nox in all its splendor, but for a moment, Baelath was aghast. Built upon the land where the river forked, the city sprang up from the ground. Gray-brick walls, standing well over a hundred feet high, though still smaller than any Great Tree back in Blaonir, enclosed the city and ran along the edges of the river until it met at the stone castle. The structure jetted up from the ground, reaching high into the sky. Three golden points arched their way up, each one containing elaborate windows and balconies. Ledges ran along the battlements, where Baelath could see men walking back and forth, and at each corner, a watchtower was built overlooking the city and its people. Purple and black cloth hung from every opening along the front, and every guard standing along the walls was wearing the same colors.

Baelath couldn't have dreamed something like this, and he slowed his pace to better take in the view. All he'd ever known were trees.

He could see a portcullis to the east of the city and the bridge that connected the road from the forest to the city. It was already a busy area, with many coming and going, mostly traveling along the road, some heading southward. A few walked toward them but stopped and walked down to the river, which seemed calmer the closer they got to the castle than it had been when they first came upon it a few hours ago.

They made their way to the bridge and tried to blend in with the crowd. They had reached the gate, pushing those ahead and being prodded by those behind, when the crowd ahead slowed and halted. Baelath peered around those who stood in front of him and saw that everyone was halted by the guards who protected the entrance. They were stopping everyone for a second or two, giving them a quick once-over, then letting them pass.

Evelyn and Baelath looked at each other, wondering what the guards were looking for—if indeed it was them. Not knowing what to do, they just continued along their path, trying to hide within the crowd as best they could. Finally, they reached the guards, two big men, with shoulders as broad as a doorway. They looked like they were being forced to stand in the hot sun all day, and they made quick work of letting people by, elves and men alike, not caring who anyone was or what anyone was doing, their eyes fixated on the top of everyone's heads.

But Baelath couldn't help but feel as if the two guards eyed Evelyn and him more suspiciously, especially when one of them made direct eye contact with him. They were just about to pass—Baelath's eyes were trained ahead—when their halberds swooshed down and blocked their path. Baelath felt every nerve in his body tighten at that moment, and he was just about to dart away from the crowd when a voice rang out behind the guards, telling them the way was clear, and the two annoyed guards lifted their weapons and let them pass without incident. Baelath hurried past and walked up to the heavy iron gates, where a sign hung above it, reading The Elven Gate, and they passed through it and entered the city of Nox.

People were walking everywhere—humans mostly, some elves, even a few dwarfs could be seen. Children ran up and down, playing with others who ran after them. At first, they passed by what looked to be homes, but with a closer glance, they seem dilapidated. Barely held together, some leaned one way or the other; some were missing parts of the home altogether, and the wood itself seemed rotted. Families still enjoyed them, though, as evident by everyone's laughter and jubilant tones that filled the air.

With every intersection they passed, the buildings became nicer, and the music grew louder. Soon, they were walking next to shops, inns, and taverns that all seemed up to standard for the glory that Nox was. Brightly colored signs swung in the wind; people were out on the streets, trying to sell their goods or crafts; and everywhere you looked, the purple-and-black–colored banners waved in second-story windows. Baelath became lost in it all, stopping to smile as the children wove around his legs, and he grew interested in whatever a random person tried to push on him. He even bought a trinket to remind him of Nox, after he was gone. Nothing special, just a little statue carved to look like a soldier and painted black and purple. It was then that Evelyn cried out—he hadn't noticed the two River Elves that were walking directly toward them.

"They found us!" she gasped.

Whipping his head around, he saw two elves running toward them. Without a second thought, he grabbed Evelyn's hand and began to run through the crowded streets of Nox.

Chapter 3

Swooping through the streets, they hurried by confused bystanders, and a few of the guards curiously looked on as well, but no one made any attempt to stop or slow them. Weaving in and out of the crowd, they fled into the market circle, where it was even more crowded than the side streets. There were carts of bread and vegetables, and stands of exotic-looking fruits in all different shapes and colors—orange and red balls, bunches of long yellow and green curvy-shaped fruits stuffed into a basket. Meat shops littered the area as well, filling the air with the smell of charred meat that initially made Baelath gag. He buried the uneasy feeling in his stomach and continued to pull Evelyn through the crowd, bowling over onlookers, eventually making his way to the other side of the market circle.

Looking back, he saw that his pursuers were getting clogged up in the swarm of masses, unable to run through the ones that Baelath and Evelyn had knocked over, and the innocent shoppers who came to help them started gossiping about what the commotion had been. When one of their chasers knocked down a lady who was cautiously carrying a stack of bread over to a table, they used the slight distraction to duck down a random side street and raced along its path. Buildings flew by Baelath's line of vision and rickety old signboards blew in the breeze above him. They made their way into a more rundown part of the city, and even while sprinting down the cobblestone streets, Baelath could notice the shape the buildings were in. He knew they only had a few seconds to get somewhere before they would be spotted again, so they scampered into a small building. A faded green sign, splintered in three different places, hung above the door, reading Three Foxes Tavern, and they quickly shut the door behind them.

Baelath saw that this was not one of Nox's most popular places. The walls were stained with what looked like blood, pieces of the ceiling were missing, the lighting was almost nonexistent, with only two lamps in the entire place, and the windows were too dusty to let in even a little sunlight. He counted only six people inside. Three were conversing at the bar, one man standing behind it, wiping down a mug, while the other two held drinks in their hands. Another man looked passed out in a chair at a table by himself in the front left corner of the room. Two others sat in the opposite corner, in the back of the room, playing some sort of game, but their gazes were on Evelyn and Baelath. The man sitting on the right seemed to quickly move pieces around the game, but it was too dark for Baelath to be certain of what he saw.

"Can I help you?" the bartender asked. He had set down the mug he had been wiping and now looked at them intently. The other two men at the bar had turned in their seats and also looked curiously at the two elves who had just barged into the place. "Well, can I?"

"Umm, yes," Baelath said nervously. "Just ale for us at the moment, please." He and Evelyn sat at the far end of the bar, away from the two men, who still eyed them steadily. The elves grabbed their drinks, and Baelath set two coins on the bar.

The bartender scoffed as he picked up the coins and went back to wiping the mug he'd set down. After a few more seconds of silence and keen stares, the murmur picked back up. The two men went back to their game, and the three at the other end of the bar went back to conversing. But Baelath stood as still as a statue, eyes fixed on the door, waiting for it to burst open at any minute, expecting to see the two other elves who had chased them standing in the doorway.

The minutes passed, though, and the door stayed shut. Letting out a sigh, Baelath relaxed and sipped his drink. The taste was much harsher than what he was accustomed to, but once it went down, it left him feeling warmer and calmer than he had been. After taking a couple of sips more, he had allowed himself to breathe and slump in his chair when a loud yell rang out inside the tavern.

"You been cheatin'!" screamed one of the men at the table. "I had you beat, but now I lose? Only thing make sense is you cheatin'."

"Well, that's just absurd, my good friend," said the other, his rough face sporting a smirk underneath his beard. "You played a good game—no doubt about that—but in the end, it just wasn't enough." He stood, collecting his winnings. "Maybe another day you'll best me, but alas, we must be on our way." Turning around, he ran his fingers through his golden hair; his arms were as wide as logs. His shoulders were so broad that Baelath thought, *I wouldn't be surprised if he has to walk through doors sideways.*

The other man stood up as well; he was a small little thing compared to his opponent. Dirty brown hair, gray in his beard, almost feeble-looking. Wrinkles enveloped the man's face and hands, and he had a few teeth missing as well.

Men and their battles with age, Baelath thought, and he wondered what it would be like to have your body begin to decompose. *Such a shame that they lost their beliefs.*

"I won't be losin' to a cheatin' fool. You give me back what's mine," barked the old man. "You hear?"

Everyone had gone silent, even the bartender.

Suddenly, the feeble-looking man whipped around and stared at Evelyn and Baelath. "You twos was helpin' him, weren't you? Come in here makin' distractions," the old man spat. "That was when I started losin'. Right after you came in." He rapidly crossed over to where Evelyn and Baelath were sitting. "You owe me money for your cheatin'."

"You lost, old man. Move on with the day, and learn the valuable lesson I taught you just now," said the golden-haired man.

"You're next," said the feeble man, pointing back at his opponent. "But first, I'm gettin' what's owed to me from your partners, here."

Before Baelath could defend himself, the old man socked his jaw with his fist. The impact knocked Baelath off his seat and onto the floor. For a few seconds, nothing moved and silence gripped the room. Then, without warning, a commotion broke out, with Evelyn throwing a punch of her own, knocking the old man back a few steps. He quickly regained his balance and unsheathed his dagger, but the golden-haired man came up from behind him and tried to spin him around. The old man was too jumpy and anxious to be completely spun around. He had flung his dagger hand at the bigger man, slicing the skin along his forearm, which soon was covered in blood and dripped heavily onto the floor. The *pat-pat-pat* of blood splashing on the floor could be heard, even over the fighting.

In that moment, a man stepped from the shadows in the back; he'd been hidden from Baelath the entire time. He had wavy black hair, smooth skin, and a young long face. His black cloak whipped in a frenzy as he tackled the old man, colliding with a now-staggering Baelath as he tried to recover from the old man's punch. All three crashed to the floor, the dagger still gripped in the old man's hands. While Baelath was tangled with the other two, he tried to pin the man's hand that held the dagger, but the wheezing old man tried to plunge it into the younger man's ribs. Instead, it met Baelath's hand, and the knife drove into his flesh.

Pushing away from the pile in desperation, Baelath tried once again to get back to his feet, but a lunging figure smashed into him, and he felt the dagger pierce his leg. Yelling in agony, Baelath grabbed the old man by his shirt and tossed him across the bar, as glass shattered everywhere. Baelath hobbled over to where the man was trying to crawl away. He lifted the man once again, but the man went limp. Baelath dragged him to the door to toss him out, but instead of being limp, the old man quickly broke Baelath's grip and head-butted him on his nose. Baelath cupped his hands over his face and felt the blood pool in his hands. A blind rage gripped him then. Shaking in anger, he revealed his sword.

The old man was too caught up in himself or was blind with age because he seemed not to see the sword at all. He sprang at Baelath, dagger held high above his head, but before his arm swung down, Baelath plunged his sword through the old man's gut, driving it with a ferocious anger until he felt the sword rip out the other side. The old man's eyes grew wide with disbelief, mouth agape, drooling blood. He slumped to his knees and dropped his dagger, hands trying to grasp his killer, but he could only fumble at Baelath's cloak.

It was in that man's final moments when Nox's guards burst in. Four tall men, all clad in light armor, each one with a purple-and-black sash around his waist, witnessed the final moments of the scuffle, and all saw the sword, still in Baelath's hand, inside the now-dead old man. They quickly swarmed Baelath and dropped him to the ground, pinning him easily. Baelath could hear the bartender passing out directions to the three guards who had been involved, and soon Evelyn was thrown down next to him, as were the golden-haired man and the slim-looking one with black hair. Their hands and feet were bound, and Baelath's wound was hastily wrapped before they clamped chains on him. The guards removed Baelath's and Evelyn's weapons and loaded the elves into a cart with locked bars. They grabbed the packs that Evelyn and Baelath had carried and placed them in the front of the carriage.

Before anyone could say anything, the guards threw a blanket cover over the cage, draping them in darkness, and as the dust rattled off it and fell into their eyes and mouths, the two elves instantly coughed and gagged.

Why does their dirt taste so bad? Baelath wondered. *Even the air here is worse than the forest.*

With a sudden jerk, the cart wheeled away, with Baelath dwelling in his subsiding anger. The darkness left him alone in his thoughts, but he could hear Evelyn breathing next to him. The cart rolled its way, twisting and turning onward through the city. Finally, after an hour or so, it came to a halt. Baelath heard a door closing and chains rattling below him. When the cover was pulled off the cart, Baelath saw that they had come inside an empty room, but he soon saw the bars and the cage in the back. The guards forced them inside, though the large man with the golden hair made it difficult on them, and they were shackled to irons that connected to the wall.

"Where are we?" Baelath asked, but none of them answered. In silence, the guards locked all four of them into place, locked the cage door, wheeled the cart around, and pulled it back through the door. With a final bang of the door shutting, and the click of a lock locking, they were left alone.

"Are you OK?" Baelath asked, turning to Evelyn, who seemed shaken still.

"Why do you keep killing everyone?" she muttered. "Look where it has gotten us this time. Imprisoned in a foreign place, where who knows what will happen." She turned away from him and sat on the ground, sighing. "Just leave me alone."

"Whoa!" said the golden-haired man. "That's not the first man you've killed? You're lucky you've made it alive this far. Usually, known murderers are killed on the spot in these lands. The king doesn't stand for it anymore."

"It was an elf I killed before, and it was back home," replied Baelath, now turning to face the man. "And I didn't murder anyone this time either, or did you forget the dagger he cut you with and stabbed me?"

"Ah, that was nothing. I've taken worse than that before, some from the old man himself," said the large man, shrugging his shoulders.

"And besides," Baelath said, ignoring the man's comments, "if it wasn't for you, we wouldn't be caught up in this at all. I saw you switch something on the board when we walked in, and then the man accused us of helping you."

"That was just taking advantage of an opportunity, and I didn't think he would catch on. He wasn't a sharp one, that guy. Wasn't the first time I swindled him, although it looks like it was the last time." The golden-haired man chuckled. "Guess I'm going to have to find a new patsy."

"If we get out of here," said the younger-looking man, speaking for the first time.

"What makes you say that, brother? We didn't do anything, just a little brawl in a tavern. Wasn't our first, that's for sure," replied the large man.

The other one didn't say anything but instead sat cross-legged on the floor, staring off into the distance.

"Well, where are my manners? Let me be the first to apologize," the large man said, turning back to Baelath. "My name is Jax, and this here is my brother Max. We are mostly farmers, up there in the Greenhills, but I find myself more of an adventurer than a plain old farmer when visiting the city, and the taverns are, well, usually, a nice place to play a little close to the dangerous side. But you two ..." Jax gave them another close look and slightly chuckled. "You both come scrambling in, looking like you're hiding something or from someone, and then before I can find out what you're about, you shove a sword straight through an old man."

"That was your fault," muttered Baelath. "If you hadn't been cheating the man and just had accepted a loss, he would still be alive, and the four of us would be on our separate ways."

"But I did cheat, and I did get caught. And you did kill that man, so here we all are," said Jax, smiling at Baelath.

He is right. A tiny thought crept into Baelath's head. *You're nothing but a killer now.* The thought kept coming back, over and over again, to the point where Baelath began to shake with anger. *You're wrong,* he thought. *It's only been in defense of lives and always will be.* Nothing spoke back to him.

They all sat in silence for a few hours, watching the light that crept inside from the cracks in the walls slowly dim until night overtook them. Baelath couldn't see anyone, but he reached through the air and touched Evelyn softly on her arm. He felt her jerk away at first, but then felt her hand entwining with his, their fingers interlocking. He felt bad, guilty, for allowing her to come with him. She should be back home, enjoying the fruits of another great hunt, and he wished he too was back home, lying under the trees of Blaonir. He thought of the hunting grounds to the south of Mellom Elvene, and he thought of the grass he would lie back on and how at first it pricked his back, but after a while, it grew quite comfortable. He thought of the colored leaves—bright yellow and dark orange, vibrant green and rusty brown, twirling together straight upward until they seemed to explode above him into perfectly cut shapes, each hanging by a thread. He thought of climbing a Great Tree with its thick branches and how rough the bark felt against his skin. He thought of the view from up top and looking at the moon hanging low in the sky and seeing the treetops sprinkled in starlight. He felt so far from home, and he thought of how foolish he felt for trying something that he was unprepared to undertake.

But his thoughts kept going back to the old man and his gaping look as his life slowly trickled away. He felt sorrow for the old man and ashamed of himself. He promised himself that if they got out of this alive, he would return home, even if it meant dealing with his father's shame and disappointment. He knew he couldn't put Evelyn through something like this again—chained to a wall and locked in a cage.

Just when he accepted his fate and started to doze off, the door creaked open, and three guards entered the room, two of them holding torches. The other clearly was their commander. His armor was lighter, and he wasn't wearing a helmet at all. His short white hair came to a point in the middle of his wrinkled forehead, and even in the dark, Baelath could see his beady green eyes fixed on him. He stepped into the cage and approached Baelath, his cheeks sporting an even whiter stubble than his hair.

"This one," the commander barked, and the other two unlocked the chain Baelath was hooked to; then they grabbed him underneath his arms and proceeded to carry him out of the cage.

"Where are you taking me?" Baelath growled. He tried to squirm from the guards' grip, but it was too strong to even slow them down, and he was ushered outside.

They made their way across an open courtyard, though Baelath couldn't see much in the dark night except the city's lights off in the distance. They led him to another door on the opposite side of the yard, and again Baelath was carried inside, this time to a hallway with stairs. Climbing for what felt like forever, they reached the top and turned the corner. Walking down another hallway, they made their way to the end and stood facing another door, one painted purple with two black lines running up and down its length. The commander knocked once and opened it, and the two guards pushed Baelath inside and shut the door behind him.

The room was magnificent, the most eloquent room Baelath had ever seen. Golden lamps lined the walls, and plum-purple banners hung over the windows. The black carpet almost completely covered the room, leaving just the small outline of smooth stone along the edges. A table stood off to the side, holding glasses and a jar of liquid that oddly resembled what Baelath had drunk at the tavern earlier that day, though it looked much cleaner than what he'd had. In the back of the room was a desk of the finest timber. It glowed red in the lamplight, illuminating what looked to be small embedded embers, like it had been plucked straight from the blacksmith's forge. Stacks of parchment littered the top, and two chairs covered in fine purple linen stood in front. Two people sat at the desk, one behind in a large black-and-purple metal chair, and one in front. The one behind the desk wore a golden crown that encircled his head and came to a single point above his slightly wrinkled forehead; at the tip was a black jewel so dark it seemed to cast a shadow from its perch. The man looked to be middle aged, with a hardened face and a pointed chin with a reddish-brown beard from ear to ear. It wasn't a long beard, but it was somewhat bushy and unkempt, but his hair seemed to be kept nice, as it was slightly long but slick and shiny in the damp lighting. He was wearing a long, flowing purple robe with a black outline along its seams and a touch of gold embroidered into it. He stood from his chair when Baelath entered the room, and while he wasn't a large man, like Jax from the tavern, he had a larger-than-life feel to him.

The other person in the room Baelath recognized as his father.

"Ah, you must be Baelath, whom I've just heard all about," said the bearded man with a bright smile etched on his face. "First, let me say what an honor it is to meet you. I've known your father here for a while now—well, for me anyway." Chuckling, he came from behind the desk and over to Baelath. "Also let me apologize for the unfortunate incident that happened earlier today. My guards tend to get overzealous at times."

The man reached out his hand for Baelath to shake, but Baelath just looked at it for a few seconds, an awkward silence setting in. He looked over to his father, who had yet to stand or even turn in his chair. That's when he shook the man's hand.

"Why, you must forgive me. Where are my manners?" the man exclaimed. "My name is Rodrigo, and I am King of Nox and the Greenhills."

"Glad to meet you, King Rodrigo," Baelath said, still looking at his father. "But I still don't understand why I'm here."

"Yes, yes, yes, again I apologize for what happened. Had I known who you were and what exactly went down at the tavern, this whole situation could have been avoided," King Rodrigo said, walking back to behind his desk and sitting in his chair. "Murder has a very strict punishment for those who practice it here within my walls, and it won't be tolerated."

"I was defending myself," Baelath broke in. "I was attacked and wounded. What happened was completely justified."

"The injury will be taken care of by our best healers, and it's a shame you were caught up in this ordeal. Here, on your first visit to Nox, you were caught up in a tavern brawl that led to murder," said the king. "Luckily, it wasn't just you in there, or my hands would be tied." The corners of his mouth rose slightly, as though he tried to suppress his smile. "You see, I cannot let a crime go unpunished."

Realizing what King Rodrigo had said, Baelath grew slightly angry. "So the two men I'm locked with in your cage—are they the ones who go to trial?"

"Like I said, some punishment is needed. No one will miss or think twice of a couple of farm boys from the hills. Your friend and you will be allowed to leave the city tomorrow night. After the trial, of course."

"The *mock* trial," snapped Baelath. "So because of who I am, I get to go home, while they get to spend the rest of their lives in a cell?" He burned his gaze at his father.

"Home?" interjected his father, finally turning in his chair to stare back at his son. "You don't get to come home. After what you did, it wouldn't be allowed. Even if I wanted it."

His words stung Baelath more than the dagger that had pierced his leg. The pain of not seeing home again, not seeing the trees or hunting through the forest hurt him more than anything he'd ever felt, and that was clear by the expression on his face.

His father swooped up from his chair and crossed the room, his face wreathed with anger. "You killed three of my Watchguard—my captain, no less. In our own land, where elven blood hasn't been spilled in hundreds of years. You're lucky I'm here, for if you were anyone else, you would be left to rot in the cells you found yourself in. I pity you now, leaving behind a trail of blood wherever you go," yelled his father, his voice boiling in fury.

"We were attacked in the middle of the night," Baelath said, raising his own voice but not even coming close to his father's tone. "If they had just come to capture us, then it might be a different story, but they didn't. And if I hadn't done what I did, then Evelyn might have been hurt, or worse."

"I don't care what your excuses are," the elven king said, barking louder than his son. "You shouldn't have been in the position to be caught anyway, making a scene, leaving home like you did. And twice they found you, and it took killing them for you to escape."

"If I'm not allowed home, will you at least let Evelyn back in?" asked Baelath. "She didn't do anything wrong. It was me who killed them, only me. And it was me who killed the man at the tavern, not the brothers, and especially not Evelyn."

His father looked at him for what seemed an eternity. "No," he whispered. "Her fate is now tied to yours, for better or worse." And like that, he turned to walk toward the door.

"What are we supposed to do if you banish both of us?" asked Baelath, a hint of desperation in his question. "Hide while your Watchguard scours Arcane for us?"

His father half turned back to him, but didn't look directly at him, his head pointing downward and his gaze even lower. "Finish what you've started," he commanded, and like that, he walked out the doors, which looked to be made from the same wood as King Rodrigo's desk that basked in glowing embers.

A guard swooped in quickly to close them, and his father was gone.

The king of Nox and Baelath both stood there in silence for a few moments, both staring at the door, then the king stood again and walked over to stand next to Baelath.

"So the trial will happen tomorrow at some point. All four of you will be charged guilty and brought back to your cell to spend the remainder of your lives, *but* later that night, a guard will escort you—and your friend, of course—to the city gates, and you will be allowed to leave unharmed," said the king, just like his father did when discussing plans over the countless dinners he was strung along to. "Although I do advise you against ever coming back here, for I cannot be lenient a second time, and I've made that very clear to your father."

"How do I know you will let us go after you saw my father banish me from my homeland?" Baelath questioned, wondering if he could trust this man.

"Whatever you have between your father and you is of no concern to me, and I would be a fool if I imprisoned the son of the elven king," said Rodrigo. "But I have to appear to uphold the law to my subjects, and we don't want anyone finding out that the elf king's son came into our city and killed a citizen. Rumors are a nasty thing in cities, and elven trade is a thing I'd very much like to keep intact and peaceful. Come now. It is getting late, and I have a trial to prepare for tomorrow. Get some sleep; by tomorrow at this time, you will be free."

And with that, the king yelled to the commander, who came back with his two guards, clapped Baelath in irons, and brought him back to the cell, where Evelyn and Jax were waiting for him. Max was already sleeping, though Baelath couldn't tell until Jax said that he was. The brothers told her they would help them survive the wilderness, once they were let go.

Jax said they would probably just be banned from the city. "But after five or so years, they let you back in."

Once the guards locked Baelath back in and left them alone, Baelath told them everything that had happened, except for the trial being a mock trial and that Evelyn and he would be allowed to go free, while Jax and Max would not. He didn't want to anger Jax right now; he was too exhausted to fight that large of a man. Evelyn told him that she had explained their reason for leaving Blaonir, and the brothers had told her they would help them survive the wilderness, once they were let go, which Jax confirmed with a nod.

They didn't speak for long, but Jax told them a peculiar story after Baelath asked how he had gotten so good at sleight of hand, able to switch pieces on a board in the blink of an eye.

"It's an interesting story," Jax said. "One that began after our first crop run to the city with just my brother and me. We were sitting in that same bar you found us in, and some hermit-looking man came up to me and asked if I wanted to learn a new game." He turned his head upward to the left as he thought of the memory. "He first taught me the game, which I learned quickly, but then he showed me the tricks I know now, but it was not an easy task to learn them. Especially because he kept rapping my knuckles with his walking stick. And this wasn't a switch stick; this was as thick as a branch and heavy as one too. By the end of the first week, my knuckles were bloodier than a newborn baby." He chuckled at his own joke before proceeding. "But after the second week, I had it perfected, and then he told me to keep coming back and that one day, he would show me another. So for the past seven years, we have waited in that rundown tavern, waiting for the old man to show up. 'Keep coming here until the king gives you a gift; then you will know what to do,' he would say at the end of every day. Now, though, I might have to wait a while until we can come back. The king usually banishes murderers, although he forgets the peasants after a few years."

Baelath wondered what odd type of man would teach a boy those things. After a while, he sat on the ground with his back to the wall, staring into the empty abyss of black that engulfed them, and he drifted off in his thoughts.

Gray smoke filled the air around him, twirling and collapsing inside itself. Four shadowy figures knelt next to him, two to each side, all with their heads bowed. He could see dark swirls of movement in the smoke, leaping and hurrying past. Then slowly, a soft hiss filled his ears, and everything stopped moving. A path of smoke cleared, and something terrible emerged. Its face was white, but no features were clear except the red tears that streamed its face. Walking slowly over to Baelath, dragging what looked to be a red sword, though it was black smoke that made the shape, this evil creature continued by him and the rest of the kneeling figures. It circled behind them, and in an instant, the sword of smoke came crashing down on the kneeling shadow to his right. He could see the anguish and heard the screams of those who knelt next to Baelath, but above it all, he heard a worse sound. A deep, booming laugh, softly at first, barely noticeable within the screams, but soon it filled the air and vibrated the ground until Baelath couldn't take it anymore and collapsed to the ground, writhing in pain.

He snapped his eyes open and shot up from the ground he was lying on. Sunlight had filled the room. He was back in his cage. Evelyn slept next to him, as did Jax. Only Max was awake, sitting cross-legged in the middle of the cell, looking right at him with his violet-tinted eyes.

"Bad dream?" he asked, not altering his gaze at him.

"You could say that," Baelath replied, standing on his feet now.

"I didn't even know elves slept. I thought you just meditated or something," said Max; his smooth face didn't wrinkle under the thought.

"We sleep the same as you, eat to live the same as you, and we even breathe the same air as you," said Baelath. "There is little to no difference between you and me."

"I know you can see farther and hear better than all other races. Climbing and running, you are faster than the average man, though some men can beat your elves. And you move quietly too but probably not quieter than me," said Max. His eyes still were fixated on Baelath, making Baelath feeling uneasy. He wished Evelyn would wake up so he could have someone else to talk to. "You're not the first elf I've met, but you do look different than him. His skin was lighter, white almost, and his hands were claw-like."

"You're describing a Dark Elf, while I'm a River Elf from the Blaonir Forest," said Baelath. "How did you end up meeting a Dark Elf?"

Max nodded his head toward his brother, who was still asleep on the ground. "You think that old man was the only one my brother swindled? We come into town once a month or so, and he always looks for the easy target."

"And you?" Baelath asked. "You just follow him around? For what? Protection?"

"Yes, quite unfortunately." A quick smile flashed across his face, yet Baelath got the impression that it was a place of sadness, not happiness, that brought a smile to his young cheeks. "It seems I've made it my habit to make sure my brother comes out alive, though it's becoming increasingly harder of late," said Max, finally breaking his gaze with Baelath and watching his brother sleep.

They sat in silence for a while before Evelyn finally woke and sat up. She looked over at Baelath, who smiled at her. Her brown skin shimmered in the sunlight that broke through the windows. Her shoulders rose rhythmically with the slight hiss of air that came with each breath as she began to awaken from her sleep. Her viridian colored eyes swept over him like an ocean's wave when she caught him smiling at her. She did not return the smile; rather, a look of annoyance vibrated from her. She did walk over to him, but not before brushing her hair over her ear. Her eyes wouldn't look at him in this moment.

"How late is it?" she asked, gazing toward the entrance where the cracks let the morning sun flicker in.

"Don't know," he said, looking at the door. "But I'd like to get this over with as quickly as possible."

"You should wish that these moments last as long as possible. It could be the last time you see daylight," said Jax, now stirring from his sleep. "But while you do enjoy them, could you do it silently? Your conversations are interfering with my ability to soundly sleep." A half smile crossed his face.

"Sorry to disturb you," Baelath sniped. "But every moment here is a moment wasted, and I fear I didn't have many to begin with."

"Jord will be fine," Evelyn whispered, putting her hand on his shoulder. "We will get him; I promise."

He knew she was only trying to make him feel better, yet somehow it did. She had always been able to calm him, even when they were kids. His anger or frustration would get the best of him, and there she would be, soothing everything over, relaxing his emotions. He never quite understood how she could do that.

The door opened, and the guards walked over to the cage and shackled them again and led them out the door. They walked out into a magnificent courtyard draped with purple flowers. Now in the daylight, Baelath could see the entire courtyard in all its splendor. It was a circular area, much like the city itself, with doors like the ones they had just walked through encompassing the walls around them. A patch of grass was in the middle of the area, and a great fountain stood in the center, spraying water upward. They walked along the edge of the courtyard that was already filled with dozens of spectators, with eyes trained on them.

They reached the entrance of the castle and climbed its steps. They passed through the doorway, after having been prodded by the guards behind them, and stumbled into the entrance hall. Here, there were more purple flowers littering the inside, with black banners hanging beneath them. Paintings of men, all wearing the same crown Rodrigo wore last night, lined the walls, their eyes seemingly following them down the hall. Finally, they reached two closed doors made of the same wood as the King's desk, brightly burning red. They stopped for a moment, and the guards swung the doors open, and Baelath's breath was taken away.

Inside the room, opened to where he could not see the top, was blackness. The windows in the back let all the sunlight in, illuminating the entire room. Black pillars lined the outer edge of the room, spiraling toward the sky. The floor was made of a purple stone that sparkled in the sunlight, giving it a shimmering glow as they walked down the steps in front of them. In the back stood a throne as grand as he had ever seen, made of pure gold. It rose higher than the two surrounding chairs, each made of the red wood he often had seen, and the throne too held a similar-looking jewel to the one the king wore on his crown, coming to the same point that its counterpart resided in. And on the throne sat the king of Nox, Rodrigo, wearing a marvelous purple robe that masked the stone in the floor, with a bright golden trim outlining the folds and flaps. It rose to his neck, where then it flowed down behind him, a black garment wrapping his back. Two men occupied the chairs beside him, both wearing purple robes but with black outlines instead of gold.

They were brought down to the middle of the room, which was filled with people dressed in fancy outfits. Purple dresses of all shades, it seemed, and black suits scattered the upper level between the pillars. The chatter from their whispers floated down and became a buzz in his ears that drowned whatever thoughts he might have. They went down the steps, where four of the prisoners stood. The men and women who lingered there wore clothes of many colors. Blue and green, red and yellow, and there were a few in white as well, but they all wore the same purple sash around the front of them, shoulder to waist. None down here spoke; rather, all eyes were fixed upon the four in chains.

Baelath could feel everyone's sharp gaze as they stood in the center of the room. The king motioned to someone, and a small, feeble-looking man shuffled his way to the king and stopped just in front of the steps leading up to the throne. He turned and unrolled the small parchment he held in his hands.

"These four have been charged with murder and conspiracy to commit murder. The justice officials will hear all the evidence that has been acquired and will base their verdict on it," the feeble man wheezed. He rolled up his parchment and shuffled back into the crowd.

"*First witness!*" bellowed the guard who stood on the steps near the king.

A different guard walked up in front of the king, the one who had taken them from the tavern and into the cell. "When I arrived at the scene, I saw the old man lying dead on the ground. Four people stood around him, one carrying a bloody sword. I was then told of what had transpired, so I arrested all of them," the guard said. "Two of them, the men, tried to fight and resist, while the other two, the elves, made no attempt to hinder me or my men."

"What's this?" growled Jax, standing next to Baelath. "He's painting *us* to be the guilty ones? We had nothing to do with it."

The king nodded and thanked the guard, who bowed and walked back to his spot, guarding his prisoners. The king motioned again, and the guard yelled for the next witness, and the doors swung open behind them. This time, just one guard walked with a nervous-looking fellow. Baelath recognized him as the bartender in the tavern, and he did the same as the guard had—he told the story of what had happened, starting from when Jax and the old man started playing the game. He spoke of Baelath and Evelyn bursting into the tavern and causing a scene. He said they just sat there, not making any disturbance, but lied about the fight. He said the old man tried to leave peacefully when he won the game, but Jax wouldn't allow it, that he tossed the old man into Baelath, who pulled his sword out but was only trying to defend himself and Evelyn.

Baelath could do nothing but lower his head, for he did not want to gaze at anyone, not while this was happening right in front of him.

"Lies!" bellowed Jax. "These are lies, and this is a mock court. I've been on the other side, up there next to those very same pillars," he said, pointing upward. "And I've seen what a mock court can do."

"You will be *silent!*" yelled the king, standing from his throne. "You speak again, and you will spend the rest of your days in the black cells."

"I'm already being set up to go there anyway," Jax spat. "Yes, I cheated the old man in the game, but I did not kill him. Killing him would be like killing a customer, and I don't like losing money."

The murmur grew loud through the crowd, with everyone on the higher levels whispering to their neighbors, while the ones who stayed down below let out gasps and pointed at Jax.

"Take them away. I've heard all I need to hear," barked the king, climbing down the steps and trying to regain order in the room.

The brothers were dragged by the guards, both fighting with what little movement they could muster. Jax kept yelling at the king, at the guards, even at Evelyn and Baelath. Max kept quiet but glared with a vicious anger at Baelath.

Baelath couldn't take it anymore. "It was *me!*" he yelled, turning to the king. "I killed that man, and I acted alone. He was a fool, so I took his life. These men did nothing, and they should be freed."

The king turned to Baelath, who couldn't tell if there was a smile or pure rage across the king's face. The room had gone dead silent, as if, all of a sudden, everyone else disappeared.

"Then you shall have your wish. Tomorrow morning, they will be allowed to leave, as will your companion, but they will spend the night in lockup for their outbursts during this trial. And *you*, my elven friend, will spend your life locked in the cells, where you will never be seen again." And with one more final glare at Baelath, the king turned and left the room through a side door. The crowd immediately picked up its murmur again.

The guards came and led them back through the main doors and into the hall with the paintings. They passed into the courtyard, which had filled with even more onlookers, each eager to get a look at the murderers.

The sun hung directly above them, its light cascading all around them. A bright shimmer reflected off the pool into Baelath's face, but he thought he saw two elves standing near the back; once they got closer, he couldn't see them any longer. The four of them were brought back into the cell and chained up. The guards were rough with Jax, who had kept fighting with them during the walk back.

After the guards left, Jax directed his fury at Baelath, cursing him and blaming him for trying to get them locked up. It took a few minutes until he finally calmed down enough for Baelath to explain what had happened—that King Rodrigo and his father had planned to place the blame on the twins, citing their low-level status as farm boys, while the king was to fake the imprisonment of the elves, knowing full well he would set them free at night. Baelath told the twins that the king couldn't risk war with the elves or even disrupt the "precious" trade between them.

"I'm sorry I didn't say anything till now," said Baelath. "But if I had, who knows what would have happened? We might not have even made it to the trial."

"Who knows what will happen *now*?" Evelyn said softly, standing off to the side.

It was anyone's guess as to what would come later, given the expression on the king's face; he would surely be angry. But if Baelath took all the blame, and both the king and his father said he wouldn't be held captive. Then, surely, they would all be allowed to leave in the morning—although something said to him that wouldn't be the case.

The waiting set in, and the day dragged on. Shadows grew longer until the light disappeared altogether, and night set in. Flickers of moonlight shone through the cracks of the door, and soon they all felt the effects of another long day. Jax was the first to doze off, followed closely by his brother. Baelath looked over toward Evelyn; he barely could see her outline. He wondered how she felt about everything and if what they were doing was the right thing. He had no idea what the morning held for them, yet if he had just kept his mouth shut, they would have been on their way, leaving all this behind them. Still, it would have haunted him, knowing those two would suffer in his place.

He turned his thoughts toward Jord. He started making a list in his head of the places where Jord could be—although he could not think of any place other than Morketrekk—when the door sprang open, and five guards shuffled in, stirring the brothers from their sleep. The guards unlocked them from the wall and started herding them into the courtyard. Jax struggled against them at first, and so did Max, but soon enough, they were pushed toward the castle entrance. They walked through an empty courtyard this time; only the splashes from the fountain made noise on this calm night. The moon was full and everything basked in its white light. Shadows danced as the clouds rolled overhead, and the nine of them strolled forward. They went through the same motions as before, walking through the hallway and into the throne room where their trial had taken place earlier that day. But this time, they didn't stop there; they walked toward the back corner of the room to another side door. The guard who led them knocked on the door, then motioned the four of them inside.

Baelath was first to walk up to the door and push it open, leading them into another room, where a throne stood in the back, but no chairs were beside it. There were tables behind it with many objects, both large and small. Oddly, it also contained their gear and the packs the four of them had when they were arrested. Two men stood in the back of the room; one was King Rodrigo, but Baelath did not know the other, though he'd seen him earlier at the trial, sitting next to the king.

The four of them approached the king, who now saw them as they stood side by side in front of his throne. He walked over to his seat and glared at Baelath for what seemed like an eternity, with only silence echoing all around them, like all the air had been sucked out of the room. Then the king smiled at them and let out a hearty laugh that cut through the uncomfortable silence.

"Baelath, my boy," boomed the king. "What a magnificent play you made in my court today. You left me speechless, and trust me, it's been quite some time since that's happened. Isn't that right, Samuel?" The king turned to the man standing behind him.

"Yes, yes, that is correct, my liege," Samuel quietly said, staring curiously at Baelath. "I will leave you to your business, then." He gathered his belongings and scurried out the door.

Once the door was closed and just the four of them stood alone with the king, Baelath took a couple of steps closer to Rodrigo, not knowing what was going on or why they'd been brought here. Before he could open his mouth and ask anything in particular, the king raised his hand to eye level, stopping Baelath in his tracks.

"You must all be confused as to why you are here before me, at this time of night, no less. And before I answer that question, first I need a couple of questions of my own answered." The king gave a stern look to Baelath. "First, why did the two of you come to Nox in the first place?" he asked, motioning toward Baelath and Evelyn. "Second, how did the four of you come together? And last, what is the plan *now*, if I let you go?"

For a second, the four companions stood silent. Baelath looked at the others, who looked back at him, waiting for him to talk first. Looking back at the king, Baelath began telling the entire story, starting with the discovery of the ancient tree and the gathering of all the important elves in the Blaonir Forest. He talked about Evelyn's and his escape and getting separated, finding the sacred lands of the elves, the confrontation with the Watchguard, and how they chased them all the way through the streets of Nox, and how they had tried to hide in the tavern. He explained in more detail what exactly had happened between him and the old man who accused him of cheating, and how the twins had intervened.

"And then the guards burst in, and from there, you should know the rest of it," said Baelath, as he finished his story.

"Hmm, very good, yes." The King nodded. His gaze turned downward, like he was trying to hear a distant sound just on the edge of the horizon. "That is indeed an incredible tale, and it does answer a couple of my questions, but it does not answer my last one," the king said, now looking back at the companions. "What is the *plan* now?"

"What it was when we first started," replied Baelath. "To rescue Jord."

"But you said it yourself that you don't know where he is. How do you plan on rescuing someone if you don't know where he is imprisoned?" asked the king.

"I have an idea," said Baelath. "Only one person would kidnap a friend of the elves."

The king shot a look at Baelath, as if that last statement annoyed or amused him; Baelath couldn't tell.

"The Dark Elves."

The three men looked confused, as though Dark Elves weren't real.

They don't know the history of the elves, thought Baelath.

"Well, it looks as if you do know where you're going," said King Rodrigo. "Maybe you don't need my gifts after all."

"Gifts? What gifts?" asked Jax, who now eyed the king suspiciously. "Is it like the gift you tried to give to my brother and me in your mock trial? You know, where you pronounced us guilty without hearing a word from us?"

"Again, let me apologize for my behavior earlier. When an outsider— an elf prince, no less—breaks a law, it makes dealing with it a little trickier. And hopefully, my gifts will make up for my incuriosity." King Rodrigo stood from his throne and walked over to the tables behind him. He picked up a shield, lifting it with a grunt and carrying it on top of his outstretched arms. He strolled down in front of Jax and presented it to him. It shone silver with a golden edge; a blood-red ruby was plunged in the middle of the shield, surrounded by six white diamonds. A black strap hung from underneath it, almost dragging on the ground. The most interesting thing about it, though, was that it looked brand new. No rust, no dents, not even a smudge on its surface.

"This shield was made from the finest of materials, crafted by the most skilled dwarfs, and it has protected many kings, both dwarf and man. It was given to the third King of Nox, King Santiago, for his bravery helping the dwarfs against the goblin raiders. It has been passed down from king to king for hundreds of years, and now, I pass it to you. Wear this shield, and you shall never be struck down." And the king placed the shield in Jax's arms and walked back to the tables.

He came back down, this time holding a wooden bow, which looked to be made out of driftwood, and one pure-white arrow. He stepped in front of Max and handed him the bow and arrow. "This is the king's bow. It was a gift from the first elven king to the first king of Nox, King Leonardo. It was made from the bark of the tree that now sits in the middle of Mellom

Elvene, and the arrow was crafted from the stones of the Zoe River that flows through this entire land. It signaled an alliance between men and elves and established Nox as its own kingdom. Its string has been pulled by every king of Nox since then, and now you will pull the string. Use this bow and arrow to strike the darkness from your enemies, and bring them into the light."

Again, he turned and walked back to the table, and once again, he walked back down to them, this time standing in front of Evelyn. "I indeed do not doubt that you are a warrior and could hold your own with anyone in this room, maybe even the best of all of us," the king said. Baelath thought there might have been a soft twinkle in his eyes. "And a weapon might do you good, but I also detect that you're probably the most astute of the group. And knowing that, I believe I have the perfect gift for you, my dear." He opened his hand, and resting in it was a black key, dull and brittle-looking, and he handed it to Evelyn. "The first key ever made in all the land, and never has it been placed inside a keyhole. It was forged in the fires under the Eastern Mountains, during the time when dwarfs and goblins worked side by side in the furnaces. This key will open any door that stands in your path, but be wary, for it can be used only once. May this let you get to where you want to be."

One last time, he strolled to the tables and grabbed an object. Returning, he stood in front of Baelath with a piece of parchment in his hands. He handed it over to Baelath, who turned it over to reveal a map of the land. A quick scan of it revealed the outlines of the major areas that he knew about, including the Blaonir Forest, the Greenhills, the Golden Plains, and all four mountain ranges. But the most interesting part lay in the middle of the Dark Woods outline, where a little dot was marked, and underneath, it read *Jord*.

"This is a map of all of Arcane, and since you are guiding this little group of yours, what better gift for a guide than a map," said the king. He smiled and folded his hands together as he stepped back from Baelath. "Now, legend has it that this is the first creation. By whom is unknown, but this isn't just an ordinary map. No, this is a special map with all sorts of enchantments woven in it. Elven enchantments, and dwarven enchantments, maybe even goblin too. I cannot tell. Never lose this or let anyone else have it, for in the wrong hands it can be dangerous. This wasn't passed down to us or given as a gift. No, this right here—this is man's first possession, if you believe in its lore. Nevertheless, it wasn't given, but it was a right to own it. I haven't the slightest idea how it came to be in the treasures of Nox, but there it has laid for hundreds of years. And now I gift it to you, Baelath, in the hope that you will right the wrongs that I bestowed upon you, upon all of you. May you find whatever it is you seek when you read this map."

"Why are you giving these to us?" asked Baelath.

"That, my friend, is a long story," said the king. "One that started when I ascended to the throne. On the first night I was king, I was lying in my bed, lost in thought, when I was startled by an old man lounging in one of my chairs. I demanded to know how he was able to get in without being seen, and I was just about to call for the guards when he said something that froze the words in my mouth."

"What did he say?" asked Jax.

"Those words were for me," the king replied, without so much as a glance at the large man. "I will share the last bit of information that he gave me. He told me to pass a law expelling murder from the kingdom. He said that after a decade of trying to enforce the law, it should finally be the normal act in the city. Only when that was true would my kingdom know peace, and I would live on the throne until I died an old man. After the decade passed, Nox did know peace, and so I honored his last advice. He said that the next time the law was broken—after the decade, of course—instead of imprisoning them, I was to reward them with these gifts. He said it would either be two of you or four. It was the only thing he was unsure of. I tried to pour some wine and ask which gifts he was referring to, but when I turned back from the pitcher, he had disappeared as easily as he had appeared. I had almost forgotten about that night until I thought I saw that man in you during your speech. That's when I knew he must have been talking about you, Baelath."

Baelath stood in shock as he tried to process this information. Someone had known he would be here, had known he would commit murder, and had known he would face the king. He wondered who could have known that.

The king took his seat upon the throne and looked back at the four of them, each still contemplating their gifts. "And now, I believe the show must end for us, and I will be true to my word and let all of you leave unharmed. My guards will escort you to the western gates, where you can either follow the road or travel the hills, but make sure this is your final hour within the walls of Nox. Remember, Baelath, you are supposed to be locked inside the dungeons, and I have a reputation to uphold." And with that, he motioned them out.

The twins went through the door first, then Evelyn. But Baelath lingered a little longer, still staring at the map. He looked up toward the king, who was looking back at him with his kingly smile. Baelath bowed his head slightly toward him. The king nodded back, and with that, Baelath turned and exited.

Outside in the larger throne room, the guards were waiting for them, and they were led back out into the courtyard, where a cart was waiting to take them away. It rolled them through the streets of Nox in the dead of night, with the sounds of the squeaking wheels echoing through the city. The twins and Evelyn talked of their gifts from King Rodrigo and what they meant or what they maybe could do with them, but Baelath stayed quiet, his mind still stuck on the little dot on the map reading *Jord*.

What could that possibly mean? He needed answers but didn't know where to look. The king had made it very clear that this was their last meeting, and his father had banned him from his home, so where could he look? His mind still was lost in thought when the cart came to a sudden halt, and the doors opened. They were ushered out through the gates; two guards stood on opposite sides, looking as though they might have been asleep but snapped awake when they heard the cart approaching. Once they were past them, the gates were slammed shut and locked. They had nowhere to go but forward, leaving the city of Nox behind them.

CHAPTER 4

BAELATH STARED OUT at the open land before him. The black of night slowly faded into a dim gray, and the first glimpse of the sun's rays rested on the horizon. In one direction, the road beyond the gate wove quietly southward toward the city of Sol, and in the other direction lay the Greenhills, rising up from the land in the distant horizon. They had to make a choice: either follow the road to the next city of man or travel the hills. Neither seemed too exciting to Baelath; he knew both had their dangers. Following the road to the next city could lead to another altercation, for men seemed to be quick to temper. Yet traveling the hills would surely be slow, and the path seemed quite unclear. Having never traveled through hills before, he was sure it would take some time. The forest had some slight hills but nothing like what stood before him now.

"So where do we go from here?" Evelyn asked, her brown skin blending in with the night like she was only a shadow, though Baelath could see her eyes perfectly. He was still pondering her eyes when Jax turned and spoke to them.

"Max and I need to return home first if you want our help navigating across the land. Mother will be worried sick if we don't stop by to see her."

"Where is your home?" asked Evelyn.

"In a tiny village out in the Elysium Valley," replied Jax, pointing northwest toward the hills. "It's only a few days' travel, especially without pulling the cart, though Mother will be angry with us for losing it. From there, though, we can set out, and if I'm not mistaken, Max here knows a shortcut to the river crossing we need to reach, if we plan on getting to those Dark Woods you talked about."

"And why do you wish to help us?" asked Baelath, his eyes narrowing. "Especially after I almost got you locked up for life just because I am an elven prince."

Jax turned to his brother, and Baelath saw his shoulders droop a little, but he quickly turned back. "That may be true, but we are also free to leave because of you. You could have let us rot while you walked free, but you were willing to sacrifice yourself, and I'll be damned if we weren't willing to do the same" Jax's chest expanded with each word. *Maybe he isn't such an ingrate after all.* "Besides the crops are all turned in, and we are now banned from Nox, for the time being at least, and we are in need of a little adventure. It's the least I promised for my little brother." His hands ruffled Max's already messy black hair, trying to get his brother to smile with him.

"Well, then, it seems the decision has been made for us. We will travel the Greenhills and not the road, though I feel the road may be safer," Baelath said.

"Not when you're with Max and me," boasted Jax. A half smile cracked his face. "No place safer than these hills when we're around."

And so they began to walk north, leaving the road behind. As Baelath turned around to get a last glimpse of Nox, the first city he'd seen, he spotted a large raven, just turning its gaze from the group as it soared back toward the night sky in the far west.

The land stretched out before them, and Baelath felt the patted-down grass beneath his boots, no doubt worn down by the many travelers who made their way to Nox and back, most to sell their crops, since apparently all there was to do in these parts was to farm, according to Jax. Jax spoke of the places in the Greenhills, from the great village of Noxville, which lay a half day or so outside of Nox, to the haunted hill from which no one returned. But mostly, he spoke of his home in the valley—how the mornings were always shrouded in thick mist that kept crops vibrant. "If you sit on top of the hill overlooking it at dawn—well, let's just say you may never see anything as beautiful."

The land began to slope upward as they approached the first hill. It was mostly dirt beneath their feet now, and Baelath could feel the sunken footsteps of the thousands of travelers who had climbed this hill. It took them an hour to reach the summit, and what Baelath saw was a sight to behold—such wonderment to his eyes that he almost shed a tear. The land seemed to roll before him, rich with a grass so green it looked like it reflected light. Streams and woodland were scattered along the sides of the rolling hills, and the water glittered in the sunlight. Across the valley were more hills, much bigger than this one, and in the distance, he could see others striking up through the low-hanging clouds. He saw the valley floor littered with small hills themselves, creating little pockets at the base of them. He could see hills on top of other hills. Perfectly rounded hills, some bare and some covered with trees, and then another mound rising from the middle of them. It all looked so surreal to Baelath that if anyone had tried to describe it to him before he left Blaonir, he would have laughed at them. Now that he saw it with his own eyes, he knew he could also never properly explain it to anyone else back home. *Not that I ever could now,* he thought. *This is my life now, wandering the land, once Jord is freed.*

Climbing down proved much easier than climbing up, but reaching the bottom only meant another to climb. Up they went, and back down again. The path was replaced with the tall, vibrant grass, almost herding them in, causing them to walk in pairs, the brothers out front and the elves following. After three more hills, the sun started to lower in the sky, and the brothers decided to stop and rest. Baelath was confused at first, but one look at Jax and he knew.

"I need to eat something," panted Jax, whose color seemed to drain from his face even more. He leaned up against a tree and took a drink of water, while Max brought over a red, circular-shaped item with a small brown stem popping up from the middle, holding one little green leaf. "Ah, a tasty apple, how I've missed you," Jax said. "How I long for Ma's home-cooked meal. Oh, let me just say—you two are in for a treat." His eyes now closed, and his nose pointed up, like he was smelling something in the air.

"Elves don't eat much. Just the few things we grow in the forest and trade with travelers who come," said Evelyn, not at all impressed with the talk of a cooked meal. They were used to hunting and enjoying dinner over a late-night fire.

"Hmm, I've heard elves didn't have to eat at all," quipped Max from behind him, still rumbling through his pack.

"Not all you've heard about elves is true, as you may come to find out," replied Baelath, a smirk creeping across his lips. "Yet it seems the same cannot be said for man."

"Don't rush to judgment," Max replied. "For we may surprise you before the end."

They continued their banter about men and elves for a little longer before starting out again, their bags feeling heavier than before. The sky had begun to turn orange and purple with the fading sun, and the bottoms of the hills were cast in darkness. But if you were standing on the top of one, you could still see for miles around you, with all the hills stretching out from the black below them. Baelath was the first to the top of this last hill, and when he looked down into the valley, which seemed wider than any before, he could see little torches burning brightly, illuminating small buildings gathered in a small semicircle with a small stone fence encompassing it. He could see people walking around too, quickly being bathed in the firelight as they passed each torch. He could hear some crying out for their children to return home, their voices traveling on the thin air up the hill, while others laughed and sang out in the dusk. Baelath even heard some music floating up toward him, somehow soothing him, and he let a small smile creep onto his face.

"We have seemed to reach Noxville and not a moment too soon, for the residents are weary of travelers at nighttime, though I'm sure the gatekeeper wouldn't have a problem with us. No, not old Johnny," said Jax, who had strolled besides Baelath. "Come, let us get there before true dark overtakes us." And they began their descent down the hill into the village.

Moonlight showed them their way down, though not without graceful steps, but soon they came to the gates of the village. Baelath, even in the dark, could see that these were not nearly as grand as the city's gates. These were just two wooden planks connecting a stone fence that came chest high, and some parts were falling down or crumbling. Only one man sat on a stool outside the gates, looking as if he was dozing. The wisps of his white hair swayed with each bob of his oval-shaped head when he heard the four of them approaching. Startled, he shouted out to them, hands grasping a rusted, old, short sword that was stuck inside its scabbard.

"Relax, Johnny, my boy," called out Jax, as he boastfully made his way toward the old man, head held high and arms stretched forward. "It's just your old friend, Jax. You remember, don't you? I have some companions with me, more than just my brother, but don't be alarmed. We are just passing through and need a place to sleep for the night."

"Aye, I remember you and your brother too," the old guard grumbled, seeming none too pleased that they had woken him, even though it was still relatively early in the night.

Johnny, the gatekeeper of Noxville, eyed them suspiciously but agreed to allow them in. He even agreed to take them to one of the village inns, where any traveler could sleep for the night for a fair price, although Baelath wondered how fair. After handing a couple of gold coins into Johnny's wrinkled hand, he let Johnny hobble out in front to lead them through Noxville.

Johnny only talked to Jax, though, asking how his trip had gone, how the market was, what was selling and what wasn't—mostly small talk—but once Jax mentioned they planned to travel back home, Johnny's face grew serious.

"You'd best be careful. I've heard talk of goblins coming from the north," Johnny told them, a stern look in his eyes. "A weary traveler or two, nothing more, but that's how news comes here. A tale or two at first, but soon everyone is talking about it. I keep a keen ear—ha, I dare say—for I'm afraid in these times."

"How far north?" Jax asked the gatekeeper. "Where did these tales come from?"

"I'm not exactly sure how far north, if at all it was, but these travelers came in from the eastern path, probably the Rocky Valley. Their boots were thicker and seemed more worn down than the farmers down here." Johnny seemed to forget his darker tone from earlier and went back to the happier gatekeeper who talked of the good old days. "Well, anyway, this is it. Make yourselves at home. I'm pretty sure it's empty for the night. Just remember to be careful if you're still heading north," he whispered before he turned and shuffled back to his post, presumably to return to his nap.

The four of them entered the inn, a medium-sized gray-stone building with a wooden door that barely hung on its hinges. Stepping inside, they saw that it indeed was empty, as the gatekeeper had said. Just the innkeeper and the cook were still milling around the room. It was a big room with ten to fifteen tables lined up against the outer walls, and at the other end of the room was a fireplace, with stacks of neatly cut wood piled next to it. They started a small fire and sat at the tables closest to it.

Jax went to talk to the innkeeper and then came back to his chair with his new shield laying against it. Max went to ponder his bow. The silver of the string still shone even in the dark of night. He looked over at Evelyn, who placed a string through the key she got from Rodrigo and tied it around her neck. Baelath watched them looking over their gifts from the king, all the while with the map in his hand. *Why did the king give us these specific items? Does he know something we do not? How could he, though, when the day before today he had not even known he existed. Maybe it was just a goodwill gesture for his earlier actions.*

"Can you believe the markings on this?" asked Jax, who was intently inspecting his new shield. "Some seem to be hundreds of years old, yet the finish on this feels brand new." He kept running his hands over the engraved markings that covered the shield. "I wonder what they mean."

"That is how unused shields are supposed to feel," sniggered his brother, whose own hands were fondling the king's bow and its bright-white arrow. "This bow, though—you can *feel* the years inside it. Its wood has been smoothed by being gripped thousands of times, and its string is perfectly in tune with the handle, having been plucked beyond count," Max said, turning the bow over and over again in his hands. "What about you two?" he asked, nodding toward the two elves. "You don't seem displeased with your gifts, but neither do you seem particularly fond of them."

"I am indeed fond of my gift, and I shall never remove it," Evelyn proudly said, holding the necklace she'd made that had her key dangling from it. "The king saw in me what the three of you lack—foresight. You face whatever is in front of you, never backing down. But there will come a place and there will come a time when our weapons are useless, and then, this key—this key will be the most dangerous thing we have. To go somewhere where we are not supposed to be yet need to be—why, that's the greatest gift of all."

Baelath listened to them talk, but his mind kept wandering back to Rodrigo and his parting gifts. All he had been given was a map of the land, yet he knew he didn't fully understand it. There seemed to be something else with a deeper meaning than just a map. Why did the king warn him against letting it fall into dangerous hands? Surely a map wouldn't do much harm. He unrolled the map and began looking it over again, trying to focus on the different mountain ranges that stretched across the paper or the rivers snaking their way through. But his eyes kept coming back to the little black dot, sitting inside the Dark Woods area, marked Jord. *How does it know where to find him? Is it a trick or a lie?* he kept asking himself. So many thoughts—his brain felt like the inside of a beehive. No matter how hard he tried, he couldn't stop the questions from popping up again and again.

The night wore on, and soon the others left for the room for which Jax had paid but not Baelath. He kept mulling over all the questions and events. He knew his adventure was just beginning, yet it felt like forever ago that he had begun. This uneasy feeling kept him up throughout the night, and eventually, the first rays of the sun began to creep over the surrounding hills and cast the valley into a grayish light. Hoping to clear his head, Baelath decided to get up and take a walk up the hill, hoping a clearer view would shake the pieces loose in his mind so he could start to put the puzzle together; maybe he'd even stretch his legs a little. He quietly left their sleeping area, walked outside, and was greeted by the damp of a cool morning and a calming silence. He already began feeling refreshed, like a bear waking from its slumber. He started up the path to the northern part of the valley, wanting to see what lay ahead of them on their journey. He could see the village more clearly, now that it was daybreak. The sun was now peeking over the hill's crest, like a child trying to hide from his parents. He almost expected to see a smile on the sun once it fully broke into view, but knew how absurd it would be. Baelath couldn't help but laugh. He walked through the surrounding farmland and could see where the crops had grown earlier. Old stalks of wheat lay on the dirt, and other stems and leaves littered the fields. Jax had said it was harvesting season and the land was mostly bare now, with just a few areas where some still were untouched.

It took an hour to make his way to the top, maybe less, as he wasn't good at tracking time. He stared out to the north at first, watching the clouds roll by overhead, but eventually, his gaze was westward, as if he was trying to see the forest where Jord was held. But all he saw were the rolling hills that surrounded him, some alive with the thick grass swaying in the morning breeze, and some etched with woodlands, like small brown patches sewed into the fabric of the land. He could hear streams trickling nearby and the small creatures that hurried down to them for a morning drink, and he could hear the birds calling to one another. He sat down in the middle of an open field and soaked in everything that he could. He basked in the world around him that was untouched by anyone and let the feeling of complete relaxation wash over him, melting away any worries or concerns he had just had. This first moment of being alone, overlooking the world, was enough to calm Baelath, and he felt himself slowly drift off.

He woke later and found Evelyn sitting beside him, she herself staring into the beauty of the land. "How long have you been sitting here?" Baelath asked.

"I followed you out in the morning," she said, smiling slightly at him, just enough to make her dimples visible. "I waited until you slept before I sat here, and at first, I was confused why you chose this spot, but once I came, I understood."

They sat in an easy silence as the sun climbed higher into the light-blue sky. Low-hanging clouds rolled in the distance, looking like small puffs of smoke gently floating away from a slow-burning pipe. Baelath and Evelyn sat with her head on his shoulder and his arm around her.

"We need to be on our way. I feel as if we are wasting precious time," he said. He didn't want to but knew they didn't have all day. *One day, we'll go home and spend our time doing nothing. I promise,* he thought. And he would make sure he held to that or else he would be completely lost. "I hope they know that shortcut they keep talking about, though I believe we would have been safer on the road. We could outrun the rumors that would chase us—and the Watchguard, for that matter—but I fear these hills. They settle at the bottom of them, but it is much easier to run downhill than it is to travel uphill, if attacked. And not only are they at a disadvantage, but they have no defenses. It's an amazement that these villages are still standing and haven't been burned to the ground. We've been told in countless stories of the damage that goblins can cause, and we both saw the desolate area of Blaonir."

"We should reach their home tonight, and then tomorrow, we will be on our path again. No need to worry. Besides, we're going to need all the help we can get if we have any chance of succeeding," Evelyn said, trying to reassure him. "Look, here they come now." Evelyn pointed, and indeed the twins were making their way up the hill. They could see Jax's beaming smile, even from a distance.

"Shall we set out?" Jax said once he and Max reached the top. "If we make good time, we might be there before nightfall."

"Then let us be on our way," Baelath said with a forward gesture of his hand. "Lead the way."

They began the descent down the hill, heading deeper into the Greenhills.

They had been walking for a while—up and down many hills and through small patches of woods that stretched through the hills; crossing small, peaceful streams and meadows that abounded with color and next to fields growing their crops—and the sun was halfway to its highest point. Here or there, they would pass a traveler or two or sometimes a farmer out in the field. Most just gave a nod and a hello, but sometimes they would make small talk, and it all seemed to be about the same thing. Goblins. Either an attack on a faraway village or about finding one lurking and having to run from it before they viciously attacked. Whichever it was, the twins did not take kindly to the idea, and Jax turned frenzied after the last farmer told them how the goblins were burning villages and farms and how, on a clear day, you could see smoke rising in the distance. Most farmers didn't seem too concerned, believing that they were too close to Nox to be truly threatened.

When they arrived at the next village just after midday, the mood had swung, with Jax now brooding with anger.

Well, if he was angry before, thought Baelath as they broke the hilltop, *he's about to be enraged.*

The sight that greeted them in the village—which was about half the size of Noxville and even more unkempt, with no gate or wall protecting the place—was not pleasant at all. It almost made Baelath ill, and then the smell actually did make him ill. After wiping his mouth, he saw tears rolling down Evelyn's amber-colored cheeks, and Max looked like he'd been hit by a bolt of lightning. Jax, though, looked ready to chop an entire Great Tree down in seconds.

Painful screams and uncontrolled sobbing filled the air below them, almost drowning out the cawing of the vultures that lingered above. Men were scattered everywhere, some whimpering against walls, while others wandered the streets, staring off into nothingness. Tents had sprung up all around the village green, and in between the rickety wooden buildings, white tarps, covered in bloodstains, looked like weeds growing in a garden. Women were running from one tent to the next, carrying blood-soaked rags with them and pots full of water or blood. Children were in the fields, digging graves for the carts full of dead men and women who were hanging, uncovered, off them. The images grew worse the farther they walked, bad enough to almost make Baelath turn around. Discarded limbs that were too damaged to save lay against buildings, and the sounds of bone being sawed slowly through, followed by the crisp hiss of flesh being seared, echoed from inside inns and homes.

But the worst was the screaming. It never stopped and vibrated the world all around them. Some were quick but piercing as the dying came in and out of consciousness; some were dull but mind-numbing, as if the noise still reminded them that they were alive. Some just droned on, blending in with the rest of the noise.

"What happened?" gasped Evelyn, eyes open wide in shock and horror of the carnage around her.

"Come, let us find someone to ask," Jax said, still vibrating with anger.

And so they ran down into the village and searched, trying to find someone who wasn't dying or trying to stop someone from dying. Finally, they saw an old man sitting on a tree stump outside a tent, alone, staring up the hill in front of him.

"What is going on?" asked Jax.

"Goblins," he muttered, his eyes never wavering from the hill. "Goblins from everywhere. Fire and death, they brought, and the night was ablaze with it. Fire and death. Fire and death." He kept repeating the words, over and over again, until they grew into a faint whisper and he stopped speaking altogether, but eyes still did not waver from the northern hill.

Baelath felt sympathy for these men, like he knew somewhat of their pain. Long ago, goblins had taken his mother before he could remember who she was. They had destroyed a part of his family and his home, and now they were destroying a part of his friends' home. For too long, Baelath had left his vengeance buried, for too long he had not taken revenge, for too long had the crime gone unpunished. But no longer.

He turned to the others with a fire burning in his chest. "They will pay for what they've done, and they will be driven out from this land before more harm comes to it. They will answer for their crimes." He spoke with a trembling and strange anger that he didn't know from where it came.

"Yes!" exclaimed Jax, unleashing his sword from its scabbard. "I will drive this tip through any goblin we see, until the last of them are gone."

"An entire village got overrun by them!" cried Evelyn. "What chance do the four of us have?"

"None," answered Baelath calmly. "But an army does."

"Look around," said Max, now stepping up to the three of them, his face still not quite over the sights. "These are the men of the Greenhills, and while we don't back down from a fight, we aren't trained. We are unequipped and probably outnumbered. This is no army, and even if it were, it is in no condition to fight now. So whose army would you bring with you?"

"The king's," said Baelath, smiling ever so slightly.

"The king's?" replied all three of them.

"You heard what he said—we are not allowed to go back," said Jax.

"And besides, you are supposed to be chained in a cell somewhere, deep in the prisons of the castle. How would it look if you just strolled up to the city and through the castle doors again?" said Evelyn, overlapping Jax.

"What makes you think he'll even help?" Max laughed over both of them. "He isn't exactly gracious to his farmers, as we're all aware."

"Because this is his charge, his land. He will defend it," said Baelath. "Come, let us go to Nox, but swiftly now."

They gathered their gear and found two horses tied to a post. They asked a nearby villager if they could borrow the horses, and after haggling with the man and Jax anteing up a few coins, they mounted the steeds. Jax and Evelyn climbed on one with a luscious black coat that shone in the sunlight, and Max and Baelath were on a brown-and-white spotted gelding. Baelath didn't like separating from Evelyn, but the elves had never been taught how to ride on horses, though Baelath did remember riding a horse once with Jord. But the twins had been trained since they could walk to ride horseback, and each held the reins while Evelyn and Baelath sat behind them. And with a loud yelp and a kick, the four flew off, away from the village and back toward Nox, back toward the king.

The scenery blew by, whizzing as they crossed the streams and through the woods. Hills took moments to get over, and soon enough, they were racing through Noxville. Johnny the gatekeeper gave them a confused wave as they passed. Not long after, with the sun still hanging above the clouds, trying to break through like a chicken hatching from its shell, they came over the final hill and saw the city in the distance, its walls safely enclosing all its inhabitants.

Then Baelath considered his plan—it was overzealous, and he had no idea how to gain an audience with the king, let alone make it into the city. Still, he had to try; he couldn't continue, knowing hundreds more would be slaughtered, not when he knew he could help.

"So," said Jax, bringing his horse to a halt. "What is the plan from here? We simply cannot ride two horses into the city without being stopped, and I know of no hidden entrance."

"Look." Baelath pointed ahead down on the hill. A group of travelers were making their way toward the city, a band of men and a couple of mules pulling a few carts behind them. "We shall mingle with them and hopefully slip in unnoticed," he told the others.

And so they raced down toward the group, catching them in a matter of moments. Jax had to bribe one of the men to overturn his goods from his cart, making room to smuggle the four of them in, and he was still mumbling about it when they slipped under the cover. The cart lurched forward, and it jerked and rumbled the entire way toward the city, only getting slightly better once they reached the road. But they soon stopped, and Baelath could hear the guards talking to the men.

"Why is this one covered?" a guard grumbled, his footsteps growing louder.

They were bringing in three carts, and two of them were full of the farmer's crops, each uncovered. The third one, where they all were hiding, had a tarp covering it and tied securely down. At the time, they had been in such a hurry that they just needed a quick way in. Now, Baelath could see how foolish it was, rushing in headfirst. They'd been gone all of two days; of course the guards were still on alert.

"That there is … is nothing, um, just our … our own provisions we need for our trip," one of the farmers stammered, almost seeming to question his own answer.

"Untie it," snapped the guard.

"Sir, that would take some time to loosen all those knots, and we must reach the market quickly or miss out on a spot to sell our goods," another farmer said.

Baelath could hear the sound of a sword unsheathing, and a wave of terror washed over him. He had no idea if the guard knew they were under the tarp or if he was threatening the farmers. He was frozen in his spot, crouched underneath a tarp in a farmer's cart, wondering if they were about to be blindly stabbed. Then a loud *thwack* came, and the strings fell away, and the tarp above them loosened. Baelath used this chance to catch the guard by surprise. Before the tarp could fall and uncover the four of them, he sprang up and whipped the tarp with a loud crack, covering the unsuspecting guard and slamming him to the ground. Three more guards came rushing over, but Evelyn was already there to meet them, and like a graceful dancer, she maneuvered around them with ease, striking quick blows to their heads and knocking them out cold. In seconds, it was over, and four guards had been knocked to the ground. The three farmers looked on in shock. By now, a crowd had gathered. The guard who Baelath wrapped up was beginning to stir and uncover himself, and so Baelath ran back to the cart to grab his things. He grabbed Evelyn's hand, and they started pushing their way through the incoming crowd.

Now other guards wandered over, having seen a large crowd gathering at the gate and wanting to disperse it. The second that the companions emerged from the crowd, they saw two other guards walking toward them. At first, the guards made no change in their movements, but then, they seemed to recognize the four of them and hurried in their direction. The four of them turned and broke into a run, with Evelyn leading the pack.

Again, Baelath found himself running through the streets of Nox. This time, it was men, not elves, chasing them. Winding and weaving through the side streets that were becoming too familiar to him, he could tell that Evelyn was leading them toward the market stands because they were mostly running east. They darted in someone's house—bursting in on an unsuspecting family who were preparing for their evening meal—down this street, then back up this one, darting down another, and sweeping across more. Soon enough, they burst into the market area, and instantly, Baelath knew it was a bad idea. Dozens of guards were posted, and they easily spotted four people, two elves and two men, who looked like they were on the run.

They group tried to turn around, but already, four more guards were converging on them.

"We need to split up; one of us just needs to reach the castle," panted Evelyn, with her eyes narrowed.

"I don't think it'll work," said Baelath, seeing no escape. "Let us instead get captured, and then we will get our audience—hopefully." He added that last word quietly. He dropped his gear and held his hands slightly up as he slowly walked toward the approaching guards.

Once again, Baelath and the others were shackled and taken away in a cart that rumbled through the city. They all sat next to the same people that they had before.

"Well, this is strange," said Max, noticing the similarities too.

"We've come a long way in these past few days, haven't we?" Jax said with a chuckle. "I just hope this one has relatively the same outcome as before. Maybe faster, though. I'm not sure I could spend a whole day sitting in a prison cell."

Minutes later, the cart lurched to a halt, and they were unloaded from the cart. But this time, they weren't locked in a room behind bars. This time, they stood in front of the steps to the plum-colored castle doors with the gold-plated knobs. At the top of the steps stood King Rodrigo, dressed in his finest black robe that barely brushed the ground. It almost looked as if the robe was made of diamonds, for the light reflected off it and illuminated the air all around him. His crown was perched perfectly on his head; the white glove on his right hand held a gold rod as tall as the man holding it. The tip came to a flat circle with elongated points encircling the top. His face looked older and darker than the other night in his throne room. His eyes narrowed when he saw Baelath approach, a stern look replacing the warm one. He held his arm forward and beckoned them to come up the steps. The moment they stepped forward and began to climb, the King turned and walked back inside, and the guards surrounded them as they continued to climb the steps. The doors were left open. The hall was lined with men and women who Baelath thought were in the king's court, for he recognized many faces from when the trial took place. They entered the larger throne room, where the trial had been, with the same three men sitting in the same chairs. This time, more guards could be seen lining the walls, and more people filed into the room behind the prisoners, cramming the room to its limits.

The four of them, still shackled and bound, were brought in front of the three men. The king sat in the middle, and each of them had a guard standing behind the chairs.

"So it seems you did not enjoy my cells," spat the king, glaring angrily at Baelath. "And you three—you were told to never come to my city while I am king, yet here I find you, breaking a prisoner out and disrupting my streets again."

"We did not break—*oomph*," was all Jax could say before a guard drove the handle of his sword into his gut, dropping Jax to the floor in agony.

"I wish not to hear your lies all over again. You have disobeyed me, and you will pay the price," said the king, eyes still fixed on Baelath. "I tried to be nice. I tried to go easy and give you a break, and you betrayed me. Well, no more. The four of you will rot in the deepest dungeon we have, where neither sun nor water can reach."

"You have no authority to pass out such a sentence. We are elves, and only by elves will we be judged," said Baelath, taking a step toward the king before a guard shoved him back.

"Enough of your words. You think I care if you are some elf from a land I have not even seen? As of this moment, none of your kind knows you are here, and none will seek you here." The king broke his gaze with Baelath and looked around the room to his audience.

"You may have no care that I am just an elf from a land where you will never step foot, but we step foot in yours, and word will spread that you took an elf without addressing our king, and then they will come, whether I am alive or not!" Baelath's voice grew louder so that all in the room heard him.

"No one will miss an elf. That much I promise," the king said, smiling confidently.

Do I dare to reveal any more? Baelath wondered. He wasn't exactly sure who was listening to these trials. If the wrong people found out that the elvish prince was on a journey, he might lose whatever hope of secrecy he had begun with. But he knew the king would not help him again, and his father was long gone by now, leaving Baelath to his own destiny—good or bad. He had only one move left, and if he wanted to leave here tonight with the king's army, then he had to say it.

"And what of an elvish prince?" asked Baelath.

In that moment, the king snapped his eyes toward him, burning with anger, his mouth crooked.

"I am the son of our king, King Daelon. My name is Baelath, and I am elf royalty. If you pass your sentence, then the entirety of the elven army will descend upon your precious city, and we may very well burn it to the ground."

The crowd gasped at this, as none had known who he was; they had thought he was most likely a fugitive from his own lands, which wasn't entirely incorrect. But now they knew an elvish prince stood within their halls, and he could not be brought to their justice, at least not without talking to his king.

Those in the room sat in silence, no one moving, all too scared of what the king's reaction would be, but none could have guessed what the king did next—he burst out in laughter, and all the rage drained from his face. He looked like a young man again, the one Baelath remembered, as if the years disappeared with his smile. The crowd began its common buzz again upon the king's booming laughter. Some scurried away, while others leaned in close to their neighbors. All of them were talking about Baelath, about the king of Nox laughing with the elvish prince.

"You played me perfectly again, my friend," King Rodrigo whispered to Baelath as he strolled down to him, his red beard glowing in the sunlight that beamed in from the floor-to-ceiling windows. "Come, let us talk in private now, away from prying ears and eyes." The king motioned to the guards to unchain the four, and he walked through his side door and into the small throne room. Following him, they found the room looked exactly as it had before. "So what makes you come back here, embarrassing me and ignoring my wishes? Do you not like the gifts? I thought they were perfect gifts, suited for each of you."

"It is not that, my good king," said Max, who slightly bowed when he spoke. "Your gift is a treasure, and we treat it like so."

"So I ask again—why are you here?" The king looked at each of them in turn.

Baelath spoke first. "We were traveling north, through the Greenhills, when we came to a small village. But a village it was not at that moment; it was merely a camp for survivors and wounded. And a grave for the dead. They were from a distant village, farther north, and they had been attacked by goblins. And they were not the only ones in these past few weeks, if the stories are true, but they are the ones we saw. And what we saw would weaken the heart of the most courageous, for pain and death encircled us with every step. Cries of agony filled the air, and the smell of blood and seared flesh filled the nostrils. We could not continue forward in good faith if we did nothing. We needed to try to help. And you, the king of these lands we walk upon, could help us the most."

The king sat in silence for a moment, and the four of them looked at each other, wondering what he was thinking. Moments passed before the king stood and spoke to them. "I certainly don't diminish your experience, but I get reports of goblin attacks many times throughout the season. Goblins roam the hills as much as men do, and I just do not have the forces to defend those lands. I choose to leave it to those who make their homes out there."

"But they do not have the training. They don't have the resources or the equipment to handle any attacks. They're just farmers," cried Evelyn, almost to the point of tears.

"These two are *just farmers*," said the king, motioning toward the twins. "Yet they seem to be capable of much."

"With all respect," Jax said, "we are not like most farmers. We have made ourselves strong, ever since we were young. Most don't have that privilege."

"I'm sorry that they are powerless, but I simply cannot have an open war on the goblins, not without the other cities' support," the king said somberly.

"If the powerful shun the powerless, then what is the use of power?" asked Baelath, looking directly at the king. They continued to stare at each other for many moments until the king let out a heavy sigh.

"Again, your wisdom shines through you, Baelath, and you have humbled a mighty king," said Rodrigo. "You shall have your wish—somewhat, for I will spare a garrison of fifty men, commanded by one of my best, Captain Bazir, to accompany you in driving back these filthy creatures." He sat down on his throne. "Now wait outside the walls at the western gate. This time, I hope you heed my words and never come to this city again, for destruction of your little quest will follow." And with that, he motioned them out of the room.

They waited outside the gate, as the king had directed, watching as the sun dipped below the horizon, its last rays streaking into the blood-red sky. Night was almost upon them when the ground rumbled beneath their feet. Baelath was wondering if some sort of disaster was about to occur— would the city's walls come tumbling down on them?—when suddenly they were encircled by many men on horses. The garrison had arrived, and once Baelath and his companions were settled on the extra horses, they set out toward the looming hills. Each man held a torch, so the light joined together and cast visibility into the darkness that lay before them. Again, the lands passed beneath their feet as they galloped up and down the hills. Baelath kept looking upward, seeing that nothing lay between them and the night sky on this cloudless night. Stars shone brighter than any fire, and the moon cast the land in pale white. They rode on through Noxville without so much as a glance at anyone.

Before the moon reached its highest position, they arrived at the village where there were the survivors of the goblin attack, but now it had grown exceptionally, with tents filling the little valley floor and springing up on the sides of the hills. Screams randomly pierced the night air, leaving all who heard them to speak in a hushed whisper. The smell of charred flesh and dried blood littered the air, but still the garrison rode on. They went up the north side of the valley to the top of its hill, giving them a perfect view of the chaos that had erupted during the day. That was where they stopped and set up their camp. Baelath looked out into the world in front of him, breathing in the crisp night air. Nothing much had changed in his view of the scenery, but somehow Baelath felt different, as if the world was an endless landscape he couldn't have imagined when he was living in Blaonir.

The garrison was busy setting up their tents and making fires. Baelath watched as a couple of scouts fled into the darkness in different directions, quieter than the wind that followed them. His three companions walked up beside him and settled down for the night. Jax was the first to sleep, but the others sat up late into the night, mulling in silence. Max plucked the string to the king's bow as he sat by their campfire, his eyes fixed on the arrow at his feet, which reflected the moonlight. Evelyn sat next to Baelath, her fingers playing with the grass to keep her hands moving. They both stared off into the distance, each wondering what lay ahead, until sleep overtook them.

Dawn was breaking, and the men began to stir. They cooked their breakfast and drank their morning tea. Baelath sat up and woke the others, for there was a commotion throughout the camp.

"What could possibly be happening at this hour?" muttered Jax, still half asleep.

"I'm not sure, but I intend to find out," said Baelath, walking toward the center of the camp, where the commander's tent stood. Evelyn and Max followed closely behind.

All around them, men were packing the tents, stamping out the coals to their fires, dressing in their armor, and sharpening their weapons. Some quickly finished their morning meal, while others tended to the horses, making sure they were fed and watered before they were saddled. By the time they reached the commander's tent, some were already mounting and forming their ranks. They had just about reached the fold of the tent, when out stepped a man clad in bright silver armor, with a purple cape perched on the back of his shoulders that flowed to the ground in elegance. He towered over the rest, even Jax, and his body was almost square, much like his face. A crooked nose hung above his bushy white mustache, and whiskers burrowed out from his gaunt cheeks. His short gray hair waved in the morning breeze, and his stout face grew annoyed at the sight of the three of them strolling toward his tent.

"We have found *your* goblins just to the northeast of here. My man said a count of two dozen or so," he sneered. "Such a pathetic waste of my time, this is. You sorry sack of farmers couldn't even handle a few goblin raiders? This should be over before nightfall."

"Sir?" Max piped up, stepping slowly forward. "My village is not even a half day's ride from here. Once you've completed the task, we would love to show our gratitude and throw a celebration in your honor, if you would allow us. Then, tomorrow you can return to Nox as champions over the goblin horde."

The commander studied this for a moment, then smiled. "Yes, a celebration would be good, I suppose," he said, laughing. "The men could use a night of pampering. We seldom get any time off back in the city, always on guard. We shall see you tonight, then, by nightfall. But now, we ride, and you may take the horses you rode here to reach your village. Go and make your preparations, *farmer*." And he strolled off to his horse.

"I'm coming with you," Baelath insisted.

The Captain stopped in his tracks and slowly turned around. "Fine. I'll take you and the other man," he barked at them. "Someone's got to lead us back to this village of theirs." Captain Bazir pointed to Max. "Gather your gear, and wake the other one. We leave in five."

Baelath quickly ran back to their campsite and woke up Jax, who somehow managed to stay sleeping through all the commotion. They gathered their gear and loaded it on the horse with Max and Evelyn, who were about to make their way to the twins' home. As they were ready to depart, Evelyn drew close to Baelath and pushed something into his hands.

He opened his palm and saw one of her rings.

"Come back," she whispered. She ran her hand through her hair quickly, and then she jumped on the horse with Max. With a swift kick, the horse darted forward, and Baelath watched as they rode off into the valley.

A horn blew, and suddenly the garrison was on the move. Baelath quickly climbed on the saddle behind Jax, and soon they were tailing the others. They rode hard and fast for a few hours, making quick work of the hills as a steady trail of dust flowed behind them. Baelath was beginning to question if Captain Bazir had been given the wrong information when the garrison suddenly slowed and lightly trotted for a few minutes until they reached the top of a ravine.

Baelath looked out as the ground before them dropped and opened wide, almost like the two hillsides surrounding the ravine were once one before being cracked open like an egg. Both sides were covered in thick woods with a dark-green foliage. A small stream crept toward the edge and flowed over into a rocky pit below, giving off a light mist that caught the light just right to cover the pool in a majestic rainbow. The stream then trickled and snaked its way through the wooded area and finally emptied into a small lake at the other end. The men decided to stop here for a bit of food and rest before climbing down, but no sooner than they had dismounted than a hushed murmur swept through the garrison. Everyone stopped moving and then slowly moved to the ground.

Wondering what was happening, Baelath crawled forward and peeked over the edge of the small cliff and looked down. A few dozen goblins had emerged from the woods and sought the water that puddled up at the base of the waterfall, with more still creeping out from the woods. They seemed to be unaware that fifty men with arrows loomed above them, and soon the goblins were surrounded on three sides as the garrison spread out on the hilltop above, all eyes trained below. With one wave from the commander, the sky was laden with arrows. They flew high into the air, and in one seemingly everlasting second, the arrow tips dropped, lurching forward. Soon, the ravine was filled with screams and screeches, and more arrows followed, their shadows dancing across Baelath's face. It felt like a lifetime, yet in the next moment, all the goblins lay dead, arrows littering the ground next to them. And in them.

It took a while to climb down and make their way through the woods that spread through the ravine, but they emerged from the last line of trees and witnessed what they had done. Baelath counted up to thirty goblins but stopped counting after that. He couldn't keep looking at them, their faces twisted in pain and shock, but he made himself stare at their corpses, an abomination of the land, with their pointed chins, wide noses, and ears that had no symmetrical features. Boils covered their faces, with some looking like they were going to burst, while others already had burst and were oozing a yellow pus. Black, beady eyes stared off into nothingness as Baelath walked past them, and some eyes followed him wherever he went. They were not tall creatures of any sort, the tops of their heads coming up maybe to his waist. They had long nails, almost clawlike. Each goblin looked slightly different from the others, yet somehow, they all looked the same. After a while, the faces seemed to blend together, and Baelath couldn't tell them apart—just dozens of the same dead goblin.

The commander came over to talk to Jax, but Baelath was too far away in his mind to listen. His fingers fumbled over Evelyn's ring as he took a seat against a tree. *I am coming back*, he thought. *But will I ever be the same after seeing this?* He looked up and saw Jax walking toward him.

"You OK?" Jax asked, a worried look on his face. "You seem out of it."

"Something isn't right," Baelath said. "This doesn't seem like enough goblins to do the damage we saw back at the village. It took the garrison—what?—two minutes to wipe them out? I know farmers aren't fighters, but I'm sure they could have stood up to this."

"I guess we'll never know. It's over now. Come, let us go to my village. I heard my brother is preparing a feast." Jax helped Baelath to his feet.

Baelath took one last look at the massacre and then mounted behind Jax. Together, with the garrison in tow, they headed off to Jax's village. They rode out of the ravine and turned west, heading up the hillside. They passed many more ravines and woodlands, streams, and open plains. Finally, as the sun was sinking into the horizon, they peeked over their final hill and saw what Baelath assumed was a village, though this looked nothing like the village that housed the remnants of the goblins' attacks. It looked more like a huddled collection of shacks, like someone had built them in a day. The fence for the livestock either was broken or nonexistent in most areas. There were no roads, and there were barely any paths, half of them already were overtaken by grass. A few torches were placed outside what Baelath assumed was the only inn, and some houses hung lanterns outside their doors. Even in the twilight, Baelath could see more animals than people dwelling down below. A small dust cloud gathered as everyone went about their evening chores.

By the time they reached the bottom of the hill, Baelath could see that all the people had gathered outside, ready to welcome them in their village square, which was just a patch of dead grass surrounding a water well, and reward them for their deeds.

Yet something inside Baelath wondered if he and the others truly deserved such a welcome. Something didn't feel right. *Why didn't any of the goblins in the ravine carry weapons? Surely, they would have had weapons to drive those wounded men from their homes, yet not a single sword, bow, or club was among the fallen.* It was strange to hear about, let alone see, a goblin party not carrying some sort of weapons, like they were on an assignment or mission of some sort. *But what mission could a goblin have, other than absolute destruction?*

The villagers cheered when they spotted the men riding down into the valley, and the children came racing up to meet them, flowers in hand. A hero's welcome, it was, one as grand as Baelath had ever seen, even from his time with his father, touring through Blaonir. They rode on through the village, waving and shaking hands with all they passed, and at last they came to the village square, and he saw Evelyn standing there. She was next to Max and a middle-aged woman, slender but built tough, she was, with bright blonde hair and emerald eyes.

"Mother!" yelled Jax, hopping down from his saddle. "Have you heard? We killed all the goblins."

"Yes, I did," Jax's mother said. "And that's not all I've heard, Jackson." She glared at her son. "How was the city? And your friend at the pub you always gloat about beating? How is he?"

"Right, yes, I suppose you heard about all that," replied Jax, throwing a quick glance at his brother. "What's done is done, I suppose, and anyway, we've made some new friends. I see you've already met Evelyn, and this here is Baelath."

"Hello, how—" said Baelath.

"*Ma'am,*" she quickly interjected. "Hello, *ma'am.* But come, no need for such necessities out here. Let us eat and show these soldiers how we farmers celebrate in the hills." And so the five of them went off to their house, while the men went about drinking and feasting in the square with the villagers, who had joined them. Music filled the air, and as Baelath looked out the twins' tiny window, he saw girls grabbing different soldiers by the hand and pulling them up to dance, while the boys sneaked around and drank behind the adults' backs.

The twins' mother talked to Baelath and Evelyn about their home and their farm, and Baelath told her all about Blaonir and Mellom Elvene. Soon, the sun disappeared, and the moonlight replaced it. The laughter and singing grew louder outside, but the celebration was only just getting started. Jax explained that farmers celebrated, danced, and drank better than anyone, but still, Baelath and Evelyn stayed inside, talking to the twin's mom. She wanted to know everything about them because she had never met an elf before.

Somewhere along the way, the conversation turned to why Baelath and Evelyn were on their path, and how they came to meet the twins, and all the occurrences afterward, all the way to this point, goblins included.

"And he even got the king to give us some fancy gifts," said Jax, returning through the door. A heavy sweat covered his forehead, but he had the grandest smile Baelath had ever seen.

"Gifts? What kind of gifts?" their mom asked.

Before any of them could reply, they heard a loud smashing sound from outside, and the four of them rushed out to see what the commotion was. Once out of the house, Baelath saw that a drunken man had thrown another drunken man through someone's house wall, and now they were brawling with each other while onlookers cheered and hollered. He ran over to break it up, and it took the twins' help to get everyone to calm down.

That's when Baelath saw it—a most frightening image to behold.

On top of the hill that they had ridden down, there burned a few torches, enough to be seen but not enough to attract unwanted attention, especially not with the celebration. Baelath watched in horror as the fires were put to the surrounding trees, which sprang to light with flames. Then, slowly at first but soon at a rapid pace, the hills became ablaze, and the night glowed as the flames flickered high into the air. It was like day had come again, as the entire valley floor shone with a luster. Looming on the top of the hills, hundreds upon hundreds of goblins had gathered, all with weapons and torches in hand, and whatever stood in their way was met with one or the other.

A sharp cry rose out from the dead of night and pierced the smoky air, and a few moments later, Baelath watched as the fires descended from the hilltops. The goblins had come that night.

CHAPTER 5

BAELATH WATCHED AS goblins poured down the hills, streaming toward them with ferocious speed, lighting the grass and every tree ablaze, casting them all into what would soon be a raging pit of flames. Without thinking, he took off running, heading toward the commander's tent, which was propped in the middle of the field next to the crossroads. He ducked and dodged his way through the ones who were still celebrating their pathetic victory and, when he finally reached the commander, he was deeply in his cups in front of a small fire, still boasting about the events in the ravine to a small crowd of villagers, most of whom were young women.

"Captain! Goblins!" screamed Baelath, rushing over to their campfire.

"Yes! Goblins! How we smashed them against the mighty fist of Nox and scourged the plague of them from these lands," exclaimed the commander, his eyes barely open. "Victory to the king!"

"Victory to the king!" the others responded, a dozen or so arms with mugs shooting into the night air.

"No! There, look!" Baelath pointed to the raging fires consuming the hillsides. "Goblins on the hills!"

Everyone's gaze followed Baelath's arm, like one would follow a path on a map. At first, a silence swept over the onlookers, but it soon erupted into yells and screams as they began to topple over each other, with everyone running in opposite directions.

At that point, everyone who had been celebrating saw the vicious fire spreading all around them, and most saw the goblins crawling down into the valley. Captain Bazir tried to bark orders, but between the villagers

84

and incapacitated men, very little got done. A small group had managed to gather around their commander, and with a mighty yell of *"Charge!"* from the commander, the small band of soldiers raced out to meet their invaders.

Baelath somehow found himself following them. He unsheathed his sword and gripped it with a sudden rush of anger that he could feel bubbling to the surface. His walk hurried as the men rushed out in defense of the small village. Suddenly, Max and Jax dashed past Baelath. Jax held sword and shield, and Max was loosing arrows into the flame-lit night sky. But nothing could slow the onslaught, and the first wave of goblins quickly overtook the small group of defenders, like water rushing over sand, cutting down the captain and his few men in moments, leaving nothing between the horde of goblins and them. All three froze in their tracks but quickly spun around—they didn't want to just be another line in the sand as the wave crashed over it.

Baelath ran toward the other end of the village, where Evelyn was. She was herding villagers safely away from the danger, sending them southward toward the other refugees. Baelath watched, stunned, as home after home lit up in flames, and people were burned or slaughtered by these ferocious goblins, who seemed to smile and laugh whenever they struck someone down or ripped their claws down their victims' backs, whether man, woman, or child. Soon, the only shacks left were the ones on the edge of the village road, where the twins lived.

"Mother!" Jax cried out, and Baelath spun around and saw the twins' home erupt in dark-orange flames. Both of them took off running to the house, and the elves followed. Once they reached the house, they were instantly set upon, and Baelath tried to hold their ground to give the twins the time they needed. His sword clanged against weak metal, and most enemies' weapons were destroyed on impact with his sword, but there were still too many goblins, and both Evelyn and he were pushed back inside the burning house.

The twins frantically searched for their mother, running from room to room in the billowing smoke, but she was nowhere to be found. Now the flames were licking inside, and pieces of the roof and walls started to fall in. Baelath stood his ground at the door. Evelyn brushed beside him, but he knew it wouldn't be long before the goblins poured in the home.

"We need to make a break for it. We can't fight them all," Baelath said.

"We need to find our mother," Jax yelled, knocking another goblin off his arm.

"We'll find her out there, but we must look swiftly."

Jax led the way, and he ran at full power forward, his shield extended outward, and he bowled over three or four unsuspecting goblins. Baelath was next, and he flew out of the doorway, jumping over Jax's battering ram. He swung his sword down through one goblin and parried the sword of another. His hands became a blur as they struck through goblin flesh. His sword dripped with their ooze, but for every goblin he dropped, at least two more took its place. He saw that Evelyn was right by his side, beating back the small goblin party that was around him. Max was the last to leave the burning home, just barely escaping before the house collapsed. He raced out into the night, screaming to find his mother, while he shot arrows from his bow like bolts of lightning. The other three held their own for a nice amount of time against the incoming goblins, but again, they had no hope to last for more than a few more minutes, as wave after wave crashed into them.

"Jax!"

A cry went up in the night that froze all in their tracks. Jax spun around and saw his mother, clutching at her chest, the blood already seeping through her fingers. Two goblins had come upon her and were lashing her flesh with their sharp stone axes, slicing her open with every whack. Jax stood in absolute horror as his mother was killed in front of his eyes, but in the seconds that he froze, a dozen goblins grabbed at him and swarmed over him, bringing him to the ground. For a moment, Baelath watched as Jax was trampled, disappearing underneath a wave of enemies. But then, just as Baelath thought he was watching his friend die, a shield erupted from under the pile, and a few goblins were sent flying through the air. Jax forced his way to his feet, smashing or slicing all who stood before him. But the damage had been done.

Max came running over, shooting down the few goblins who remained fighting them, and he saw the horror that had happened. In absolute despair, he could only look at his mother's body, lying in an ever-growing pool of her own blood that shimmered in the light from the consuming fire that occupied the village. A hundred or more goblins ran through the streets, burning all that remained, which, at this point, wasn't much. All had fled or died, and all of the homes were on fire or destroyed. Nothing in the village would survive the night.

Evelyn grabbed Jax and pulled on him, trying to get him to come to his senses, while Baelath did the same to Max. It didn't take long before they were attacked again, and the twins fought with an anger that Baelath had not seen before. The group of goblins that had come upon them turned around and ran back to the main invading party, and Baelath used that moment to pull the twins back.

"We need to get out of here," Baelath said. "Going where the others are going will not help Jord. We need to flee to the north."

The twins nodded in agreement. There would be time to mourn later on, but they first needed to survive the night, and that would not be likely if they stuck around any longer. And like that, they slithered off into the darkness that danced along the edges of the firelight, heading up the hill to the north. Although Baelath and the rest tried to flee the smell of charred ashes and burning flesh that followed them like a stray dog, it lingered in their nostrils well into the night.

They traveled for a few hours, hoping to create as much distance between the goblins and them as they could, but traveling by foot in the dark was not an easy task. Many times, they were tripped by a hidden root or a hole in the ground; even the slope of the hill would throw them off. There were a couple of times when Baelath heard Jax tumble to the ground, cursing each time he clambered back to his feet. Finally, once the black of the night went away and was replaced by the dull gray of morning, they stopped for a while to rest and hopefully sleep.

None of them slept, though, as they all lay on their backs, staring into the ash-colored clouds. They could still see the smoke of last night's encounter rising into the sky. They could barely eat, as their nostrils were stained with the smell of burning flesh. The blood-soaked images still ran rampant in their heads. After a while, they set out again, heading north and traveling light and as quickly as they could, weaving through valleys and across small streams, climbing little ravines and hill ledges.

No one talked the entire day, with Jax charging ahead of the rest, anger and anguish in every step. Max followed slightly behind with a more somber walk, barely lifting his legs, head bowed to the ground. Baelath was behind them; he felt terrible for the twins but still was determined upon his course. It was sad for them, but Jord remained imprisoned, and he had to get him out. *It's the only thing that matters*, he thought. He knew they would have done the same if they were in his situation, if it was their family in chains. But it was exactly because of *his* situation that they had watched their village and their mother fall to the swarm of goblins. *If only the king had believed me and sent more men to defend.*

They stopped again around nightfall, mostly from pure exhaustion, as they had been traveling since the night before with few if any stops. And again, they sat in silence. The mood was a mournful one, with no one looking at each other. They all stared into the fire until only embers were left, and the dark began to swallow them whole. Finally, Baelath had enough of this situation.

"I am sorry for what happened last night. I wish the king had taken me more seriously about that threat, for this could have been avoided." His tone was somber but firm. *I need them in the right state of mind, not this dejected look they wear on their faces.*

Jax slowly raised his gaze from the ground. "Avoided? Avoided, you say?" His words were almost growled. "This all could have been avoided, had you not decided to return to Nox to ask for *His Majesty's* help in the first place. The goblins would have left our tiny village alone, and our mother would still be alive."

"We did all we could," said Evelyn, her voice breaking. "None of us wanted that, and we were trying to help you."

"How were you helping us? You led an army of goblins to our doorstep!" yelled Jax, now standing over the fire. Max jumped up to try to calm him, but Jax just shrugged him off. "Also, did I mention you've gotten us arrested not once but twice? One where they tried to pin a murder on us!"

"And if it wasn't for me, you would have been blamed and be rotting in some dark cell by yourself!" Baelath yelled back at him, jumping to his feet in a fury. He could feel the blood pumping through him and his anger rising within. Without thinking, his hand grasped his sword that still swung on his hip, and he unsheathed it just enough so everyone heard the sound of it.

"Enough!" screamed Max. *"This* is where we are now, and *this* is the path that is set before us." He stood between the two of them, shoulders squared and chest puffed out. He looked comical, standing in between the

Jax's buffed body and Baelath's tall frame. "We made our choice, brother, back at the tavern, when you interjected us into their lives. Those decisions you made in those moments entwined us to them until the end. We're a part of this now, in victory or defeat. The safe return of their friend or a sword shoved through our backs—we are with them. We may have lost our family, but we have gained friends. And sometimes, friendships mean more than family; sometimes, friends are all we have."

Silence crept between the four companions, as each one pondered their thoughts. The moon shone brightly this night, and the land was filled with its white light. Baelath could see the outer edges of the woods on the opposite side of the valley. He could see the shimmer from a stream that trickled from the woods and meandered down the hills.

Where are we, and where is Jord? Baelath wondered. He couldn't help but pull out his map and look at the tiny dot in the middle of the Dark Woods labeled "Jord." *If that's where he is, then that's where we'll go.*

"Here, let us rest now," Max said, lying down on the ground. "Tomorrow, we will find the road."

"Road?" asked Baelath. "What road? You said there's nothing but hills out here."

"It's a hidden road, one that was used many years ago but now is almost gone, disappearing under the weight of time and nature," Max said, with a little mystery in his voice. "But I will tell you all about it tomorrow—if we find it." And he turned over and went to sleep before Baelath could offer a rebuttal.

Baelath couldn't sleep, though. Last night's events still rumbled around in his head. He listened to Jax snoring deeply and Max breathing in the off-beats of his brother's snores. Evelyn barely made a sound, but he could detect her exhales. They were so soft that he first thought the wind was playing tricks on him, but when he listened hard enough, he knew it was her, maybe he always knew. Soon, his eyes began to grow heavy, and he found himself drifting off.

He dreamed of a golden tree standing in the middle of an open area. A shadowy palace loomed in the background, and five figures strolled forward from the smoke and huddled around it. The tree began to morph into a sixth figure, taller than the others. The ones that huddled around now started to drift away, while the larger one came toward him, its hands outstretched, and he soon started to feel cold. Within that moment, though, a fiery figure rushed up beside him, and he could feel the warmth return inside, a weird hint of pride bubbling beneath his surface.

But a bright flash blinded him for a few moments, and when his vision returned, the cold set back in, and the fiery figure was gone. He looked around and saw the others were walking away, all but one with their backs turned. It was just him, all alone now, and he didn't know if he was ready to accept that. Confused and scared, Baelath began to back away, but then the world around him disappeared, and the ground crumbled under his feet. He tried to run away, but it was in vain, and soon, he found himself falling into a hole where he had been standing, falling deeper and deeper until all light escaped him and blackness overtook him. He closed his eyes, waiting for the impact of the ground to come, but it never did. He soon found the feeling of falling left him completely, so he opened his eyes.

He was standing on top of a red mountain ridge, looking down across a valley; the land was covered in white. Off in the distance, a tower rose from the land—nothing spectacular about its appearance, but he could feel the menace within it. Terror gripped him as he began to descend the mountain. He found himself at the base of the tower in the next moment, looking up to all it offered, and he only felt dread now, like he knew that by being here, something terrible was going to happen. The only choice, however, was to enter. He went to the doorway and threw it open with a bang and looked inside. Nothing but a void stared back at him, so he stepped inside with trepidation. He was greeted by high-pitched laughter, and he saw a powdered white hand reach out to him from the darkness. He went to grab it or defend himself from it—he did not know—and the moment he felt his hand touch the enormous reaching white hand, a flash of white light filled the room, and he saw the evil that dwelled in this place. It made Baelath want to claw his eyes out; it made him want to be hung from a tree limb. Everything horrible that Baelath could imagine flooded his mind, and it was enough to almost drive him mad, but it was over in that instant.

He woke to find Evelyn shaking his arm; her emerald eyes looked worried. The brothers were standing a few feet back, looking on with curiosity. It was morning now, but a grayness had overtaken the land.

The sun was hiding behind the thick, dark clouds that hung overhead. He could feel the chill of the air with the wind whipping all around them.

"You were screaming and holding your hands over your ears," Evelyn said to him, concern still etched across her face. "I was worried."

"Just a bad dream is all. Nothing to be concerned with," he said, grabbing her hand to help pull himself to his feet.

"I didn't know elves had nightmares," Jax said. "It's like every preconceived notion we had of elves ends up being wrong. So far."

"Come, let us head out, now that we're all awake," Max said, looking out toward the north. "I'd like to be on the road by nightfall."

They quickly packed up their camp, doused the embers, rolled up their sheets, and headed down the hill, bearing north. A slight drizzle had begun, glazing everything around. The twins' mood seemed a lot better than what it had been over the past few nights. Jax was already back to his smiling ways, and his charm crept back into the conversations. Max was leading them, diving headfirst into their expedition, and he too seemed slightly less on edge than before. Baelath even caught a glimpse of a smile from him when Jax told a joke.

Baelath still had questions about this supposed road that lay somewhere out in the middle of the hills, and he figured he could ask them, now that the tension and anger had dwindled. He hurried to approach Max. "So, what is this road we seek?"

"It's called the Lost Road," Max said, eyes still glued forward. "It was the road that the Old Kingdom used for travel. It connected everything and everyone back in the olden days, and every creature used it, or so it is said. I'm not sure exactly what happened, but the kingdom fell, and man was driven out from his lands. Over time, after new settlements arose and turned into the cities that we know today, the road was rendered useless and all but forgotten. Soon, without travelers using it daily, nature crept in and took over. If you look close enough—and know *where* to look, of course—you'll find the outlines of where it once was. We can use it to cross over the Zoe without going through any cities. After our last encounter, I too would not trust any city."

"How far does it go?" asked Baelath, amazed by this information. He wondered how he had not heard of this until now. *What else wasn't I told?* he thought.

"I'm not sure," said Max. "I've only been west to the haunted hill and east to your forest."

"You've been to Blaonir?" Baelath asked in amazement.

"Just the edge, to the end of the road. Then I turned back, for the feeling I had when I was there shook me to the bone." Max's voice trailed off, as if his memory had returned him there for the moment.

The companions continued their travels in the gray morning. Every once in a while, the sun would sneak through the clouds and bask them in light and reflect off the mist-covered land, though seconds later, it would disappear again behind the clouds, and the travelers would be covered in a dull gray once more.

Morning soon turned to midday, yet not much changed around them. Hours passed by, some in silence and some listening to Jax tell stories of old. He told them of Prince Xidor and how he had built and ruled an ancient city—he had fought hundreds of goblins, always by himself and always surrounded.

But it was Jax's last story that grabbed Baelath's attention.

"Xidor was the greatest who ever lived. He was the best fighter, the best hunter, the best rider, the best talker. I heard he even tamed a dragon."

"A dragon?" both Evelyn and Baelath said, jaws dropping.

"That's right, a dragon, the only one to ever do so," Jax said.

"I thought they were just in stories and didn't really exist," Baelath said, almost not believing himself when he said it. *There really must be a lot I haven't been told.*

"That might be true, or it might not be. But you don't get the title of *Dragonlord* by taming horses, do you? No, you don't. You get called Dragonlord by taming a dragon," said Jax, laughing at his own joke. "Now, what happened, no one truly knows. Some say he flew off to faraway lands when the kingdom fell; some say he fell in battle; some say the dragon eventually turned on him, and he was devoured. Whichever the case may be, he was never seen again in these parts, nor have any dragons been spotted since those days."

"But the road is," interjected Max, pointing down below to the bottom of the hill they stood upon.

At first, Baelath noticed nothing different about the valley floor, just more tangled and overgrown grass that sprang up over the vines, which choked the land underneath. But then he saw it—a small path that twisted and turned along the base of the hill, with patches of rocks outlining parts of the trail. As they followed Max down the hill, the rain began picking up from the soft drizzle they had experienced all morning, and now it started pouring down on them, soaking them to their bones very quickly.

"There's some shelter on the road, only a few leagues or so ahead. We can stay there for the night and wait out the rain, hopefully." Max had to nearly scream at them to be heard over the sound of the pounding rain.

They began to hurry, almost running now. Max was out in front, followed closely by Evelyn; she moved faster than all of them and would have led the way if she had known the path. Baelath trailed her, trying to keep the rain out of his face but failing unequivocally. Jax was last in their travel line, trying to lug his great sword along his hip and the shield across his back. The gray light slowly turned darker as night began creeping in, yet the rain continued to pour harder than ever, turning the dirt to mud and slowing their progress to a difficult walk.

"Over here!" yelled Max, shivering, and he darted off to the side and disappeared behind a wall of trees.

They followed him behind the trees that stood on the side at the bottom of the hill, and to their shock, a hole opened on the side of the hill—a small cave that looked to be carved out. It wasn't too roomy with the four of them inside it, but it was enough to get out of the rain and build a small fire, though it did take longer to get it going because the wood got wet in the storm. After a few tries, Jax got it going, and the fire gave off a warmth that relaxed them all for a bit. The four of them laughed and joked, told stories of their youth, and talked of the hope of tomorrow.

Outside, the world was black and cold, with thunder and lightning cascading across the night sky, but inside their little cave, it was bright and warm, and the four of them were able to sleep soundly, strangely enough.

The morning greeted them with more rain and a looming fog that hovered in their faces. Dark clouds still hung overhead, bearing down on them with an anger that Baelath had never seen the sky possess. They huddled in their cloaks, trying their hardest to keep the rain and wind out, and set themselves upon the path, with Max still leading the way.

Around midday, the rain finally broke, the clouds rolled away toward the east, and now the sun was able to shine down, making the soaked land sparkle beneath their feet. The road twisted and turned between the looming hills, which seemed to have grown larger and with much more foliage than before, as if man had not come this far yet. Baelath could see the wildlife returning from their holes and hideouts, now that the rain had stopped. Little creatures ran up and down the trees, and birds flew overhead in the bright blue sky.

Max told them that they would be traveling along this road for a few days, and at some point, it would take them to the Zoe River. But after crossing the river, they should only be a day out of the Dark Woods, where Jord was being held.

If the map is correct, Baelath thought grimly. Using this opportunity of good weather, he pulled out his map and looked at it again, just to be sure. Nothing had changed, of course—just a black dot in the middle of the dark elf fortress labeled Jord. *But what does it mean?* Why could he see where Jord was, yet nothing else was visible on it? The lands were labeled. The Greenhills and Blaonir Forest had markings, and Nox was labeled as well; the wetlands south of the forest were there, as well as the Golden Plains to the west. Mountains were sketched out too, with the Eastern Mountains right above them and three others to the west. One was in the north, another was in the middle, and the third was toward the southern parts of the land. Rivers snaked across the map, with the Zoe running from the eastern portion of the Northwest Mountains, running diagonally southeast, until it reached the eastern shores and passed through the southern part of the Blaonir Forest, but there were many others than Baelath had never seen or heard of before—the Ner River and the Bios River, to name just two.

After stopping for an hour to eat and rest, they set out again, this time with a more cheerful feeling than the day before, now that the rain had stopped, and the sun smiled down on them. Max had told them while they ate that by tonight, they would reach the farthest west he ever had traveled, to the hill that none would walk upon, and that tomorrow, they would be in unknown territory to them all.

"Why will no one walk upon the hill?" asked Evelyn, once they were walking again.

"There's an old story that some hill is haunted, and spirits of the dead wander there. I have seen the hill but never traveled to it," Max replied, still looking ahead.

"Then how do you know if it's haunted?" asked Baelath. "If you've never been there, how could you possibly know?"

"I know people who have been there, and they are never the same again. They are more distant to those around them than they were before they went up that hill. Something about that hill changes you, and we have to walk right next to it," Max said, not amused by Baelath's attitude. "I have no clue if the stories are true, but I intend *not* to find out."

The sun was beginning to sink, and the shadows were growing larger, but finally, after the road climbed up a small, rounded hill, they spotted a larger hill in the distance, rising up in the middle of an open valley, like a pimple on a smooth cheek. The hill was surrounded by a looming fog, almost like part of the hill itself, and it didn't spill out into the land at all, leaving the meadows around it with a barren feel.

"There she is," said Max, looking out toward it. "We need to get around it as quickly as possible. I don't want to spend any more time near it than we have to."

And so they set out toward this supposedly haunted hill, following the road as it stretched toward the northern side of it. Nature had almost completely taken over their path now, and their feet constantly became tangled in weeds and brush. Still, they pushed on, coming around the eastern side of the hill. By the time they finally reached the northern side of it, the sun, unfortunately, had dipped low to the horizon, making traveling farther almost an impossible task, and so, much to Max's dismay, they began searching for a place to camp for the night. They watched as the sun finally set behind the hills and darkness impeded their sight.

"Here should be good enough for the night," said Max, setting his gear down and perching himself against a tree. "We'll head out around dawn tomorrow—get an early start and away from this place."

"I agree," said Evelyn, looking around cautiously. "I feel uneasy."

As soon as her words left her mouth, a loud sound exploded from the tree above them, and Baelath felt his heart skip a few beats. Luckily, it was just an owl hooting at them but not angrily, as Baelath would have expected it to do, with four creatures invading its home. It felt more like a warning of some sort, but the owl did not stay long; it dropped from its perch and flew off into the damp night.

They built a small fire and cooked a stew with a few pieces of bread and cheese, just enough to satisfy their hunger, though barely. The four companions sat around the fire, talking and joking, until the moon, just a sliver of a crescent, hung directly above them. That's when Max said they should try to get some sleep. Tomorrow, he wanted to cover the rest of the road and maybe even reach the river the day after that.

Baelath lay on his back, gazing at the stars that shone above. His mind drifted from thought to thought, reliving the past few days over and over again. *Have I made a mistake? I know it's the right thing to do, but is it the right way?* He couldn't help but continuously ask those questions in his mind. It was then, in the dead silence of the night, that Baelath heard a soft chattering in the distance. He sat straight up and perked his pointed ears, trying to gather as much of the sound as he could. It was growing louder now, and he could hear the snapping of breaking twigs and the crunch of weeds.

Evelyn must have heard it too; she sat up, looking at Baelath, a quick look of fear across her face in the fading light of the embers. They climbed to their feet and gathered their weapons—Evelyn with her short sword, and Baelath with his blade.

They woke the twins, trying to make the least amount of noise as they could, which proved almost impossible with Jax. By the time they sat up listening, the sounds were almost upon them, coming up from the path they had been traveling only hours ago. Max readied his bow, and Jax raised his shield in front of him, his sword hiding behind it, ready to strike.

Baelath could now make out the sounds—they sounded of goblin voices, three of them, unless he was mistaken. Memories of the night when hundreds of goblins flooded the twins' village and burned everything rushed back through him, and for a moment, he was shaken by fear. Then he realized that these three goblins stood no chance against the four of them, especially since the goblins were—at least to Baelath's knowledge—walking unaware into their hastily thrown-together trap. They were close now. *They have to be just around the edge of the hill*, Baelath thought. And in a few moments, the goblins would have a taste of their own medicine.

Then, as if it had been sucked out of the world, all sound stopped, and nothing moved, not even the tree branches that had been swaying in the breeze. An eerie silence surrounded them. Only the sound of his pounding heartbeat, ringing in Baelath's ears, comforted him. Moments passed, and no one dared to move or breathe, and they could not make out or hear any movement toward them. *Maybe they turned around or headed off in a different direction. Maybe they too were stopping for the night, just on the other side of our area. Maybe nothing will happen on this night,* Baelath thought, though even in his own head, a voice laughed at him from deep in his mind.

Just as Baelath finished his thought, three goblins came stumbling into view, walking in single file, directly toward them. Even in the darkness, Baelath could see that they were misconfigured from where he stood. Their faces, each a different shape in the shadows of the night, were more grotesque than what he remembered. Boils covered the majority of them, and different sections of their bodies were oozing a thick, bright-yellow liquid that could easily be seen in the dead of night. The stench became unbearable, the closer they got, and they were closing the gap quickly now, maybe twenty yards away but still rumbling forward, still right toward them.

Baelath was wondering how long he and the others should stay there before attacking and if the goblins would even see them before their attack, when he felt a whoosh of air against the side of his face, followed by the sound of a plucked string. A second later, the goblin out front keeled over, dead, with an arrow sticking out the top of its head. For a moment, no one did anything; everyone was paralyzed in shock. Then, like a flash of lightning streaking across the sky, Jax sprang forward with his sword held high, slashing the second goblin, who was still frozen in fear. The third goblin finally gathered his wits and took off running into the woods that grew on the hill. Baelath gave chase, quickly catching up to the slow-moving goblin. Max ran off after them, running a few steps behind Baelath, trying to nock another arrow. He was fifteen paces behind the goblin, now ten, then five. The goblin was just out of reach to Baelath. It had stopped halfway up the hill, turned, and swung its hammer, but all Baelath saw was a flash of rusted silver as it whipped into view—and Baelath's world turned black.

Baelath opened his eyes and was greeted by a gray morning. Another chill was in the air, and the sound of the wind whipped all around him. *Am I just outside the Misty Valley? Was everything just a weird dream?* He sat up, rubbing the front of his forehead, and saw that the goblin he had chased was tied to a tree. He realized he was on top of the hill now, not at their camp at the bottom, back near the road. Sitting up, he spotted the twins huddled by a fire, fumbling with a long piece of rope, apparently trying to get it knotted. Evelyn was on the other side of the clearing, walking gracefully along the side of the woods.

The twins saw that he was awake and walked over to him. Max had a cut along his face and dried blood covering his neck and staining parts of his black cloak.

"You finally awake there, Baelath?" Jax boomed across to him, slightly laughing. "Got clocked good there, didn't you?"

"Is that what happened?" asked Baelath. "I barely remember."

"After we killed the first two, you took off running at that creature over there," Jax said, his voice showing disgust when he mentioned the goblin. "You were close to getting him when he turned and whacked his hammer upside your head, and you dropped straight to the ground. Max thought you were dead, and he too tried to get the filthy creature, and you can see how that ended." Jax pointed at Max's cut face and laughed again. "He again tried to run, but by then, I had caught up, as slow as I am. Stupid thing thought it could take me on, one to one. It ended quickly, and I was about to kill it when Evelyn stopped me. She said we should take it captive. Like a *prisoner.* Like we once were, just a few days ago. So here we are, our guide knocked out and my brother's face slashed open, and a nice *goblin prisoner.* She said we should wait for you to wake and decide then, though I don't see why. Now that you are awake, and we've told you what happened, what do *you* decide?"

Baelath's head was spinning. He looked over at the goblin twisting in his knots. Evelyn was still on the other side of the clearing but beginning to walk back toward them, her head still hung low. He stood up and had started to head her way when the goblin hissed at him.

"Kill me now, and be done with it, *elf,*" he growled at Baelath. "I refuse to be captured by your kind."

"Shut your mouth," Jax said, giving it a quick kick across its face. "You'll do what we tell you to do."

"You would give up your life, rather than live with hope, however distant it may be?" Baelath asked, walking over to the goblin. "No second chance? No praying for an escape or, by some chance, a release?"

"I would rather die than live under an *elf's* rule, and if I had killed you last night, I would die in honor, for ending an elf's life is the greatest hope our kind can have," the goblin growled, hissing between each breath, its eyes filled with unyielding rage.

"What is your name?" asked Baelath.

It answered by spitting blood at Baelath's feet. "I will never give you my name, for you are below me. I will go to my death with my honor intact." A sly smile stretched across the goblin's twisted face.

"Let's kill it and be done with it," growled Jax, growing angry with the lack of a decision.

"No," Baelath said. "There's no reason for him to die."

"Excuse me?" Jax said, spinning around to face Baelath. "Was *your* mother slaughtered by goblins?"

"She was," said Baelath. "After I was born, goblins invaded our land again, and she went to fight alongside my father, our king. She never came back—that's all I was told. So yes, I know your pain, but this one didn't do it, and killing him won't bring anyone back."

"But it will put a smile across my face to see it dead, and I intend to have that happen," Jax spat at him, raising his sword slightly.

"He will go free. We cannot not take him with us, and we aren't going to kill just to kill," Baelath calmly said.

"Says the one who kills old men in taverns—or do your rules not apply to you?" Jax said, almost yelling now.

"I have no rules. We are all free to make our own choices," Baelath said. He walked over to the creature, intending to untie him, but before he could reach him, Max raised his bow and pointed an arrow directly at him.

"I'm sorry, but I don't agree. He dies today. He dies now," Max said, holding his aim.

Evelyn had finally made her way back to them and was confused by the situation. Her face showed both shock and anger, like she couldn't believe what she was seeing. "What's happening?" she asked, her hand hovering over her sword that rested in its scabbard.

"We're ending a life," said Baelath. He dropped his head and walked away from the twins, with Max still pointing his bow at him. "Do what you must, but I will not be a part of it. Come, Evelyn, let's leave them to their horror."

Evelyn and Baelath walked back over to where they had made camp last night, after the events that had caused Baelath to lose consciousness. They began gathering their gear.

The twins took the rope they had been knotting and wrapped it around the goblin's neck. They released him from the tree but kept him bound by his hands and feet and dragged him to a low-hanging but sturdy branch. Throwing the rope over the branch, Jax grabbed the other end, and, with a good heave, lifted the goblin off the ground. It garbled and squirmed in the air, trying to get air into its chest, but the more it struggled, the harder Jax pulled. The goblin's eyes bulged from its sockets, and blood ran out from them, leaving tears of red streaming down its cheeks. Its twisted face became less horrific and more scared as it felt life slowly drain away.

Baelath couldn't tell if it was spit or yellow ooze, but whatever it was it came dripping from its mouth as it finally stopped moving—just a small twitch here and there. The eyes were fully rolled into the back of its head. After one more good tug from Jax, and the goblin just bounced in midair like some sort of rag doll, he dropped the rope, and the goblin crashed to the ground, sprawling in a pool of its own blood and ooze. When the twins walked back over, Jax had a smile on his face, but Max looked like he figured out that the price paid wasn't worth it.

"Lead the way," Baelath said to Max, holding his arm out to beckon him forward.

"Just follow the path until we reach the river," Max said, but still, he took the lead, with his brother behind him.

Evelyn looked over at Baelath with a mix of sadness and hope; then she too set out down the hill back to the road. Baelath looked back toward the dead goblin one more time, and pity somewhat overtook him. He tried to push it out of mind and followed his companions down the hill. When they reached the bottom, an eerie thought crept into Baelath's mind. He realized they had spent the night up on top of the haunted hill of the

Greenlands, the one place they didn't want to go, and they all had come out changed from who they had been, for better or for worse.

They traveled in silence, with Baelath listening to the sounds of the land—the rush of water flowing off the hills in small streams; the chirps of small critters, scurrying across their path and into the woods that enveloped their travels. The sun rose higher in the sky, but it hid behind a wall of clouds. Gray and heavy, the thick clouds loomed above them, like a bird hovering over a tiny worm that poked its head out from the ground. Soon enough, the gray turned black, and rain pelted them again, with a more ferocious anger than yesterday.

Baelath couldn't see past his outstretched arms, and when he tried, the rain would splatter across his face until it was unbearable to continue looking forward. Still, the four of them pressed on, their eyes looking down toward the road, which had turned to mud. The rain poured on into the night, and the four of them could find no shelter from it. Resting just made them feel worse, so they continued on their path, trying to feel it out in the dead of night. Many times, someone would slip on the wet ground or run into a tree, but after more than half the night gone by, and after what felt like little—if any—progress, the darkness receded and a light gray washed into the sky.

The rain did not stop, though, and Baelath soon lost track of time. *Is it morning still, or is it closer to night now?* There was no way of telling; the rain was unrelenting, and Baelath became worried that the rain might defeat them and wash them away or eventually flood the valleys and drown them all. Maybe they would just walk forever, lost in the hills on a road that went nowhere, blinded by a pounding rain.

Wouldn't that just be fitting? he reflected. He thought he was doing the right thing by trying to rescue Jord. He thought this was what heroes did—that they saved the ones they cared about. But each step grew harder than the last, and if the terrain and weather didn't kill them all, then surely something unseen, something unknown to Baelath, certainly would spell the end of him or his friends. *Or Evelyn*—that last thought struck him like a hit from a mountain ram's horn. Losing her, or anyone, because of him and his foolish mission would be a blow that he couldn't see how to recover from. *I didn't ask any of them to follow me; they just did.*

Night rolled in again, with rain still falling, but this time, Max was able to find shelter in another small cave carved in the side of a small hill. They built a fire, just small enough to cook another pot of stew, and got some much-needed rest.

Dawn hadn't come yet, and the night still lingered outside, but Baelath decided to get up and climb to the top of a hill, just to see how far they had come or how far they had yet to go. The rain had finally passed, though its effects lingered everywhere. It was impossible to walk without stepping through puddles, and where there wasn't a puddle, it was a slippery step on the grass. But finally, Baelath made it to the top, just as the sun peeked over the horizon—and that's when he saw it in the distance. An abandoned city in ruins was surrounded by a mist, and the clouds hung low over it, cloaking it in a deep white fog. Still, Baelath could make out the outlines of great stone structures poking out from the haze, rising in the air. Chunks were missing from it, yet it looked like a city that man had made, one of stone and brick rather than of wood. *Have we come so far south in the rain that we have stumbled upon one of the five great cities of men?* Rushing back down, he woke the rest of them and brought them to the top of the hill to see for themselves.

"That is not one of the five," Max happily said when he reached the top. "Those are the ruins of the great kingdom that ruled the land before the fall. Of course, I should have known." He slapped himself on the forehead. "It makes perfect sense now."

"What does? What do you mean?" asked Evelyn, her fingers fumbling with her hair.

"The road! It was built a long time ago—this, I knew—but I can't believe I didn't figure it out before." Excitement crept into Max's voice.

"What are you saying?" asked Baelath, relatively confused by Max's excitement.

"The road was built *from* the city, connecting the forest to the city, then the city to the river, and we are in the middle, at the ruins. If we want to reach the crossing, we're going through these ruins,"

"Well, let's go, then. With every day that passes, time grows more urgent to us." Baelath started down the hill toward the ruins. *I don't think they understand my urgency. They will, though, soon enough, even if I'm the one to shake it into them. Jord's life may depend on it.*

It only took about an hour to reach the outer edges of the ruins; with every step closer they took, the stone structures grew larger. They pressed on into the fog, letting it wash over and blind them. Baelath could barely see his friends when they entered. Instinctively, he grabbed hold of Evelyn's hand, squeezing it as if he was afraid that the slightest loosening would tear them apart forever. When he saw what he had done, he quickly let go.

Just then, a devastating roar erupted over them, shaking the ground and vibrating the loose rocks on the stone structures that jutted from the fog, causing them to pour down like ice breaking in a thaw. When the dust settled and the echo silenced, Baelath saw his hand was wrapped around Evelyn's again.

CHAPTER 6

SILENCE FOLLOWED, AS if all sound had been blown out like a candle from the devastating roar. No birds chirped; no critters scuffled along the hillsides. The four of them sat frozen in uncertainty and fear, but with no other choice—the ruins were too large to circle around, and Max was unsure if they could find the road again if they left it—they continued, the fog still consuming their sight. Baelath hoped it would lift soon so they could figure out how to get through the ruins with as little delay as possible, but his hopes had fallen short this past week.

The fog did not let up, but soon, Baelath could see the outlines of large, half-collapsed stone structures surrounding him. He felt the path go from grass and dirt to a paved stone beneath his feet, and then from the flat stone to chunks of rock, both small and large. Boulders blocked their path from time to time, and when that happened, one of them would scurry up to the top and survey the land, hoping to get a glimpse ahead or to make sure nothing was following them. They frequently turned back and found another route when one road led to a dead end, all of them following Max's lead. With all the twists and turns and the doubling back that they had to do, Baelath soon found himself lost. He wasn't sure he could find his way out of the ruins.

They wandered around in the fog, and time seemed to stand still and speed up in the same moment. Baelath lost count of the steps they'd taken, and all the turns they'd made would have made anyone dizzy. Finally, they came to an area where the fog seemed to be lifting, and eventually cleared away as they progressed deeper. The sun beamed down on them from directly above, and they all felt the midday heat wash over them, almost as if a wall of fire had scorched the land, as they exited the fog, with dew still dripping off them. And now, with his vision clear for the first time since they entered the ruins, Baelath could see everything around him.

A thick layer of dust covered the ruins, and crumpling structures were packed in around them. Large and small, narrow and wide, each falling building looked different from the last. Stones were piled at their bases, and random junk littered the rubble—broken chairs and table legs, picture frames, and trinkets stuck out from the rocks, and Baelath wondered how long it had been there, untouched by anyone and forgotten by the world.

"Where to now?" Jax asked his brother, his own eyes searching wildly.

"A river runs through the middle of the city. When we cross that, we will be heading toward the western side, and if I'm not mistaken, another road should pick up there, and we can follow it to the crossing," Max replied.

"We're not even halfway into here?" cried Baelath. "How big is this place?"

"The kingdom was the largest ever built. To this day, none has eclipsed its size," answered Max, almost proudly, as if he were a part of this vast wasteland.

"If this was a kingdom at one time, how did it become this?" Evelyn asked in awe, amazed by the ruins around her.

"No one knows exactly, for most perished here, and those who survived are long dead," Max said. "Many tales have been told of what happened here, though the story changes every time you hear it. Some say a great battle was fought to the north of the city; some say a terrible storm ended its reign. I heard one story that was truly terrifying, though it seems the least possible explanation. To me, the storm seems the most reasonable reason for what happened here."

"And what is the story you heard?" Baelath asked.

"I've only heard one person tell it," Max said. He stopped in his tracks, as if trying to remember something he never thought he'd have to remember again. "I met an interesting old man while wandering the hills a couple years ago. He leaned on his staff as he talked to me all day and night, telling me everything about these ancient ruins that he knew, and it was a lot because his story started from the first stone that was set until the day it became devoid of life. He told me of a sorceress who came from the dark and how—"

A raging roar interrupted Max before he could say anything more, this one louder and more intense than the one before. They seemed to be getting closer to it—or it was getting closer to them. Baelath did not know which one. The ground shook beneath them, and the piles of rubble began to shift, covering and uncovering more lost items. Then Baelath heard the loud cracks of stone splintering from above. He looked up, almost not believing what he saw. Large pieces of the buildings were breaking off and falling all around. Stone crashed into stone, and more pieces tumbled down toward them.

The four of them scrambled away as quickly as possible, like bees from a knocked-down beehive, each in their own direction, trying to get out of the way of the rocks falling like rain upon them. Shards of colliding rock fell down like hail on Baelath, leaving him in a bloody mess from dozens of cuts, but he managed to escape the larger boulders that smashed to the ground, encasing him in a cloud of dust. Baelath leaned heavily against a wall, choking on the dirty air, waiting for it to clear. He heard Evelyn coughing ahead of him, and he began feeling his way toward her. As the dust began to settle and his vision cleared, he found her huddled in a doorway along one of the nearly fallen buildings.

"Are you OK?"

"Yeah, just a few cuts," she said as she brushed off the debris. "Although not nearly as bad as you. Are *you* OK?" She looked worried as she eyed the multiple cuts on his body.

"I'm fine; don't worry about me," he said hastily. "What is that, though? What's making that sound?" He turned to look back at the damage that had been done.

"I have no clue who or what is making those sounds, but regardless, we need to leave this place. Did you see where the twins went?" Evelyn asked, now rising to her feet.

"No, but they can't be that far off," replied Baelath, peering toward the other side of the newly formed rock pile. "Come, let's see if we can find a way over to them."

It proved difficult to make their way through the rocks, like trying to dig through a wall, one stone at a time, and soon, they decided to head in the direction they had been heading before they were split up by the storm of rocks. Maybe they would find the twins there, waiting for them to catch up, but Baelath couldn't help but wonder if that was the last time they would see their friends.

They figured they could go back to check on the other side of the debris pile, but they found themselves blocked off from going forward toward the twins. It looked as if a building had fallen over on its side, and now, just a wall of rocks remained. They turned left—that was the only option they had, other than turning back—and again, they found themselves in a maze with walls of rock running between woven paths of the remnants of a city long since forgotten. Left and right turns, dead ends and forks in the path—endless choices in an endless maze. The sun had begun to sink dangerously close to the horizon, and they were no closer to finding the twins, let alone reaching the other side of the city.

"Here," said Evelyn, stopping against the rock wall. "This wall looks small enough to climb over. Hopefully, we'll be able to see where we are, or better yet, see Max or Jax."

Baelath quickly scaled the side of the wall, not caring about the scrapes he gave himself in his hurry, and pulled himself up onto its ledge. The sun hung even lower now, casting long shadows. Baelath mostly saw what he had expected to see—endless rows going up and down, left and right, some blocked by the fallen rock and some open, all of it looking like a dried-up river delta. But he did notice something strange off to the left. Tall outlier buildings stood in a square, almost like they were guarding something, but what was weird about it was that the buildings had gigantic holes in parts of them, like someone, or something, had carved out rigged circles.

Baelath wanted to see what those buildings surrounded; he wanted to see the secret they kept. He and Evelyn started walking and climbing along the top of the rock wall, slowly twisting and turning his way toward the buildings. He was about halfway there when his questions were answered. Another roar went out, and almost shook Evelyn and him off the top of the wall. They both steadied themselves on their hands and knees. Baelath could feel its foundation shaking, and they watched as pieces of far-off buildings rained a rock shower in its wake. Baelath wondered if the twins were underneath any of those rocks or if they were somewhere safe—or if they had been crushed under the first pile of rubble, and all this was frivolous. He never intended for all of this to happen to them.

And then Baelath watched in utter disbelief as a large boulder erupted from one of the tall buildings to which he was headed, creating another hole just like the others. The boulder was flung high into the sky, only to come back crashing into other buildings, which created more showers of death from above. Following that, with Baelath still in shock and lying stomach down on the top of the shifting wall, he heard a voice. It was a deep and booming voice, yelling from within the square. *Jax*, he thought. *Jax is over there!* He looked back at Evelyn and could tell she thought the same thing. Scurrying back to their feet, they set off on a dead run, heading toward the large buildings, heading toward the place from which a boulder had been thrown.

They ran along the rock wall and had jumped onto another when it buckled beneath their feet. It felt like forever to Baelath, trapped in his own thoughts, but he knew that it wouldn't be too long before they got there. Sure enough, he soon was running between two of the large buildings, inside their shadows, feeling like a fly in a spider's web. Once upon them, Baelath saw just how large these buildings were, and he had no words to describe them. He stopped for a moment, in awe, before continuing on.

He and Evelyn finally reached an end to the rock wall they'd been running on and saw that an old courtyard sat surrounded out of view, with a river running in the middle of it. But that was not what caught their eyes.

An creature unknown to Baelath stood along the patches of dead grass and weeds; it stood nearly ten feet tall and was nearly three feet wide. Two horns bulged from its scarred head, curving upward toward the sky. It had a snout or some other type of nose, and the eyes glowed red. Black fur covered its face, neck, and hands, but the rest of its body, from what Baelath could see, wasn't fur-covered. Although mostly covered by armor, it looked to be regular flesh underneath, maybe a little thicker than most. The armor looked worn out, barely held together. It had the appearance of having looked spectacular at one point, but now the hinges were broken and held with rope. Rust crept up from all sides, leaving the middle sparkled in dust that shone in the dim light of the sun that peeked its way through into the square. Dents littered the chest plate; it seemed almost ready to cave in on itself, if it hadn't once already. Baelath assumed its boots had armor on them as well at one point, but now, just leather remained, and that too seemed to be falling apart.

Baelath could see loose-hanging chains that seemed to be infused with the creature's skin, draped across its arms and legs. In its hands, it gripped a rusty and dirty battle ax that looked to be the size of a small man or an elf. And every breath it took released sparks, and tiny flames shot from its snout. Most incredible of all was that on the opposite side of the courtyard stood a tiny, stout man. His hair was cut into a mohawk, as orange as flames in a campfire. His face and body were tattooed everywhere, and a large beard hung below his chin, blazing in the same color as the mohawk. His hands held a battle ax roughly the same size as his opponent, which was almost twice the size of this man.

For a second, the world stood still. Nothing moved, the breeze died, and everything fell silent, waiting for the moment to happen.

Then the half-sized, elderly, orange-mohawk-haired man boomed to his opponent, "My name is Grul, and I've come to kill you. How do you answer?"

The creature answered with a flaming snort.

The little man flexed his muscles, ready to charge forward. "Prepare to die!"

And with that, they charged forward, each raising their axes behind their shoulders.

With a mighty crash, the two combatants collided in a shower of sparks, their axes meeting each other in the middle, giving off an electrical ring. With another swing of the axes, they walloped each other with such force that both ended up stumbling backward a step or two. The creature took a side swing toward the short man, but it was like the man knew it was coming, as he rolled forward, underneath the swing, and popped back to his feet, sidestepping a hard down swing from his opponent and quickly throwing a jab of his own that was poorly blocked. Movement to movement, it was like watching a dance. The diminutive man seemed to know everything that was about to happen and continued to be a step ahead of the creature, throwing tiny jabs when opportunity allowed.

Soon, the creature was left reeling and growing angrier with every tiny jab; it threw ill-timed swings and half-heartedly blocked incoming strikes. Finally, the creature roared again. Flames poured from its snout and mouth, cascading a fire barrier in front of it that proved enough to stop the advancement of the crazy-looking man. The creature turned around, ran to a boulder that had fallen from its roar, and heaved it toward the man, who dived out of the way. Baelath felt pieces of debris as the boulder flew by, and that left him reeling on the ground. The creature picked up another one—a heavier one this time—and was getting ready to flatten the little man where he lay.

Baelath was about to jump down from the wall, hoping to distract the creature long enough to give the mohawk man a chance, but out of the corner of his eye, Baelath saw a shimmer. He turned to see Max standing in an open archway of one of the surrounding buildings, bow aimed and the string pulled back. What had caught Baelath's eye was a silver-tipped arrow resting on the bow, waiting to be released.

At that moment, the arrow shot forward like a bolt of lightning, and in less than a second, the arrow penetrated the creature's shoulder. Baelath could hear the skin rip open. The creature roared in pain, rather than the deafening roars they'd heard before. Baelath spotted Jax running into the courtyard, sword and shield raised in front of him. The fire beast had yet to spot Jax and was still focused on the arrow in its flesh, trying to reach it with its arms.

The pain did not last long; whatever the thing had for blood was streaming out from the wound, and Baelath watched as the arrow broke apart, and the wound sealed shut. Now the monster was able to shift its attention back to its duel and saw Jax running into view of the battlefield.

"Come on; we need to help," Evelyn whispered to Baelath as she started climbing down the wall into the square.

Baelath followed her, and as he turned his head, he saw a devastating swing from the creature, aimed at Jax, who had just raised his shield in front of him before the ax would have torn him in half. Jax was flung high into the air, up and beyond the first wall of rock that surrounded the square. Evelyn and Baelath both gasped as Jax crashed down, hidden from sight. The short man regained the creature's attention, just as another arrow pierced its rib cage. Evelyn ran toward the confrontation, with Baelath closely following. The beast, roaring now and preoccupied with yet another arrow from Max, did not see them run up.

"We cannot hope to defeat this thing, at least with our lives intact," Evelyn said to the little man. Baelath now saw exactly how short the man was and knew he wasn't actually a man at all.

"I am Grul, and I will not leave. A dwarf does not run," said the dwarf. "I will stay here until it does not stand—or I do not."

But in that moment, the creature kicked a large boulder toward the building where Max was shooting. Large pieces of rock shot through the crumbling walls of the empty building below where Max stood, and the foundation cracked apart and tumbled away. Baelath could see the look of terror on Max's face, and he quickly vanished before his ledge gave way. Baelath saw the building fall apart and start to lean in on them; it was ready to come crashing down.

"OK, we can go," Grul said in response to what they were witnessing.

The three of them ran to the opposite end of the courtyard, where Baelath could see a tiny opening in the wall that seemed to lead out of the square. They were running up to a small bridge that crossed the river that flowed through when Evelyn yelled out to them.

"Stop!" she screamed, and Baelath turned and looked behind them. Max was half carrying, half dragging Jax across the courtyard, but the beast stood in between the twins and the bridge. "I'll distract the beast; you get everyone to that opening."

"No, I will distract. You help the others," Baelath said, not wanting her to face the beast alone.

"I can move faster, remember?" She smiled as she brushed her hair over her ear. "Trust me; I'll be fine. Just get the others to safety." And without waiting for a reply, she ran toward the foul creature.

"Let's go," Baelath said to the dwarf, turning back toward the bridge. "That building is coming down, and I fear the rest will follow."

They ran toward the other side, away from the creature, away from Evelyn. They did not move very fast, for the dwarf, with all his grace during battle, could not run fast at all. Baelath also was waiting, hoping that Max and Jax would catch up. Indeed, after a while, Jax was able to move on his own again without Max's help, and they caught up to the slow-moving duo.

When they finally reached the opening, the four of them began funneling along the crack that led out. Baelath turned back around, hoping to see Evelyn right behind him or at least on her way to him. She had distracted the beast and waited until they all were together before she started to run back to them. By the time Baelath spotted her, she had already crossed the bridge, but the beast gave chase and was gaining on her somehow. Its strides were huge, and Baelath feared it would soon overtake her, but at the last second, she jumped and backflipped right over the top of the beast. She landed behind it, which confused the beast; it tried to turn around quickly but only tripped over itself and crashed to the ground.

Almost without breaking stride, Evelyn continued to run forward, unsheathed her sword, and sliced the beast across its chest. It writhed in pain, as she jumped past it and headed toward Baelath. When she reached him, she collapsed into his outstretched arms, barely able to stand or breathe. She had a couple of cuts from shards of flying rocks, but other than pure exhaustion, she seemed to be OK. Baelath helped her to her feet and guided her forward through the crack, his arms wrapped around her shoulders. Together, they squirmed their way along until they were out the other side, where Max, Jax, and Grul the dwarf waited.

"So we have a dwarf now?" Jax said, smiling at the two of them when they emerged from the crevasse.

"I'd see it as the other way, human. Do you know the way out of here?" the dwarf grunted at Jax. "If so, lead on, but if not, it looks like I'm the one whose party has grown."

"Either way, we need to leave this place," Evelyn interjected, brushing the hair over her ear. "That building is falling as we speak, and the rubble will bury us if we are left babbling to each other. Let us move—and quickly."

"Come," Grul said. "I know the way to the western edges of this place."

They all fell in behind the dwarf, who led them along the broken roads. They turned and twisted around the half-collapsed relics of a lost civilization. Because the dwarf led the others and could move only as quickly as his short legs could take him, the five of them heard the final sounds of a failing foundation—sounds from which they were escaping— and turned to watch as one building fell into another and another. They soon witnessed a catastrophic disaster, as fragments of rock flew through the sky, leveling all it came into contact with. But the collisions were soon overtaken by the cloud of dirt and dust that traveled at a great speed toward them. In mere seconds of watching the destruction behind them, they were engulfed in the wave of dust that left them all choking and blinded. Baelath heard some grunts as bits of debris slammed into his friends, and he again lost sight of his companions but only for a minute this time. Soon, his vision returned as the dust began to settle, and the shattered pieces of rock stopped shifting and rolling.

"Come, laddies," Grul said, half coughing. "It's not much farther."

And so they continued their journey of escaping the ruins, following the dwarf called Grul, although half of their party was barely able to follow. Evelyn still had some lingering effects of exhaustion from her encounter with that beast, and Jax slightly limped from being kicked a few hundred feet backward, and Max had a deep cut along his arm. But even with all that slowing them down, they still made it to the end of the ruins before the sun went down.

The rocks and collapsed buildings slowly turned into patches of weeds and dirt, which were finally replaced by fields and woods ahead of them. Baelath had never felt happier to see trees again. It felt like home, just for a second, before he remembered he wasn't walking back home but in the opposite direction. Then he remembered his conversation with his father in King Rodrigo's chamber, and he knew there wasn't a home to go back to. *Still*, he thought, *it's not all bad*—he felt closer to finding Jord than he had ever had before, especially if Grul proved as strong as he looked, and he seemed completely fine after his encounter with that wicked creature.

Not far outside the ruins, they decided to camp for the night. Darkness was settling in on them, and their party was traveling wounded. Rest was needed, if only for a short time. After gathering wood and starting a fire, the five companions—two elves with two men and a dwarf—- relaxed by the fireside and enjoyed a nice meal of rabbit that Grul had prepared while the rest were gathering the firewood.

"OK, so a couple questions I have," said Jax, mouth still half full of food. "First, who exactly are you?"

"I am Grul the Berserker from Steelhold."

"OK, good to know," Jax said, nodding. "Second, and more important, what kind of creature were you fighting?"

"We call it the Kotor, or the Evil, as men would say. And the Kotor was unleashed on the dwarfs long ago, back when we still inhabited the

Eastern Mountains." Grul leaned over the fire to light a pipe that he pulled from his pouch. "That was during the days of peace between dwarfs and goblins, back long ago. But that day ended when they set that monster upon our homes and cities, driving us from the mountain and eradicating from existence the kingdoms of old," he said, before drawing another drag off his pipe. "The problem was that it didn't listen to the goblins, and soon, the Kotor tore a path of destruction wherever it went, leaving death in its wake. After decades of tearing up the mountain, it must have traveled down to the ruins we just came from and made its home. I don't know why it stopped there, but I'm guessing something about the destruction that occurred there, once upon a time, kept it drawn to it." Satisfied in his tale, he leaned back, intent on finishing what was left in his pipe.

"So, it has a name," Jax said mockingly. "Well, that's just great. At least good old Kotor is under a pile of rock now, and we never have to deal with *that* again."

"Oh, I wouldn't be too sure of that, laddie." Grul chuckled, and his armor jiggled in rhythm with his laughter.

"Did you not just witness what I did?" asked Jax, almost annoyed by the dwarf's demeanor.

"Oh, I did indeed, and just like you, I ran for my life. But you and I are not the Kotor, and it did not die beneath the rubble. No, the Kotor and I are not done just yet," Grul said gruffly, rubbing his hands together.

"I cut it across its chest before we left. I don't think it was getting back up," Evelyn said, moving closer to the fire.

"And this lad put three arrows in it, and still it continued," Grul said, pointing at Max.

"OK, OK, it may be alive; it may be dead," Jax said. "But why were you even here, fighting it? If we hadn't come along, you would be dead right now."

"Maybe, or it would be dead instead," Grul said, packing his pipe again. "One day, we will find out who is mightier—Grul the Berserker or the Kotor."

"But why were you there?" Jax asked again.

"To know that, kiddo, you need to know dwarfs," Grul said with a laugh.

"Who are you calling *kiddo*? I've seen literal kids back home who are taller than you," Jax said, raising his hands to the height of Grul's head.

"Har, I'm calling you *kiddo*, kiddo," boomed Grul, his armor rattling in his laughter. "For growth occurs only in experiences, not appearances."

"OK, enough of badgering him. I'm sure his day has been just as hard as ours," Evelyn said, putting a calmer mood over their makeshift camp. "I think we can all agree that the five of us are here and alive and *safe* because, for a time, I didn't think that would be possible again. Which brings me to a couple of questions I have for *you*, Jax."

"What would you like to know?" He smirked, stretching his arms behind his head, as if he was resting. "I'm an open book."

"How were you able to survive after that kick the Kotor gave you?" she asked, narrowing her eyes. "Also, where did you guys go after we were cut off from the two of you?"

"Well, to answer the first question, I'm not exactly sure," Jax said, shrugging his shoulders. "I simply braced for impact, leaned into my shield, and next thing I knew, I was flying through the air."

"Can I see your shield?" Baelath asked; he had become quite curious about the tale of the events.

Jax passed his shield to Baelath, who began to examine it near the fire. "As for your second question, after that pile of boulders almost crashed down on us, we tried getting to you guys but couldn't find a way. So we just kept following the path, which ended up turning north, away from wherever the two of you were. But after walking next to the rock barrier for some time, it broke down at a certain point, and we used that to help us climb to the top and see if we could make out anything from above. Max has always been good at seeing things from afar, and sure enough, he saw the two of you running along the walls, just off to the southwest of us. So we hurried after you, and again, we were blocked, so we climbed into one of those gigantic empty buildings to get a better vantage point. Next thing we see is a dwarf and that Kotor thing standing off against each other," Jax said with a soft laugh. "I didn't know what that was, or who you were, Grul. I just knew that thing needed to be dead, for all our sakes."

Baelath listened to the conversation but wasn't paying too much attention to it, for Jax's shield had grabbed his attention completely instead. After examining it for some time, Baelath could find no dents or scratches or damage of any kind to it, which didn't make any sense to him. *If indeed this was kicked by a creature that routinely throws boulders through buildings,* Baelath thought, *then any kick by it should not only kill the man but obliterate his shield.* Yet not only was the shield still completely intact, but it still looked like the day Baelath had seen it for the first time.

Then he remembered what the king had said about his gift—that enchantments were woven into its bindings—and he wondered if all their gifts had their own special enchantments weaved into the makings of them. Baelath got a sudden urge to pull out his map and look it over once again. Barely listening to the others as they conversed by the fire—Grul was saying something about dwarfen history—Baelath looked closely at his map and saw the black dot marked Jord in the same spot inside the Dark Forest. This time was different, though. It looked like little footprints were tracing themselves across the map and right to Jord, as if they outlined the correct path. It made Baelath wonder where they would be now if they had chosen the right path to begin with and had used the road instead of running into the wild terrain. *Foolish child,* Baelath cursed at himself, *how much time have you wasted?*

"Well, I don't know about anyone else, but I've had enough for one day." Baelath yawned, trying to put his thoughts out of his mind. "We can figure out what to do next in the morning, but I'm going to get some rest."

"Hrmph, yes, rest sounds good indeed." Grul puffed on his pipe. "We're gonna need it if we hope to reach the road tomorrow. From there, it's only a short trip to the Strongbeard kingdom, and after I tell them what happened here today, we will all be treated like kings, and we will feast like we've never feasted before. Oh, I can just taste it—the juicy meat ripped right from the bone—and listening to all the songs they'll sing about us, and how we defeated the Kotor."

"I thought you said it wasn't dead yet?" Jax said accusingly, almost as if he had caught the dwarf in a lie.

The dwarf got a little closer to the fire, his face breaking into a smile. "But they don't need to know that, now do they, laddie?" he whispered and then broke out into a tremendous laugh that echoed across the night sky. "No, no, no, they don't need to know, and then, one day, Grul will come back to finish the job." The dwarf lay flat on the ground and was soon snoring deeply.

The twins quickly followed suit, but Evelyn made her way next to Baelath, and the two talked. Baelath told her what he thought he had discovered about the shield and the map.

"But what does the map do, exactly?" she asked.

"I'm not sure, but I do know it's showing me exactly how to get where I want to go, and right now, that's what I need," replied Baelath, almost in a hushed tone. He thought it best if only the two of them knew what he was thinking, even if he only trusted her for the time. "I don't know what I'll say, but I'm sure the twins will follow us. I feel they're just as invested in this as we are now. But I hope I can convince Grul to help as well. Did you see the way he fought against the Kotor? If he could only do half that again, I'd still take it, for I fear we are not done fighting just yet."

"I know, but it seems every encounter grows worse than the one before it, and I'm afraid of the next encounter. I'm scared of what it might cost." She sighed and stared off into the stars above them. "Some of us almost didn't make it out alive. Can we be so lucky next time or the time after that? When does the luck run out, Bae?"

"With our friends behind us and the gifts of another, hopefully never. I know that as long as we stand together, we will have all we want," Baelath said. He paused for a moment to look back toward the fire. "We're going to get him back, and we're going to call out the king for leaving him to die, and we're going to call the Dark Elves to answer for their crime. The time to stand idly by is gone. We have passed the point of no return from this … this quest where neither of us knows when or where or how it'll end, but once it does, and if you and I are still here, then I promise we will go on the longest hunting trip we've ever had."

At that, Evelyn laughed and cried at the same time. Tears streamed down her face, and her shoulders bobbed up and down. "Yes, we will. Yes, we will," she sputtered in between her fits of laughter.

The two of them continued to laugh and talk until they both grew too tired to continue. They fell asleep by the fire, unaware of the stare from a pair of beady, lifeless eyes that towered above them on a thick branch.

Chapter 7

BAELATH AWOKE TO find his companions already up and about. Grul was stoking the fire, ready to make a mighty breakfast. He would break off into fits of mumbling in between his boasts of what they could be eating back in his kingdom in the dwarfen mountains. Jax was sitting to the side, sharpening his sword, his eyes fixed on his weapon. Baelath wondered if Jax would ever forgive him for what happened to their mother.

Evelyn was still next to him, using a damp cloth to clean her cuts and wash the dirt from her face. *Revealing the beauty that lies underneath*, he couldn't help thinking. He quickly turned his head away. *I've never thought that before.*

Baelath was just about to ask where Max was, when he spotted him coming from the north, arms filled with their flasks.

"There is a stream up there," Max explained once he had rejoined the group. "I filled everyone's flask."

"Har, and you better ration it too," said Grul, looking up from his cooking. "We won't be coming near any rivers on the way back, so the next time you can refill won't be until we reach the Stonebeards, and water won't be what you're drinking—hmph." He gave a rather empathic nod on that last bit. Dwarfs were known for their brandy and whatever else they kept hidden.

Baelath wasn't worried about that, as he knew they weren't going with the dwarf back to his lands. No, they would veer south of those mountains. The map said to continue heading west, where they would cross another river. Baelath's worry lay within what his plan was to get to Jord, and more important, on how to get back safely. They were inching closer to the Dark Forest; each passing day left less land to travel, and Baelath knew he only had a couple of more days to figure it out. But for now, the plan was to keep going, and he hoped the rest would come to him before it was too late.

Before the sun had begun to climb into the bright-blue sky, they had packed the camp and set out. Baelath noticed how flat this land was, especially compared to where they had just been a few days ago. Baelath preferred to travel like this, compared to the constant climbing up and down the hills, as lovely as the view was when reaching the top of a larger hill. It almost felt like traveling through Blaonir, though there were no trees; instead, there was a vast land of dead grass and weeds and a blue horizon. As far as Baelath could see, there was nothing else around them. Besides no trees, there weren't any crops or streams that stemmed the land. No flowers or animals, just a half-dead wasteland, forgotten by those who were left after whatever tragedy had befallen this place.

Grul led the party, with Evelyn close by, listening to all his stories. Baelath was behind them, paying more attention to his map than to them, though he did listen in from time to time. Jax was right behind Baelath, humming along in rhythm with his footsteps, which Baelath could hear had sort of a bounce to them. Max stayed farther back, bringing up the rear, his eyes peeled on all around him. He glanced back every so often, as if he half expected the beast to come up on them. The hood of his cloak hid most of his face, but Baelath spotted a look of worry when he checked on him—their gazes met for just a split second.

I'll let it go for now, Baelath thought, though he knew he should take care to remember that look. *His willingness for adventure is breaking,* Baelath thought sadly, *but there's nothing I can do right now. I must keep going.*

"*Har!* The feast will be the greatest feast you've ever seen with your elf eyes! We dwarfs know how to host a guest," boasted Grul, his arms waving wildly as his excitement grew. "Especially a fair elf maiden from the Faraway Forest."

"Is that what you call our land?" Evelyn asked, somewhat giggly at that notion. "You call Blaonir the Faraway Forest?"

"Well, what would you call it?" boomed the dwarf. "*Har*, we dwarfs live in the Bent Mountains, with a forest that is within our eyes' view. That's the Near Forest, and all the way across the land, there is another forest, where you live. So we call it the Faraway Forest. We dwarfs are not the brightest in the land; we give no fancy names to things. Well, not that anyone else could understand, *har*." He laughed, his orange beard and mohawk awash in sunshine. "It wasn't always so, though. A long time ago, since the beginning of our days, we lived in the Eastern Mountains, right above your forest. All the dwarfs, goblins, elves, and men lived in peace, and all were within a day or two travel of each other. But those pesky little goblins couldn't deal with the fact that we dwarfs were, and still are, better stone workers. Our halls were something to behold, and even these days, they will leave you in awe, but those filthy vermin wanted what we built. That is when the Kotor was unleashed, and the goblins swarmed us—thousands and thousands of them pouring into holes they dug into us from above, the sides, and even below. They slaughtered all who stood in their path and nearly drove us into extinction. They pushed us completely out of the mountain, but it did not even stop there."

Baelath now walked closer to Grul, listening to his stories, and Jax too walked behind the trio, also within earshot.

"If it wasn't for the elves, we would all be dead, *har*. Imagine that—a world without dwarfs. No, not me. But even after my ancestors were driven from their homes, fearing for their lives, the goblins pursued us across the valley. So much blood has been spilled in that valley, from that vicious slaughter to the many wars we waged, avenging those atrocities and hoping to take our home back. We dwarfs called it the Bloody Valley, but somewhere, it got lost in translation, and I hear it's called the Blodig Valley," Grul said, turning to each of them so frequently that it seemed he was turning in circles.

"The Blodig Valley! I've heard of that place," said Jax, as he turned back to his brother, who still walked back from them, though much closer than he had been before. "Max has mentioned it, that it's nothing but a wasteland, an endless land of dirt."

"Look around, kiddo, and what do you see?" Grul motioned with his hand. "Har, this is it. We're at the very bottom of the valley, and the *wasteland*, as you put it, will end soon. Those who came this way didn't make it far."

They walked in silence for a while, each lost in their own thoughts. Grul hummed a deep, low song, and Evelyn had gone up ahead, seeing if she could find the road that they should reach. Jax and Max now walked side by side. Max's eyes still peered in every direction, while Jax blissfully looked upward toward the sky.

"So, Grul," Baelath said, "why are you called the Berserker?"

"Well, I guess it's because I go berserk, har!" Grul said, laughing to himself.

"What's *going berserk*, for a dwarf?" Baelath asked.

"What's that supposed to mean, laddie?" Grul said with a slight edginess, as if he was taken aback by Baelath's question.

"How does a dwarf get that name?" Baelath asked. "I heard that all dwarfs have a slight temper and that no one should ever make a dwarf angry. So how did you get all the other dwarfs to call you the Berserker?"

The elf and the dwarf looked at each for a long minute, each staring at the other without expression. Then the dwarf broke into a hearty laughter, vigorously shaking his armor and the bags he carried.

"Har, that you heard true, laddie, that you heard true," Grul roared, clapping his hand on Baelath's back so hard that the elf stumbled a few feet forward. "When I was a lad myself, young and full of wonder, I liked to fight, especially in a chaotic fight, one where you don't know what is going on. Well, my kingdom held an event every few years—a dozen or so would step into the circle, and we'd fight. We'd fight until someone gave up or was knocked out, and some even went until their death, but it wouldn't end until only one dwarf was left standing, even if it took days. One fight even lasted over a week—*har*, a week! Can you just picture it? A week of fighting? Sounds like music to my ears, but that was before my time." The dwarf hummed a quick tune and seemed to lose himself in thought. After a minute, he blinked bewilderedly at Baelath. "What were we talking about?"

"Your name, Grul the Berserker. How you acquired that name," said Baelath, amused by Grul's perspective on a good time.

"Har, right you are, laddie, so the fighting. Yes, I participated in one of those fights some time ago, back when even entering the fight gave you honor. It was not uncommon for one dwarf to take down a couple of others on his way to the victory. What was uncommon was for one dwarf to take down all of his opponents by himself. Yet that is what I did, and it didn't even last the hour. When the fighting began, a white rage washed through me and blinded me to all else, except for my task. All I saw was whatever was in my way, and I unleashed all my fury against it. Every move as calculated, since we dwarfs take some effort to move from place to place, and I wasted none. The spectators were driven into a frenzy, and before it was over, they were all chanting 'Berserker.' And so the name stuck, and that's how it came to be," Grul said, very proud of his accomplishments. "*Har*, your friend returns, it seems."

Looking up, Baelath saw Evelyn jogging toward them. Her smile stretched across her sunlit face, and the sun made her black hair shimmer with each bounce in her step. By the time she reached them, the twins again had joined Baelath and Grul in waiting for her to come back.

"The road is just up ahead, another hour or so walking," she said excitedly. "I could see a few travelers along it, but for the most part, it seems empty."

"Har, just like I said, and from there it should be a pleasant and safe travel all the way back to our kingdoms," boasted Grul, oblivious to what Baelath was planning.

The five of them traveled together this time, not spreading out as they had before. Grul still told stories of his home and all the adventures he had been on, and the twins listened intently. Evelyn also enjoyed the conversations, laughing often at Grul's claims.

"It's true," he said. "They blindfolded me but didn't bind my hands or feet. Mistake on their part, if you ask me because I took them all out. That'll show them how to properly capture a dwarf."

As they drew closer to the road, the land became more alive, but the air became dirtier. There were sporadic trees at first, but soon they were clustered together, creating small woodland areas all around. Baelath could hear the birds chirping and cawing as they flew overhead. The five crossed tiny streams, letting the water rush up against their legs, and passed through fields of crops or empty plains of grass, which had turned to the more vibrant green that Baelath remembered, rather than the pale, dead grass they had been walking next to for the better part of a day.

At last, they came upon the road, its dirt path weaving and twisting along the land from north to south. Patches of tall grass or weeds consumed parts of it, but the outline was intact, and they plodded down a trail of past footsteps that sketched out what remained. It was empty for now, and Baelath had no intention of staying around until it didn't.

"Har, here it is," Grul said jubilantly, "just as I said it would be. Now, come, let us travel north, and we should reach the first kingdom in a couple of days." Grul waved them toward him as he began to travel up the road.

"I am sorry, Grul, but I'm afraid this is where we must part ways. I will not be traveling on the road or back to your kingdoms," Baelath kindly said. "The others may join you, if they wish, but I cannot."

"What's this nonsense you speak of?" Grul asked, slightly taken aback at this decision. "Where do you intend to go, if not to the dwarfen kingdoms? There's nothing else out here."

"A friend of mine has been captured by the Dark Elves, and I'm on my way to free him. I will continue traveling west and make my way into the Dark Woods and find him." Baelath spoke with such conviction that he noticed the twins stood a little straighter. "I thank you for all the help you have given us, and once I have freed my friend, I will visit your home and be your humbled guest. But for now, I must continue on."

"But you can't continue that way. First off, there's a river that has only one safe place to cross. *Har!*" the dwarf said.

"Then we shall find a second place or fail in the attempt. I have run out of time to waste, and I slightly fear that I have run out of time altogether," said Baelath.

"But the river isn't even the worst part, for if you are able to cross, then you will be in the heart of the Valley of Darkness, a valley so low that the mountains on either side block out all light," Grul said. His eyes darted back and forth, as if his surroundings were changing on him. "They say evil things dwell there, things that feed off fear and prosper in the dark. I have heard that your own shadow betrays you." The dwarf's eyes grew wide in fear at his own words.

"How can your shadow betray you if there is no light?" Jax asked, half smiling at his perceived clever comment.

"To enlighten you on all that you do not know would take a lifetime. Har!" boomed Grul. "But on that particular issue, I have no answer, for I avoid that land, as do all others who wish to survive."

"I hear your words and will take them under advisement, but still I must continue on," Baelath said. "As I said, I thank you for all the help you've given us, but I must brave this land, and I must do it soon, before it is too late. Go to your feast, Grul. You've earned it and much more, and anyone who wishes to join him may do so. I do not know what I'm walking into or the dangers that are in front of me, but I have no choice but to continue."

"I didn't leave home and come all this way just to leave you now," said Evelyn, enclosing her hand into his. "I'm with you until the end."

"As am I," said Max. "My bow is not finished with its enemies, and neither am I."

Everyone turned to Jax, who sighed deeply. "Though these words will probably be the death of me, I think I would already be dead about five times over if it wasn't for you, my friend." Jax unsheathed his sword and held it upright in front of his face, his shield extended in front of that, covering the hilt. "My sword and shield are my conviction, and my conviction will never break. I will be your right hand during your peril—that I swear."

"So we have all chosen. The four of us will continue, headed toward this Valley of Darkness. I wish you all the best in your travels, Grul, and hope we will meet again," Baelath said, bowing to Grul.

"Har, me too, my elf friend. Me too," Grul said, slightly lowering his head before he returned the bow. Then he turned and slowly walked to the road, turning right onto the path.

The four companions crossed behind the proud dwarf and continued straight ahead without him, walking toward the lowering sun.

They hadn't walked for more than five minutes when a voice yelled behind them. "Wait!"

Turning around, Baelath saw Grul running as fast as his legs could carry him. Once he reached them, an awkward silence passed as Grul doubled over, trying to catch his breath. "I've ... decided ... to come with you. You'll need my help."

"Just breathe first, my friend. Then say what you need to say," Evelyn said, walking over to comfort the wheezing dwarf.

After another minute or so, Grul started again. "I cannot, in good conscience, let you try to cross the river—where none of you can, unless someone built a bridge—and to travel into the valley without a guide. Well, you wouldn't last long. Not saying me coming with you will get you through. Chances are, we'll all end up dead, just won't be in the first stint. But come on, no fussin' now. Let's not make a big deal out of this."

"What about your feast? You slew the demon your people have been trying to kill for generations," Baelath said. "Don't let us deprive you of your glory."

"Ah, they won't believe me—bunch of dimwits," bellowed Grul. "I need you four to validate that, which is why I can't let you go get killed before we get there."

"I thought you said the creature wasn't dead yet," Baelath said.

"And I just told you they are a bunch of dimwits. Har! Better to say it's dead and have no more dwarfs go dying by looking for it, rather than losing another generation to the beast," said Grul, chuckling. "Once we have your friend, the six of us will return to my kingdom and become heroes and live in legend forever. But we need to get there first, so come, come. Grul the Berserker will lead you across the Valley of Darkness."

With the five of them back together, they continued westward, leaving the road and the ruins behind, and headed toward the land in between the two mountain ranges that soon came into view. At first, they were just specs on the horizon, but with each passing step, the mountains grew larger and larger. After a few more hours of travel, the sun dipped behind the now-looming mountains on their left, and dusk quickly fell on the land.

"We should camp for the night before dark overtakes us," said Baelath. His eyes peered off in the distance, searching for any unwanted followers.

"Closer, closer," barked the dwarf. "I want to cross the river by the end of the day tomorrow so we can travel through the valley during the morning, when there's a faint gray glow about the land, rather than the pitch-dark during the day—or worse, at night."

"Then let us continue, and you take the lead, Grul," Baelath said, his hands gesturing forward. "But let us make haste, for there is but little light left in this day."

And so the companions continued, and soon the sun dropped below the land, and the red glow was replaced by the twilight of endless stars. It was under this starlight that they set up camp. With the five of them working on it—and they didn't set up everything, as they just needed to eat and rest for the night—it wasn't long before they were sitting by the fire, enjoying a nice meal the Grul had cooked for them.

"So, Grul," said Baelath, after finishing his meal—and quite quickly, before the others had—"what is this Valley of Darkness that has you so afraid? I saw you stand face-to-face with a fire-breathing creature, ready to fight to the death. But now, you seem reluctant to travel it and would not be doing so, if not for the four of us."

"It is an evil land, where shapeless forms dwell, and darkness devours light," whispered Grul. His posture shrank as he spoke. "It is no place where you can stand and look your enemy in the eyes. You cannot battle there and claim victory over the fallen, for they do not fall; rather, they simply disappear, ready to strike again."

"But how does no light reach there?" asked Jax, a puzzled look on his face. "Surely there would be light from the moon, if not the sun."

"I cannot explain why the moon does not travel overhead there or why the stars go out above, the deeper you go. Maybe they are just as afraid as I am. Maybe the mountain blocks them, just like the sun," answered Grul, still munching on his dinner, with sparrow grease running down his beard.

"But how do mountains block the light?" Evelyn asked, her eyes drawn toward the dark outline of the oppressive mountains.

"Do you see how big those mountains are, little elf?" Grul boomed, bouncing up and down with each laugh. "Can you see the top of them? No? That's because no one can, and no one's been to the top either. Har! Nothing lives on those either. Not even the weeds that choke out other life can survive on that. Har! Barren as can be. To be honest, the mountain is probably more wicked than the valley, but no one travels on it. Don't be getting any ideas over there, boy elf, for the valley is as dangerous as I'll undertake. But we dwarfs—and I believe even the Wood Elves, call this the Endless Mountain, since there is no end to it, and I am almost certain it is the bridge to the stars. Har! Also, I may have forgotten to mention that the land slopes downward almost immediately after we cross the river, so any rising light passing overhead just leaves a dim gray on the very top, but soon, that'll be lost too, the deeper you go."

"I am not a fool, my new dwarf friend," Baelath said. "I know that the danger that lies ahead is beyond my perception, but so has been my entire quest. From the moment we set out, Evelyn and I have faced obstacle after obstacle, not knowing which would be the one we could not overcome. Yet here we sit, the five of us now, having beaten or escaped whatever confronted us. And I will tell you that I too am scared of our next adversary, but I would not travel this path if I did not think it was absolutely necessary. I will also tell you that I would climb to the top of this mountain here if I had to, for I will not be stopped until I see Jord again or die trying."

"That's a good speech, laddie. Har! But in the end, speeches are best left for the dead and kings," Grul said, his eyes gazing into the fire. "We warriors let our deeds do the talking."

Grul talked well into the night, mostly about his home, and he sang songs of olden times. Slowly, the fire died until just the embers glowed a dim red, and Baelath closed his eyes and listened to the dwarfen songs about the mountains and finding their way, rebuilding what was destroyed and capturing lost glory. The deep vibration from Grul's hum lulled them all, and each companion lay back and stared into the night sky.

After a while, the dwarf stopped and drifted off to sleep, well after the twins. Baelath looked over to Evelyn as she lay on her side, her black hair flowing over her neck and covering half her face. Her eyes were closed, and she seemed in a peaceful sleep, with her chest rising and falling softly and slowly. Baelath was glad his friends were able to find comfort that night and that Evelyn could rest easily, but he could not. For an unknown reason, he felt troubled and a restlessness moved through him. He knew he was reaching the end of his journey, his quest to rescue the one who had made him who he was today, the one who was more like a father to him than his own father, his friend. He was dreading these last few moments but could not explain why. He felt the shadow lurking around the corner in his mind, and with each step they took toward those woods, the greater the shadow became. Baelath knew the lore—that any River Elf that walked those woods would become a Dark Elf himself, his soul lost, but still, he'd left home. *Will the Dark Woods now become my new home? Will they be my friends' new homes too, or worse, their graves?*

Baelath's thoughts swirled until the sun broke over the horizon to the east. Not wanting to lose any time, he roused the others, and soon, they set off toward the river. Before the sun had reached its highest point, Baelath heard the sound of rushing water.

"Can't be too far now," he said to the others.

"But we still must find a way to cross," Grul answered, his voice a little hoarse after the night of singing. "The Zoe River isn't some woodland stream. Har!"

Within the hour, the companions found themselves on the banks of the Zoe River. The water was a clear blue along the edges, where dipping in just a toe would send ripples screeching across its top. But closer to the middle, the water became a white force, ripping forward in its rush across Arcane.

"See, laddie?" Grul yelled above the rush of water that deafened their ears. "Can't cross here. Have to find someplace else."

"I see," yelled Baelath, his eyes fixated on the shore across the river. "But the question becomes, do we look north or south of here?"

"South," said Jax.

"North," said his brother.

"I know the northern parts of the river better than I do the south," said Grul, his eyes narrowed as he searched up the river. "Let us head in that direction, and at worst, we'll come to the bridge crossing by midday tomorrow."

"That will not work," said Baelath, his eyes still fixed on the other side. "We cross within an hour, even if we swim across." With those words, he turned to his left and walked at a vigorous pace. Only Evelyn and Jax, with their long strides, were able to keep up with him. Max soon broke into a jog to remain behind them, and Grul, although he was in a full-out run, was easily losing ground.

But just as soon as Grul was about to disappear from view altogether, Baelath stopped and looked out across the river. "See the stones?" he said, pointing toward the water where twelve stones sat, each one larger than the one before, until the middle; then they gradually decreased in size again, forming some sort of bridge. Whether this was a natural formation of the rocks or made by someone, Baelath did not know, and he had no time to find out. They would cross here or not cross at all.

"I will go first," Evelyn said, once they all had climbed down the outer banks of the river.

"I should go," Baelath said. "I am the lightest on my feet."

"But I am the better swimmer," Evelyn reminded him, a quick smile passing across her face. "If something goes wrong, I am best suited to reach the shore again."

"Then let us hurry," Baelath said, holding his arm out for her to pass and climb onto the first rock. "But be careful."

Evelyn put her foot onto the rock and tried to wiggle it around, but it would not move. She stepped onto it and did the same thing with the next two, but again, neither one would budge. After that, she swiftly moved through the next three, making her way to the middle of the river. She stood there for a couple of extra seconds to see if that rock was indeed unmovable like the rest.

The grace she displays almost matches her beauty, Baelath thought.

She bounded quickly over the other rocks until she stepped off the last one and onto the other side. A quick turn and a wave meant that it was safe for them to follow, and follow they did.

Grul went next, although he was scared that the rocks would not hold them as they all crossed, and he took much longer than Evelyn, even with her checking to make sure all the rocks were safe. Finally, he made it across, and Jax went after that. Within a minute, Jax safely made it to the other side. Baelath thought he saw the fourth rock move when Jax stepped off it, but he saw no ripples in the water and the rock didn't appear to be swaying, so Baelath assumed his eyes were playing tricks on him. Max followed his brother, and Baelath kept his eyes on that fourth rock, but nothing seemed to happen when Max crossed it. So when it was just Baelath left, he hopped on the first rock when he saw Max step off and then onto the second and then the third.

But just as he placed his foot on the fourth, it rolled. It felt like an eternity passed as he flailed his arms in the air, hoping to grab onto something, but it was for naught, and he plunged headfirst into the icy waters of the rushing Zoe River.

The impact alone almost knocked out Baelath, and for a second, his vision went black. He could feel the tug and pull as he was being driven downstream and swept underwater in the current. He fought as hard as he could to pull himself out of it, but it was too strong this deep below the surface. He focused on to swimming upward and tried to think of himself as climbing the trees back in Blaonir, but without his feet pushing off branches, it was practically useless. *No air left. Can't breathe.* That was all his mind could think. Still, he fought and fought, and slowly, he found himself rising closer to the top. A few more seconds of his pushing upward, and he finally broke the surface, gasping for air. As he choked on the water he was coughing up and swallowing, he saw a flash of black hair whipping toward him, and within moments, Evelyn had grasped his wrist and pulled him out of the current.

He had no idea how she was able to swim through the current while holding onto him, but she managed to do it easier than Baelath could keep his head above water. It had been only a few minutes from the time Baelath had plunged into the river until Evelyn pulled him onto shore, and now, the two of them lay side by side, gasping for air, as the pure exhaustion from the event had left them barely breathing, especially Baelath, as he kept feeling water come up from his stomach. He saw that they had ended up far downriver from where the rock bridge was located, as he could no longer see the rocks or the other three, who had taken off following Evelyn along the shore when she dived in.

"Thank you," gasped Baelath, still slightly choking on water. "It was too strong for me."

"I told you I was the better swimmer," she said with that smile etched across her face. Her dimples peeked out, her eyes were radiant in the sunlight, and strands of wet hair were smoothed over her face.

For a second, Baelath felt their hands entwine, and he could have sworn that time ceased. And then it happened—something that Baelath would remember as one of the worst things he ever heard.

"Oi, you all right, elf laddies?" yelled Grul, his deep, booming voice shattering whatever moment that might have been. "I told you we should have gone to the real crossing, but no, don't listen to the dwarf who's been living out these parts his whole life. Let's listen to the elf from the Faraway Forest. Sounds good to me." His sarcasm grew with every word.

"But we're on this side now, are we not?" said Baelath, standing to his feet and looking back to the other side. "And the day has just begun."

"No, laddie, have you forgotten where we're going? The day may have just begun here, but down where we're going, the night has already started." Grul's eyes looked westward, and Baelath could now see the land instantly sloping downward, like they were standing on top of a hill, but instead of green pastures and crop fields waiting at the bottom, it was just black.

The brothers found them, and now the five companions stood like a wall along the western banks and looked down upon the Valley of Darkness. An eerie wind rose up to greet them, and Baelath felt the shiver down his spine. Still, he gathered what little courage he could find within himself and pressed forward, with the others following suit, growing closer together, each one crunched to the others' shoulders as they set off into the darkness.

"Together," he softly uttered to the others.

"Together," they calmly responded.

Within the first footfalls, Baelath could hear whispers creeping in his ear. He quickly glanced around and knew that the others could hear it too. He fought hard to ignore the whispers, but he would find himself turning his head and searching for the mysterious voices. They continued walking down the sloping land. Just as Grul had described, their surroundings grew gray as all light dissipated from the land. Soon, everything became some version of gray, black, or white, with elongated shadows stretching behind each desolate tree or barren rock.

Hours passed, and still they continued downward, almost more sharply now, as if the land suddenly ran straight up and down, and they would be forever falling in some black abyss. And then, suddenly, to their surprise, the land leveled off with just a slight downhill angle—but it was in that moment that Baelath discovered why this was called the Valley of Darkness. From the first step on the level land, he was completely encased in a world of black, where not even the stars could hope to reach.

"I have but one torch," whispered the dwarf, as if he was afraid of something hearing him. "We won't light it until we absolutely need it, when we are lost from each other or about to be overrun, OK?"

"Overrun?" whispered Jax. "From what?"

"Shadows, my lad, shadows," Grul said as he crept forward, leading the rest through the dark. "Shadows hate fire, but it will draw everything to us, so we must not use it until we are near the end, or we will have no hope of getting out."

And so they slowly made their way, oblivious to the distance they'd covered. Baelath knew that when the time came to light the torch, he could use his map quickly and figure out how to get out of this place. *If it even shows the way.*

Grul continued to move at a slow pace with his ears perked for any sign an attack by the shadows. After what Baelath could have sworn was a day of walking since they'd entered this forsaken land, Grul stopped suddenly and looked toward the sky.

"The sun has gone down; it is night in Arcane now." The dwarf's muscles flexed, and he gripped his ax more tightly. "Now the real dangers begin. Come, let us pick up the pace, yet be quiet. Something will be listening from now on, if not already."

They picked up their pace, while still trying to be light on their feet. Most of them didn't have any problem with that. Elves could walk without being heard, if they pleased, and Max was almost as stealthy as an elf. Even Grul was surprisingly nimble on his feet, even with the pace they were maintaining. Jax, though, had a hard time with soft footsteps. His heavy boots echoed in the darkness, and soon, they had to slow their pace to keep Jax close to them.

Then, with one misstep, everything started to go wrong. Jax placed his foot on a rock, but only half of it, for he quickly lost his balance and tumbled to the ground. His shield and sword banged together, echoing a clash of steel into the black of night. What followed could only be described as the silence before a storm, where the wind dies, and it feels as if all the air has been sucked out. For a brief moment, Baelath thought everything was going to be OK, and he let out a small sigh of relief. Then came the screeching.

High-pitched wails streaked across the land, coming from all directions, growing louder as more and more were added to the chorus. Baelath felt the whoosh of air as the shadows flew by them—at least, he hoped that was all it was.

Moments later, the torch in Grul's hand erupted in a bright flame, like a beacon calling out to all who could see it. To Baelath and the rest of them, it said to follow it; don't lose sight of it. To the shadows, which now could be seen dancing in between the light and the dark, laughing and smiling at them, it said, *Come.* Come to it and have what any shadow could want.

One shadow swooped down low into the light, growing larger in the fire's shadow, and headed down toward Grul, but Max, relying on pure instinct, launched an arrow at the shadow, piercing it through its evil smile. The arrow went straight through it and flew out into the night, and the shadow dissipated from their view.

"You can't kill 'em, laddie, but you sure can drive them away!" Grul screamed over the sounds of the shadows still wailing all around them. "Come, we need to run now." And he took the torch and ran ahead into the night, battle ax in his other hand, mowing down the shadows that leaped at him from the darkness.

Jax fell in behind Grul, great sword and shield raised high, slashing whatever Grul left in his path. Baelath and Evelyn moved up to the dwarf's side, protecting him from any side swipes, while Max aimed his bow up high, shooting all that dived from above. Together, the five of them moved in a tight circle, helping each other out, making sure they all left alive from this place.

No friends of mine will die here, Baelath promised himself. *Not in this dark place.*

Still, the shadows barreled toward them more and more, replacing those that evaporated. It almost became too much, as the shadows started overpowering the flames from the torch, and Baelath could feel the shadows covering and consuming him. He wasn't sure how much longer he could hold out or if anyone else could withstand it. Soon, a chill crept through his veins, and Baelath's hope and happiness drained away. For a brief moment, Baelath could see frost in his breath as the air around them turned cold, and then the flames on the torch went out in a whoosh, and only black smoke swirled up from the burned stump.

Baelath thought it was over for them, that the shadows would overtake them, and they would be forever lost in this dark land, never to be seen or heard from again. But then he *felt* the shadows leave and slither away, going back to where they dwelled. For just the briefest of moments, Baelath believed that the worst had passed, and they would soon be out of the dark and back into the light.

Then the air around them erupted into a ring of fire, surrounding the entire group in a blaze of heat. It left an area of about one hundred feet on both sides of them, and another few hundred feet in from of them was the other side of this wall of fire. Everything in between was the shadows of the flames that danced all around them, and Baelath could see them beginning to form in the middle. From that spot, the shadows grew, larger and larger, forming into some sort of *thing* that undulated in the shadows. It grew to over six feet tall and resembled a woman wearing a long, flowing, off-the-shoulder dress, with sleeves that came to tattered ends. The bottom of the dress flowed into the shadows that wisped against the ground. Her skin was a bright gray, almost silver, with black lips and black fingernails, and her cleavage was bursting against her bodice, yet it did not move up or down, for it seemed she did not breathe.

Whatever this was, it was not alive. A dark black veil covered half her face, though Baelath could clearly make out her cold white eyes that stared, he felt, directly into his soul. If Baelath were to describe this shadow woman to another person, he could only say it was the most beautiful and most terrifying thing he had ever laid eyes on. He wanted nothing more than for this entity to leave and never come back, and at the same time, he could not look away and could spend his lifetime in this spot, staring at her.

Then she screeched into the night, and her face transformed into a horrifying sight. The eyes went black, and her mouth revealed fangs, dripping in blood. She seemed to age a century as her face shrank and grew wrinkles. Holes opened up along her chest and shoulders, revealing maggots and worms slithering inside her. In the second that she did that, Baelath was torn away from what had been her beauty, and he shielded his eyes in terror. In the last moment, however, he saw the shadowy thing charging at them. Luckily, he was not the only one taken aback by the creature's wicked looks. Jax had reacted the same as Baelath and had raised his shield arm. The creature violently slammed into it and was blown back into the shadows. But in another second, she had reformed to her first state and stared directly at Jax. She reared back and screeched into the night, the ear-piercing sound driving all thoughts from their minds.

Though the sound stopped, Baelath wished for it back because the creature looked back upon them and hissed, showing her bloody fangs again. *What is this thing?* Baelath thought in horror. Then from out of the night, her voice whispered to them, yet so clear that the flames from the fire circle dipped in response to the chill that gripped the air.

"The Shadow Walker has come. Feel the wrath that all the darkness has to offer and all that the darkness has yet to give." She spoke to them as if she was standing right behind them, whispering into each one's ear.

There was a *thunk*, followed by a slight whoosh of air past Baelath's ear, and he saw an arrow rippling into the night, directly at the Shadow Walker, but she just let it pass through her, like Max was shooting at a wall of smoke. It did not deter him, and two more arrows followed—and two more again went through the Shadow Walker and flew off into the night. This time, the arrows must have angered her, as she reeled back and wailed into the sky.

"The shield, laddie, the shield," Grul shouted over the high-pitched scream that filled their heads. "Use the shield to block her while we try to find a way out of here."

Jax stepped up toward her, just as she charged in a diving swoop toward them, flying through the air, bouncing from shadow to shadow. Again, she slammed into Jax's shield and retreated, moving from side to side, looking for an opening against Jax. Jax, though, was a strong warrior in his own right, and try as she might, the Shadow Walker could not get past him. Soon, Jax was making counterstrikes against her, and though his sword passed through her like the arrows had, she clearly did not like it and fell back anytime she was struck, until the shadows formed her again.

Max continued to shoot arrows at her, and Grul threw some of his short axes, but all to no avail. Baelath did not know what to do, and Evelyn kept trying to test the circle of fire, but anytime she approached, it grew in ferocity and exploded toward her. Even when she took a running start, all she did was jump into the middle as it expanded behind itself, not allowing her any hope of finding a way out without being burned alive. She made her way back to Baelath, patting out the fires on her cloak. He was standing about ten feet behind Jax, watching him battle with the Shadow Walker, but Jax was clearly becoming tired, and Baelath became afraid that he could not hold out much longer.

"I'm out of arrows," said Max. "All I have left is that arrow that the king gave me."

"That's it! Use that!" exclaimed Evelyn, a wave of shock and memory washing over her. "Remember what the king said? Use this bow and arrow to strike the darkness from your enemies and bring them into the light. Use it!" she screamed at him.

And so Max nocked the king's gift of an arrow onto his gift of a bow and took aim directly at the Shadow Walker, who was rearing her head in another awful wail, ready to charge at a now-swaying and slightly stumbling Jax; both his arms hung heavily at his side.

It's now or never, thought Baelath. *Either this darkness will end, or we will all be consumed by it.*

Then Max let go, and instead of the thunk that Baelath would usually hear as the string was plucked, this sound was more musical, like a note from a song being played in the distance. The arrow rushed toward the Shadow Walker just as she lunged forward, and to all who watched, it felt like time became an arbitrary thought, and the arrow was suspended in the air, and the shadows swirled around in the firelight. Then the moment passed, and the arrow struck directly into the oncoming face of the Shadow Walker. It slammed in and stuck right where her nose should have been, and another wail erupted into the night. But it wasn't in anger or terror or for instilling fear or hurt. This was one of pain and, ultimately, death. A light began to fill inside the Shadow Walker and came pouring out in cracks it made along her body, burning away any remnants of her. Once she was finally gone, the fire circle died out, and Baelath thought that even some of the blackness was lifted, and maybe a tiny bit of starlight found its way down there at the bottom of this land.

Knowing it was truly over, the companions moved on and quickly felt the ground slope upward. Soon, they left the darkness behind them and entered into its gray area again. But that did not last long either; they crested the final ridge and walked back into the world of color and saw the green grass and the snow-tipped mountains peeking from the clouds to their right. Up ahead, Baelath could see the outer edges of the Dark Woods, and even from this distance, he could see the twisted shapes of the trees.

He knew that would have to wait until tomorrow, for even if he hadn't been driven to the point of exhaustion, Jax most certainly was, having collapsed onto the ground once they finally reached the top of the valley and left all matters of black and gray behind them. But Baelath too was tired and needed to rest, and Max had arrows to make, though he did find a couple of them on their way out of the fight from the Shadow Walker.

So here, on the outer edges of the Dark Woods and the Valley of Darkness, they made camp for the night and ate a little something, but most of all, they slept. Baelath could feel that his strength, courage, and the little hope he'd had was drained in that fight. Tomorrow, he knew he would have to enter the woods and somehow make his way to Morketrekk, where the Dark Elves had their throne.

Baelath quietly pulled the map out and pored over it by firelight. *That is where Jord has to be*, he thought, *and it's directly in the middle of the forest, their largest city.* He could see smaller cities dotting the woods, but Jord's name was under *Morketrekk*. It would be a perilous journey, more so than the past few he had already undertaken, but he could not stop now, not when he was so close. Jord was only another couple of days away from him now, and Baelath did not know how much time he had left before something terrible might happen to him. In fact, something terrible might already have already happened, and Baelath might be leading his friends on a doomed quest.

CHAPTER 8

MORNING FINALLY CAME, and Baelath felt refreshed. The sun shone off to the east, just breaking the horizon but high enough to shower them in sunlight. But Baelath's gaze was pointed toward the west, where the outer edges of the Dark Woods loomed like a wolf in the night. Even from a distance, Baelath could see the horrid shapes of the trees, the vicious way they bent and wrapped their branches around the others, creating a natural roof that blocked light. He could see the fog rising up, casting the trees in a shroud of mystery. Baelath stood unmoving, like a statue, his map in hand.

Evelyn moved up beside him and looked out. "We'll find him," she whispered, taking the map from his hands and rolling it up. "I promise."

They roused up the others and packed up their makeshift camp, with just Grul's grumbling slowing them down. Within the hour, after they had eaten a small breakfast, since no one was quite sure when their next meal would be—*or if they would have another*, a despairing thought among them all—they set off and left one evil land behind them to go into another. A flock of birds circled overhead—*Crows, by the look of them*, Baelath thought—but once they had set off, the murder of crows scattered in the sky, flying in random paths and directions, except for one. One bird flew like an arrow westward, in a straight line, and disappeared over the tree tops and into the fog.

No, it couldn't be. Could it? Baelath thought, his eyes following the crow. *That would be impossible, but where did all those birds back home come from? And how did the king get any message if Jord is locked away?* There

138

were too many questions without any answers, but Baelath wondered if the answer to one question was the answer to them all. *Can Jord transport his mind into birds?*

It didn't take long for them to reach the outer edges of the woods, and Baelath could now fully see the grotesque nature of this place. The trees were not like any Baelath had seen before and were almost the opposite of the trees back in Blaonir. The trunks were not the rich, vibrant, alive color of the Great Trees of home; instead, they looked and felt dead when he placed his hand on them. Most of them were an ash color, but Baelath could see some had become black, as if they'd been dead for hundreds of years yet still stood, rooted to the ground, refusing to fall over in death. Others were covered completely in green moss, but the moss itself looked sinister, a ratchet-green color compared to the bright green moss Baelath had known from his hunting days. Above, the leaves looked dying or dead, and they shivered on the branches as if they were afraid to leave the branch. Frail and brittle, they looked, the colors alternating between a deep green, a dirty brown, and a faded black or dark gray.

Baelath could no longer tell what was actually alive in here and what was already dead, and it sent a cold chill down his spine. *This is it; no turning back now.* He knew they could delay no longer, and he stepped below the tree line, walking along the fallen leaves and branches that littered the ground. He wondered how deep the pile of dead wood and leaves was below him. *How long has this place stood on the edge of destruction, yet slowly feeling the oncoming decay entwine itself in its very fabric? Was this place ever alive and vibrant, or does death just grow here?*

Once they had made their way into the first few rows of trees, the fog enveloped them, making any visual tracking impossible. Every tree looked the same, yet the woods seemed to be changing. Baelath could have sworn one tree bent in a particular direction, yet seconds later, when he looked back, it was bent the opposite way.

"Stick together here, lads," Grul growled. "Nothing but trouble lives here."

"What was that?" yelled Max, pointing off into the distance.

"What was what?" Jax asked, looking around nervously.

"I saw more of those shadow things, stalking around those trees over there," Max said, but when the others looked, there was nothing but the fog shifting along the ground.

"There," Evelyn proclaimed. "I see it." Except she was pointing in the opposite direction.

"Come," Grul said. "We must hurry along from here if the shadows can indeed travel into this place."

They picked up their pace, with Grul practically running. Still, Baelath caught glimpses of the shadows, but somehow, they were different from the ones before. The shadows that Baelath knew moved without actually moving any part of themselves, like gliding in and out of the light. But Baelath could see what looked like legs running every time he saw a shadow here.

Then, he pieced it together and knew that these were not shadows from the valley but the Dark Elves from the woods. *"Run!"* Baelath yelled, now sprinting as fast as he could and veering to the left. The others fell behind, and he soon had to stop to wait for them—and in that instant, he saw exactly what was happening. More Dark Elves had joined in the hunt and were squeezing in on them from either side, funneling them in one direction. He counted dozens on his right, and before he could even begin to count the left side, the others burst into view.

"What now?" panted Jax, as he saw what was happening as well.

"I say we fight 'em, *har*," boomed the dwarf, holding his ax in front of him, ready to strike down anything that came too close. "We can take 'em, all of 'em."

"No," said Baelath. "We can outrun them."

"I'd have better luck with the fighting, laddie," Grul chuckled. "I've got no hope outrunning elves."

"We can lose them in the fog and hide until they've passed," Baelath said, speaking to the others as well. He could hear the panic in his own voice. "It's the only chance we've got."

"Then let's go," said Max, seeing the dark outlines of their hunters closing in. "Before it's too late."

Jax lifted the dwarf onto his back. "Hold on tight," he said before sprinting back into the fog. Max followed, and Evelyn bounded after them. Baelath looked around one last time at the Dark Elves closing in on them, and then, he too ran off after the others, quickly catching up to them. He knew that they needed to get ahead of their pursuers, break off to one of the sides, and hopefully hide within the low-hanging fog for a while—at least until he came up with something, anything, other than what they had going for them now.

Every time Baelath thought he had gained enough separation and tried to veer off his straight-line course, he would see more outlines forming next to them, close enough to shoot with a bow, point-blank. It could have happened a few times, if Baelath hadn't been so quick on his feet and rolled when he saw the dark form of a bow raise in his face. Finally, after running for an hour or so, Baelath had had enough and hoped to break their line with a sharp turn left. He planned on running straight through them, hoping the surprise would confuse the Dark Elves enough for his group to get through. But the instant Baelath turned and ran, arrows spewed from the gray fog, whipping past him in every direction. It was the same for the others, stopping them in their tracks but never striking them. Baelath could see he had no option but to continue or be overrun by the mob that was coming from behind and that continued to grow in numbers. He felt there must be hundreds chasing them now, herding them like cattle. *But to where?*

He knew this wouldn't end well, but Baelath still ran with a fire in his heart and held on to that tiny sliver of hope—that maybe if he ran hard and long enough, he could reach Morketrekk before they were captured. And maybe he could find Jord before they caught him, and once he was with Jord, they could possibly escape. But that would mean leaving everyone other than Evelyn behind, probably to their doom, and he didn't think he could live with that, not after getting his friends this far.

And so, he continued on his run, allowing the Dark Elves to completely surround them, except for just in front of them. The rest of the group had figured out that they were being herded somewhere, and soon enough, Baelath and his friends broke into a clearing, with a single tree standing in the middle. It eerily reminded him of the place he had found when he was hunting on the night before he had set out from home. The clearing was almost a perfect circle, and the grass was tall in this area; it was able to grow in the sunlight rather than suffocating under the canopy of dying trees. But instead of the tree being filled with elves, like he had found back home, all the Dark Elves, hidden underneath their cloaks, were waiting around it, torches in hand, illuminating this dark land in dancing flames. They all came to a halt and stared at this bleak fortune in front of them. Baelath was soon forced to his knees, and his weapons were taken from him by some of those who had chased them here. He watched while they did the same to the others. Evelyn and Grul were to his left and the twins on his right. Jax was closest to him, and the man's face burned with anger as he struggled mightily against his captors.

Then, out from the darkness and into the light that the roaring flames provided, walked a Dark Elf, so magnificent yet so hideous in the same moment that once revealed, the world quieted and waited. Baelath could see the pure evil in his features, yet he looked soft and gentle, with the slightest twitch of his face. His bright blue eyes gazed upon them; his skin was so radiant that it seemed to glow. A long black cape was wrapped around him, but armor jingled beneath. Behind his shoulders were metal batlike wings trimmed with gold, and skulls hung from his belt, clacking together with each stride. His black hair flowed down behind him and seemed to bounce in the dying wind. His forearms and lower legs were lined with upward curving spikes, each with the same gold trim as his metal wings. A long, wide sword hung from his hip, with a black handle with a golden blade. A red glow burned from inside the sheath, as if the sword had just been removed from the fires that forged it. Once the Dark Elf approached them and stood facing the five of them, down on their knees, Baelath could see the sickening smile etched across his lustrous face.

"Well, well, well," the Dark Elf chuckled. "What a group we have here." He looked down upon each one, his cold eyes looking at each one individually, as if he could see inside to their very souls. Then he broke into a chilling laugh that rattled even the dwarf's bones. "*River Elves* in these parts? Why, that won't do at all."

"My name is Baelath, and I am a diplomat from Blaonir. I demand to see the prisoner you are wrongfully holding captive." Baelath tried to make his voice sound brave in hopes of fooling the Dark Elf.

"*You* are a rogue elf, acting without orders, causing disturbances in cities and in the countryside. Yes, we've heard tales of your adventures in Nox. You'll be happy to know that their city is under siege from the goblins, whom you aroused. But that is neither here nor there—well, maybe there, but it means nothing to us now. I've waited for this moment for so long that I won't ruin it with haste, though I am half surprised you made it this far. Still, I waited too long. And now that I have you, what shall I do with you? What shall I do indeed?"

"You must release me. I am the prince to King Daelon," Baelath replied. He thought the Dark Elf would have no choice but to bring them to the king now, but how wrong he was.

"*I* must do nothing. I have orders to bring you back, but they don't know when you will arrive. What's a day or two to them? Is it too much for me to ask for a little fun?" The Dark Elf smiled down at them, like a parent admiring a child.

"You want fun?" Baelath spat at his captor. "Let me out of these chains and fight me, and then you won't have to worry about having any fun at all." Baelath angrily raised his head to meet the Dark Elf's gaze. "Unless you think I will win, then it would not be wise for you to do so."

"Maligor the Shadowed One struck down by a lowly River Elf? As much as I would enjoy all of that, I have strict orders to bring any elves that I find to the king." He unsheathed his sword, and it glowed red in front of him, evaporating the beautiful features of the Dark Elf, while highlighting all the evil ones.

For a moment, Baelath felt terrified. Any hope that remained in him was extinguished the second those eyes fell upon him.

"Just elves," Maligor said, that bone-chilling smile returning in the corners of his mouth. "So, tell me, *diplomat*, what would you do"—he began walking in front of them, moving slowly from person to person—"when everything is falling around you?" He made his way behind them, dragging his sword along the ground, leaving a horrible screeching sound echoing into the night. "When everything you strived for is gone forever, when the air becomes tighter, choking the very breath from your throat, when all that cheerful optimism becomes lost?" Maligor now stood behind Evelyn. "Do you just breathe, let go, give in?" he said, as Baelath felt him move behind him. "Do you let all that despair you've held off for so long wash over you like a wave?" Maligor's voice now grew louder as he made his way behind Jax. "I say to let that fire in your eyes burn out, for it will do you no good here, because can't you tell?" He leaned forward to whisper into Jax's ear but loud enough so Baelath could hear it: "*It's already over.*"

Then he shoved his sword into Jax's back and through his spine, and with a final shove, it burst out from his chest. Blood spewed everywhere, as Jax gurgled, his blood pouring out from his mouth, and the night became filled with the screams of the dead man's friends—and laughter from Maligor.

Jax's dead body slumped forward, facedown on the ground. Maligor stood over his kill, and with a deep, booming laugh, he ripped his sword from the carcass as easy as if he were pulling a wooden stake from the soft dirt. The blood pooled around the lifeless body, and Baelath could do nothing but stare at it.

"I'll kill you for this," Max said, barely above a murmur. "You hear me? I will kill you." His voice was louder this time as he raised his head to look at Maligor with tears in his eyes.

"Careful, now," Maligor said slyly. "I only need the elves, and it is a long road ahead of us, I don't know how much fun I can take. I've had too much fun already, and I believe that too much of a good thing can be bad." His words almost sounded charming and joyful. "So come, up to your feet. Your nightmare has only just begun." And with that, the Dark Elves behind them raised them to their feet and prodded them forward, deeper into the woods, leaving Jax's body forever behind them.

Their forced march lasted only a few more hours, until Maligor decided to camp for the night, and the four prisoners were left chained to a pole on the outskirts of the camp. Left uncovered and under heavy guard, the four of them wept for Jax. Baelath could not express his sorrow for getting them involved in everything, for the loss of his home, for dragging them into all of this, and for leading them to their probable deaths. He began to wonder if he'd made a mistake by allowing the others to follow him, even Evelyn—the thought of her being hurt or killed was more than he could bear at the moment. The sounds of the Dark Elves' celebration were a constant reminder of the night's events, and the four stood together, tethered to a pole, each alone in their own darkness.

Hours passed before they set off again. The vibes of the joyous night before had died, and in the morning—if this was called such a thing in these lands, for the black of night had left and was replaced by the stain of a dull gray—the sounds became whispers. Baelath watched Maligor's elves slowly slip away into the trees.

Soon, a few guards came to unhitch them from their pole and marched them for hours and hours. The gray color of the land dissolved, and the black of night crept into its place again. When darkness overtook another day, Baelath and his friends again were tied to another pole in the ground. He thought that maybe if they could remove the pole from the ground, they might have a slight chance to escape. At first, he tried to pull on it, but it wouldn't budge. He got Grul to help, but the outcome was just the same. After an hour or so of being tied to the pole, the four of them all worked together to dislodge it from the ground, but it was all to no avail. The prisoners became exhausted and slumped to the cold ground, defeated once more.

"The poles won't budge," a voice boomed from the shadows. "She created them, and only she can remove them." Maligor stepped into Baelath's sight. "Don't worry; there's quite a few of them in the forest, each designed to leave someone chained there forever—to send a message, in case the trees didn't do it for you." The laugh that escaped Maligor's lips shivered down Baelath's spine. "But if I were you, I would have still tried. Leading your friends to their deaths is not something one easily would take to heart, and I'm sure it must pain you to know there's little you can do to change the outcome."

Frustrated, Baelath looked into the eyes of the Dark Elf. "What do you want with us?"

"I've already told you. I'm ordered to bring back any elves I find." The sly smile returned to his face. "Just elves, though, and there's still another day until we reach our destination. And I'm ready to have fun again."

Fear washed over Baelath as he watched Maligor unclasp his dagger's sheath and walk over to them. Baelath couldn't face losing another of his friends, not like this, not to this cruel monster that stood before them. Still, Maligor crept toward them, now unsheathing his dagger. The silver flickered in the shadows of the surrounding torches, and Maligor began to shuffle in front of each captive, baiting and threatening them with his dagger. The other Dark Elves crept from the blackness and surrounded them all again. Their stomping began to flow in rhythm with Maligor's shuffling, which soon turned into almost a tribal dance.

A death dance? Is this what Dark Elves do? Have they really fallen this far? Are they really this evil?

Then, it suddenly stopped, and so did Maligor. With his head bowed and his arms lowered, he stood directly in front of Grul. "So, it is to be the dwarf, then?"

"Do your worst, laddie. You're nothing but a coward anyway," the dwarf spat at Maligor. "You call yourself a warrior, but a real warrior fights his battles. He doesn't slaughter his foe like some sort of livestock. So go ahead, coward; slaughter me and tell yourself you were the better warrior. But I would pity you, should you ever find yourself in a real battle, in the face of a real warrior, for I would think you'd not be long for this world."

Maligor looked up, his cold eyes staring directly into the dwarf's fiery gaze. For a moment, the Dark Elf looked angry, his face clenched in a fit of rage, but then that smile returned as he crept closer to Grul. "You're right! I cannot argue with you. Right now, you are the better warrior, but what is it they say about dwarfs' beards? They never cut their beards unless they surrender and admit defeat? That sounds right, I believe, so how about it, *dwarf*? Will you admit defeat?"

"Never," growled Grul.

"Never? Even when I say I will kill your other friends and make you watch as each one slowly dies in front of you?" Maligor seemed to grow more excited by that notion than he had been at any time before.

"You said you need the elves," Grul said with a smile. "I'm willing to die for them."

"How nice; you'll die for your friends," Maligor mocked. "But what elves are you talking about? We only found one little, beardless, pathetic excuse of a dwarf. And we left him to rot in the woods, with his dead friends at his feet." Maligor was now laughing at his threat. "So, *dwarf*, I say again: tell me what it will be. Will you admit defeat and cut off your own beard, or will you watch as I kill your friends and take your beard anyway?" Maligor was now inches away from Grul's face, looking down upon the dwarf with an evil look.

Grul met his gaze with an equal look of disgust but held it only for a few moments; then his head dropped. "I admit defeat," he said sadly.

Maligor boomed with laughter, and a cheer erupted from the surrounding crowd. "You heard it here first, comrades. The dwarf loses his beard." The crowd cheered again, but Maligor leaned in toward Grul and the others, helplessly chained to the pole. "And then, his life," he whispered and smiled at Baelath. "See? Are you not having fun? I know I am." He laughed again and then, suddenly he grabbed Grul by his beard, close to his chin, and with a quick flick of his wrist, he cut the beard off the dwarf's face and held it up to another roar from the crowd. The rhythmic stomping picked up again as Maligor held the beard high over his head and began to let go of clumps of it. Grul could only watch in sadness as his beard—all his victories, all his life's accomplishments—flew away and dissolved into the night.

When Maligor's hand finally was empty, everything became quiet again, and the wind seemed to vanish as well. The Dark Elf turned his attention back to Grul. He slowly walked over to the helpless dwarf.

"You'll pay for this, I promise you," said Baelath, lunging at Maligor, but the chains pulled him back, Baelath felt his anger building inside him again, the bubbles of a furious frenzy rising to the surface.

"No, *you'll* pay for this," snapped Maligor, his eyes flickering with rage. "That is the point of all this."

Baelath stared back at him, confused, the anger dwindling inside him. He watched as Maligor twirled his dagger and raised it high over his head. The tip of the blade glimmered in the firelight as it danced high above the dwarf. A sickness washed over Baelath as the Dark Elf turned to meet his gaze, a wicked smile slashed across his face. Baelath struggled against his chains, trying to reach his captor and save his friend, but he was powerless.

Grul seemed to give up any hope, and the fire inside him seemed all but gone; his head bowed and his shoulders slumped. He seemed to all but welcome death.

But before the dagger dropped, a voice rang out in the night from outside this circle of hell that Baelath and his friends found themselves in. *"Stop!"* it called.

Maligor whipped around; the smile had vanished and a snarl had taken its place. A gap in the surrounding elves seemed to open before Baelath. The other Dark Elves hurried to move out of the way as two figures strolled into the clearing. Their black armor shone, even in the darkness, almost reflecting the moonlight. Both had silver hair that hung below their shoulders, and their helmets were pure gold with the same curved spikes as Maligor's armor. Their armor was different than what Baelath had seen before, and each wore a black robe under it. Most armor looked clunky—even Maligor's, for all its splendor—but this armor looked as if it was made into one piece, each custom fit for the wearer. The gauntlets flowed into the pauldron, which melted into the breastplate, yet with every step that the strangers took, the components moved and bent.

Once they reached Maligor and his chained prisoners, Baelath saw that both of them had bright purple eyes, drastically different from Maligor's blue, but all of them shared that same white glow to their skin.

"What is the meaning of this?" asked one of the new Dark Elves, his eyes darting back and forth between Maligor and the beardless dwarf.

"Oh, just some fun." Maligor laughed, but Baelath saw him switch his dagger to a defensive position, as if he were afraid. "Nothing you need to concern yourself with, Thane."

"It does concern me when I have strict orders to bring back the prisoners to the king, *all of them*," Thane barked. "Come, Garrus, help me free our guests."

"The king said he needed the River Elves. He said nothing about men or dwarfs," Maligor insisted, putting himself between Thane and Grul. "You can have the elves, and I'll even give you the human." He slightly turned his head back to the pole, just enough so Baelath could see the fire now burning in those eyes. "But the dwarf is mine."

"None is yours," responded Thane, who gripped his sword with defiance. "The king asked for all prisoners, and he shall get all of them."

"Well, not all," Maligor slyly said and turned his head back to Baelath to reveal that nasty smile once again. Then he turned back to the other Dark Elves and growled, "Fine. You can take them. I will still have my revenge."

"You know when you can have it," Thane said sternly. "After it's done."

Maligor turned back to Baelath and unlocked him from his chains. "And I look forward to that day more than you can possibly know," he whispered into Baelath's ear, right before he threw him into Thane's arms and almost collapsed right there. Maligor then threw the key to the other one, Garrus, and walked off into the shadows. At the edge of the light, he stopped and turned to his former prisoners. "I'll see you all again one day. I promise. And sooner than you think." Then he disappeared into the shadows with a laugh that echoed into the foggy night, His soldiers began to do the same, until Baelath and the others were left alone with the new Dark Elves, Thane and Garrus.

"Come, let's get you out of those chains," said Thane, once all had finally gone quiet and the last of Maligor's army had receded into the woods. "We are due back by midday tomorrow."

"Due back where? Where are we? Who are you?" The questions poured out of Evelyn's mouth faster than the Dark Elves could respond. "Why is this happening?" she sobbed.

"First, I apologize for not introducing ourselves. We are the King's Royal Guard, and we are here to accompany you to our king. I am Thane, and this is Garrus, at your service. As to your questions, we are due back in Morketrekk, where King Nathrak awaits you. And, my dear, you are in the heart of the Dark Woods, but surely you knew that," Thane said softly, a warm smile greeting them.

"The only place I'm going is to wherever that murderous coward went off to," Max said through gritted teeth. "Only way to stop me is to kill me."

"Murderous? We got here in time to save the dwarf," said Thane, looking confused.

"He killed another of our companions a day before you arrived," Baelath said somberly, his head bowed.

"He shoved his sword into my brother's back and left him to rot in these woods." The anger now swelled in Max's voice. "I'm going to kill him."

"I am sorry for your loss, and I am sorry for his actions," Thane said. "Trust me, Maligor is no great friend of ours, yet the king finds him … useful. When we take you before the king, you can tell him what Maligor has done. Hopefully, he will see to the end of Maligor. But for now, we must journey on." H motioned for them to walk ahead, and they quickly left the clearing and their shackles behind.

The four of them walked side by side, with Garrus leading them and Thane walking behind them. Baelath knew it would be foolish to try anything against these two, especially after what each of them had been through. *Whatever fate lies before us now,* he thought, *will be an improvement from the one we just left.* At least no one else would die because of him.

Their somber walk dragged on into the morning. Baelath could see the sunlight struggling to break through the twisted branches that creaked overhead. Grul and Max seemed to have lost hope, but Evelyn must have found hers. She was walking with a purpose, each footstep falling harder than the one before it. Her fists were clenched, and her eyes narrowed as she stared straight ahead.

Baelath grabbed her hand and pulled her back a little. "Are you OK?" he asked with a worried look in his eye.

"Fine," she quickly replied. "What makes you ask that?"

"You're practically running," Baelath chuckled. "Besides I can always tell when something's wrong."

"How can something *not* be wrong?" she asked, throwing her hands in the air. "Grul was viciously attacked, and Max lost his brother. I don't know if I could live through something like that again. Watching a friend die before my eyes." Tears began to spill onto her brown cheeks. "I want to see this king, and I will demand justice."

"Don't," Grul said. "At least not on my behalf. This is my punishment."

"Don't think like that," Evelyn said quietly. "That monster had us chained and threatened us if you didn't give him what he wanted. I don't care about your beard, Grul. You are still the finest warrior I've ever met."

"No, my punishment isn't because of that coward, nah, dearie. He just collected on the payment," said Grul, lowering his head. "It's because I didn't defeat my first monster and abandoned my quest to journey with you. It's my price for choosing happiness over duty."

"Mine too," whispered Max.

Evelyn whipped to her right where Max was walking. "Nothing that wicked creature did was your fault!"

"I feel like it is," Max said. He raised his head and looked up above him, as if remembering a time long ago. "There were plenty of times when I wished for my brother's death, times when I wished I was free from everything that was holding me down." He lowered his gaze back to his shuffling feet. "Looks like I got my wish."

"Your brother cared about you. Don't disgrace his memory by blaming yourself for this," Evelyn said. She tried to reassure him, but it seemed to do little. *Maybe I'm just trying to reassure myself,* she thought. "Nothing anyone could do."

"That's just it, though," Max said with a sigh of relief. "My brother was a lousy farmer who drank his coin away and tried to win more by scamming in card games. The times I had to bail him out, either literally out of jail or by fighting our way out, became too many to count. All I ever wanted to do was roam the lands and have the freedom to explore whatever is out there to find, but I couldn't. My brother and I had to work our farm so we could feed ourselves and Mother. And all the while, I kept thinking, hoping, and wishing that one day I would find a way out from all of that, that I could just walk the open land under my feet and live each day as an adventure." His gaze went downward, shoulders slumped, and his hands rested against his sides. "I just didn't know the price was watching my family die."

"I refuse to believe that," Evelyn said with a huff. "All of this can be blamed on one person."

"Don't misunderstand me," Max said, his gaze turning to meet Evelyn's and Baelath's. "I am going to kill Maligor the Dark Elf."

Suddenly, Garrus stopped up ahead of them, and the four companions froze in their tracks, waiting for a surprise attack. But only the wind moved around them.

"We're here," Thane said from behind them.

"We're at Morketrekk? I don't see any kingdom," Baelath said, motioning around him. "I don't see anything but woods." *If this can be called woods. This is such a sad state compared to what Blaonir is. Have the Dark Elves been reduced to this in their time away from the rest of us?*

"Through there," Thane said, pointing to the large dead-looking tree directly in front of them. "Come, follow me." He walked around to the other side of it.

Baelath followed and saw that the trunk of the tree had a large opening in it, almost like a door was carved out of it. He tried to peer inside it but could only see a pit of blackness. "What is this?"

"This is how we get to Morketrekk," Thane said, his deep-purple eyes staring into the black abyss.

"I don't understand," said Baelath, trying to follow Thane's gaze. "Where does this go?"

"Underneath, of course. To the kingdom of Morketrekk." Then Thane disappeared into the darkness.

Baelath looked back at Garrus, who nodded for him to go forward. Baelath took a deep breath and then stepped into the black pit of a dead tree in the middle of the Dark Woods.

CHAPTER 9

BAELATH COULD FEEL steps descending in front of him, spiraling him downward into the black that gripped his sight. He heard the others behind him, each of their footsteps vibrating the staircase that filled his ears with a buzz. Baelath wondered if they were being led into another trap, another prison from which they couldn't escape. For the next few minutes, he thought of all the possibilities of how to escape this encounter, how they might overwhelm their captors in the dark.

But Baelath got the sense that his friends were still weak and would easily be outmatched at this point. So unwillingly and suspiciously, Baelath continued on. A few moments later, he forgot about all of that as a small beacon of light appeared below him, and with each step, it grew until he was basking in light for a moment. The darkness faded away and what replaced it made him stare in awe.

The staircase had finally broken out from the tree and left them with an astonishing view. It was like there was a land beneath the ground, almost like an open pocket of land, deep under the dead terrain above. Baelath now understood why it looked like all the trees were dying—they basically were. Their roots didn't rest in soil but rather dived beneath it, and Baelath could see them twisting their way down from the ground above them and diving back into the dirt that lay a few hundred feet below the staircase they were climbing down. He could see more staircases in the distance and people using them, hurrying back into the land above or returning to the land down below.

Looking out farther, Baelath could now fully see the kingdom of Morketrekk and all its people going about their daily lives. Blacksmiths hammering on tools, clothes being washed, food being cooked and sold. A hum hung on the air, as hundreds of Dark Elves laughed and talked with their neighbors. It almost reminded him of Mellom Elvene in the way the kingdom seemed to breathe on its own.

At first, Baelath was confused by light down there, for it seemed brighter than above land. He looked around but saw no fires, but then he noticed it. Little flying bugs zoomed through the air, each one giving off a glow. Now that Baelath had noticed them, they seemed to be everywhere, yet they never got in the way, like two separate species coexisting in the same area, each benefitting from the other's survival. Each doomed without the other. Some would hover around; others would collect on the ground or the staircase, forming bright spots for the Dark Elves on the ground or in the air. Looking up, Baelath could even see some bugs above him, crawling along the dirt that was on top of them, the dirt that held the Dark Woods above.

By now, the others had made their way next to him, each taking in the sight, and like Baelath, they were left in a weird catatonic state.

"Come," said Thane, ushering them forward. "There will be time later to take in the view, but for now, we must continue on."

And so, their group walked down the rest of the spiraling tree staircase until they stepped foot onto the soil below. Baelath could easily feel how different it felt from the soil up above. Down here, it was rich and alive, providing a bounce to each step he took. Flowers sprung up and weird-looking crops were growing. Workers in the fields were pulling little brown balls from the dirt and placing them in their baskets. After they passed the crop fields, the village loomed ahead—stone houses sat upon the shops underneath, where the families sold their wares. Some Dark Elves would stop and look and maybe even strike up conversations but most went about their business. Horses went up and down the packed road, barely able to get through the throng, pulling large wagons behind them while their drivers shouted at those in front to move out of the way.

How do they get horses down here? Or back up to normal land? Baelath watched as little children ran and played all around. Their parents were hard at work, living normal lives between their labor and their laughter, and

Baelath couldn't help but think of home and how eerily similar this all felt. Each one grinding through the day for the same chance at happiness that everyone wanted. He looked around at each one of them and wondered, *And these people are supposed to be my enemies? How am I supposed to fight people of my own kind?*

The villagers began to take notice of them now, which wasn't hard to do with Thane marching along out front, leading them like a parade cascading through their town. Baelath could tell Thane had been a soldier in his youth, for he had seen countless other elves like this around his father all his life. But having a dwarf in their company didn't help matters. It seemed Dark Elves hated dwarfs more than they hated Baelath's kind, and soon, it felt like the entire village had gone quiet and curiously looked at their group as they passed by. Some had worried looks about on their faces, while others wore a snarl. Baelath saw some rush back inside their doors, while others hurried out of them, hoping to catch a glimpse of what the commotion was. Children stopped playing their games to rush over and poke at them before they were shushed away. Bakers stopped baking, and blacksmiths stopped hammering. A disquieting silence fell over everyone, but still, Thane marched them on, and the shops and homes began to dwindle toward the outskirts until, finally, it was just small crop fields around them again. Almost instantly, like a threat had passed through, Baelath heard the town roar back to life, each one chattering to another about the event that just transpired in their little town.

But Baelath couldn't be concerned with town gossip, and he hoped that he soon would forget it. *They don't know me, and I don't know them. I can't forget the reason I'm here.*

The land sloped downward still, and the village grew smaller in the distance above them until Thane came to the edge of the cliff. He suddenly stopped and turned around to face them. At first, Baelath was confused as to why they were stopping, but then he saw it—down below the edge of the cliff, sitting in the bowels of the valley, was a castle so magnificent yet so conspicuously evil that Baelath wondered who would build something so pure, so breathtaking, yet leave those who looked on it shuddering in fear.

The first things Baelath noticed were the towers. It looked like hundreds of towers sprang up from the ground, each twisting and turning in a unique way. The stone was polished black yet shone in the flickering light, for not many of those lightning bugs came this way, just enough to leave a lush luster along its edges. The thousands of windows that perched on each sill were painted gold, but in the front of the castle, above the staircase, which looked longer than the staircases they had used to descend here, stood two blood-red wooden doors that were taller than Baelath had ever seen before.

With the loudest click that Baelath had ever heard—for the echo shook the ground they stood on—the doors slowly began to swing open. As that was happening, Thane spun around and walked down the rocky path in front of them, bringing them from the top of the cliff right to the very first step of the castle's own staircase. It took nearly an hour to climb down and then back up to the front of the castle, but finally, they reached the doors, where two more Dark Elf guards awaited. Their armor was not quite as grand as their escorts' or Maligor's, for that matter.

Thane spun around again to face Baelath. "I'm afraid this is where we leave you. You will be led into the great hall of Morketrekk, where King Nathrak awaits you." He lowered his head a little before he whispered the next part to Baelath alone. "And I'm sorry about your friend. If only I had gotten word sooner, I might have been able to stop Maligor. I hope you can convince the king that Maligor's had his last laugh." And with those sad parting words, Thane and Garrus turned and walked through the doors.

Baelath and his friends followed behind them with their new escort, but they went straight down the large hallway, which was littered with paintings and memorialized weapons. Decorative black tables clung to the walls, and the carpet they walked on was the same red as the doors they had just walked through. The guards stopped suddenly as they came to another set of closed red doors, smaller this time though still quite large. It made the castle in Nox feel like a cottage rather than a house for royalty, and all of this made Mellom Elvene seem like just a bunch of sticks held with rope in trees. *This is how the Dark Elves live, while I had to grow up inside of a hollow tree?*

The guards knocked on each door once, and seconds later, they swung inward, giving them a look at Morketrekk's splendor. If Baelath thought they had lived in splendor, what he saw next made him feel insignificant. The hall opened up higher than Baelath could see. Long golden chandeliers, dripping with red rubies, hung from chains that dropped down from the darkness above, each holding six torches that were lit with the brightest and warmest fire Baelath had seen. He could feel the warmth the moment the doors were opened. Wide stone pillars lined the walkway, with a guard stationed by each one. The polished surface radiated a glow in the firelight; each pillar had a carving etched into it—a huge wolf, a giant spider, man-sized bat creatures. Three of them were etched into one carving, but two others, in particular, caught Baelath's eye.

The last two at the end of the walkway were very familiar to him, for he had everlasting memories of them. The one on the left side was the large minotaur that brought the ruins of a city down upon his friends and him, and the one on the right side resembled the Shadow Walker, and even looking at a wooden carving of it sent shivers down his spine. Throughout the hall, save for the pathway before them, Dark Elves wandered and murmured among themselves, their long silk gowns flowing from each of them and all in many different colors. They talked with such a frenzy that Baelath was surprised that all eyes turned to them when they walked in the doors and immediately fell silent once the group of prisoners and the guards led them down into the room. Baelath could see the gaudy silks and ostentatious jewelry that they wore on their bodies as they stared at him, like each one was trying to outshine the other with their riches or their shame; he couldn't tell which. But Baelath was more interested in what lay at the end of their walk. *Let them have their moment,* he bitterly thought. *I've only come for one reason, and I will get Jord out of here. They cannot keep a prisoner for no reason, no matter what Maligor seems to think.*

Just past those last pillars and up five wide steps sat the largest throne Baelath had ever seen. It was more than three times the height of Baelath and as wide as him too. The color of it was the same as those dead-looking trees from the surface above this kingdom, and he was pretty sure it was made from the wood of them as well. They must have made that throne before they realized how twisted that wood became when dead, compared to the marvelous red-wood trees that were found down below here. *Why wouldn't they make a new one?* The arms twisted around to form a spiral, reaching out toward whoever stood in front of the king, like they were about to wrap around your throat. Yet Baelath never took his gaze off the Dark Elf who occupied the throne.

He looked relatively old, even for an elf. But at the same time, there was a certain grace about his presence, as if he was a descendant of time itself. His hair was pure white and hung down below his shoulders, gracefully flowing in the air with each movement he made with his head as he studied the group that came before him. A vast golden crown rested atop his head; it looked to be heavier than the pack Baelath had carried across the entire land, yet it seemed to be nothing but a feather upon the king's head. His face was stern and hard, though he didn't look angry, like King Rodrigo had when they first were presented in Nox's halls, and his eyes carried a deep fire in them. He wore a light-gold suit of armor, mostly decorative wear, and a long, flowing black robe stretched behind it, with a white fur trim lining the top. A sword rested along his hip, but Baelath doubted that it had been unsheathed for quite some time. The closer Baelath got, the lighter the king's mood seemed to get. His heavy shoulders seemed relaxed, and his callused hands rested on his knees, waiting for them to approach.

When the guards reached the first step, they stopped, and without really thinking much about it, Baelath found himself kneeling in front of the king. And after he gave a quick glare to his friend, they followed suit. Then Baelath raised his head and met the king's gaze, his green eyes narrowing, as if he were looking inside Baelath. For a few moments, the room became tense. Each person was afraid to disrupt the status quo until a small, sly smile broke across the king's face, and he promptly burst into a deep, roaring laugh.

"My friends," the king boomed, rising from his throne. "Welcome to Morketrekk. I am Nathrak, King of the Wood Elves. I heard you have traveled a great distance to join us on this fine morning. You've must have encountered many great things. Come forward and speak to me of your tales."

"It is true, King Nathrak," Baelath said, slightly stepping forward. "We have traveled a great distance and have dealt with many great things, as well as some truly horrible things." Even though he could not see them, he felt his friends' movements. Tears welled in Evelyn's eyes, and she rapidly blinked before more could gather. Grul hung his head down low, giving him an even smaller appearance than being a dwarf in the middle of a room filled with elves could do, while Max tensed and shuffled his feet at the implied words of his brother's fate. "And it is truer still that I have a great desire to speak with you, for I come seeking a favor."

"A favor, you say," the king replied, a certain amusement to his voice. "And what makes you believe I'm in the business of offering favors?"

Trying to calm his nerves, Baelath took another step forward, his toes pressed against the bottom of the steps. "That is because I believe I have something to offer you, Your Majesty," Baelath said, trying to sound as diplomatic as possible.

The king narrowed his eyes toward Baelath and stared at him for a few moments, then slowly leaned back in his throne. "And what would you offer? There are few things a king needs and wants even less that I have not already acquired," Nathrak said, that mischievous smile returning.

Baelath turned back to his companions with a sad smile. He knew now that he had won, that he had gotten the king to let him make the offer. He knew he would be able to complete his quest, the one he had set out for so long ago, the one he had sacrificed everything for. He knew he would get his friend back. He just didn't know the cost yet.

He looked at the king. His smile had faded, and in its place, Baelath had put on his bravest face, trying to portray the prince that he was. "Name your price."

King Nathrak took his words in stride. His facial expression remained unchanged, and empty silence filled the hall.

Baelath began wondering what the king would ask for. *Will it be the trade agreement with the cities of men that my father held over the Dark Elves? Will it be the northern lands in Blaonir? Will I have to take Jord's place and be held captive? Will it be my father's crown? Will it be my claim to the throne in Blaonir? Will it involve Maligor?* Each thought became worse than the one before, and soon anxiety and fear spread through him.

"Before I name my price," the king said, interrupting Baelath's thoughts and pulling him back into the reality of the situation, "why don't you first tell me the favor that you've come to ask?"

"A while ago, you captured and imprisoned a friend of mine. I would like him released to me," answered Baelath, never breaking the king's gaze.

"You ask for a criminal to be released? That is no small favor here, so my price will be just as steep," the king said so all those who listened could clearly hear him. "The question becomes, *Prince Baelath*, are you willing to pay it?"

"If I can give it, then it shall be yours," Baelath replied somberly.

"Oh, but I do not want you to give me anything—just yet—but rather to take," Nathrak shrewdly said.

Confused, Baelath tipped his head to one side and pondered the king's response. "Take what?"

"Why, my daughter's hand in marriage, of course!" the king exclaimed.

A murmur broke out through the crowd. Thoughts flooded Baelath's mind. Even if he agreed to it, would his father recognize the marriage? But what choice did he have at this point? He had come so far to get here and had lost some good people along the way; he couldn't waste it all now. How would it look to say no to a king, especially when it was an offer to marry his daughter? Everyone knew you cannot say no to a king's daughter. He was pretty sure he would never leave this place if he did that.

"I humbly accept your offer, *my* king," Baelath finally answered, slightly bowing his head toward Nathrak.

That crooked smile returned to the king's face, and he rose from his throne. "Then there shall be a wedding within a moon and a feast tonight to celebrate. But first, let me introduce you to your bride, my daughter, the Princess Freya." The king turned to his right and held out his arm for his daughter to hold.

Baelath's gaze followed the king's and watched as the Princess Freya stepped out from the edge of the crowd, and Baelath could have sworn the room grew brighter behind her. A glowing shimmer trailed her elegant figure, and everything seemed to fade away around her. Her hair, as white as the first fallen snow, flowed behind her impeccably pointed ears and draped over her bare shoulders, down to her soft chest. Her skin was so transparent that Baelath could see her icy veins, yet somehow, he felt the warmth radiating from her when she crossed the room. Perfect clear-sky–colored eyes looked out toward him and then locked her eyes with his, and a tiny smile crept across her face, showing a small dimple in each of her cheeks. She wore a dark-purple, off-the-shoulder dress that flowed over her feet and slightly trailed behind her, and with each step, it gripped her figure and twisted with her hips. Baelath had never seen such beauty.

She took her father's arm and turned toward Baelath. "Father. My prince," she said, bowing her head to both of them.

"Daughter," King Nathrak said. "I would like you to meet your future husband, heir to Mellom Elvene, Prince Baelath."

For a moment, Baelath thought the princess looked sad, but in the next moment, the look had disappeared, and her vibrant smile filled the room once again.

The King raised his other hand and said, "You will have plenty of time to talk and get to know each other at the feast tonight. First, I have to deal with our other guests."

Baelath turned around to look at the others, a big smile on his face as he realized he could relax. *It's finally over*, he thought.

Grul wore a smile bigger than Baelath's, and his eyes seemed fixed on the princess. Max seemed quite content with the morning's events, and his eyes filled with wonder as he explored the room. Evelyn, on the other hand, did not look pleased but annoyed, especially with Grul, who looked longingly at the princess. Evelyn glared angrily at Grul, with her hands on her hips.

Although Baelath did not know the princess, his marrying her seemed a small price to pay to make sure everyone could go home safe and happy. But then he heard the king quietly say, "Guards," and suddenly, everything changed.

The guards standing next to the pillars came rushing down on them and held them at sword point. Max tried to slip out, but one guard shoved the pommel of his sword hilt into Max's stomach and sent him crashing to the ground. When Grul tried to grapple with one of them, the guard would have brought the dwarf to the ground, had another guard not come over and struck Grul across the face with the broad side of the sword. Evelyn stood still, her eyes never leaving Baelath. That hurt him the most. Other guards came rushing in from outside the hall, carrying shackles and chains, and they proceeded to bind each of his friends.

"What is the meaning of this?" Baelath demanded, frustration and anger boiling over him.

"Your friends have trespassed on my land, and while you did the same, we have made a deal. Do your friends have a similar deal that they can make? Can they offer me what you can? Our deal is that the prisoner I hold will be released to you, and you will marry my daughter. We did not say anything about leaving—well, leaving anytime soon—for you will stay here in Morketrekk and produce an heir. Then, you will be allowed to go home and reclaim your throne in Blaonir—with your wife and son, of course." King Nathrak's viciously creepy smile now beamed across his face.

Baelath looked over at the princess and now knew why she had looked sad for that brief moment. She knew this was about to happen, and Baelath had calmly walked right into it. He watched as his friends were dragged away in chains and pulled out of his sight, and his heart grew as heavy as it had ever been. He almost had collapsed where he stood, when Evelyn looked at him as she struggled against the guards, and he wondered if that was the last time he would ever see her. He slowly turned to stare at the king, feeling nothing but defeat. He could still hear the grunts and the gruff sounds that Grul made as he was being dragged off, swearing up a storm, his words echoing off the walls and inside Baelath's head.

King Nathrak settled onto his throne, still wearing a nasty smile. He kept nodding and acknowledging his subjects, who cheered him on. *They must hate us as much as we hate them.* Soon, his attention turned back to Baelath, who now did nothing to hide his dismay. The king slowly rose from his sovereign seat, his gaze never leaving Baelath. The king's figure seemed to have grown since Baelath first saw him, for it seemed as if King Nathrak now towered over him, looking down at him from the top of the stairs to where Baelath stood, surrounded on all sides by the guards. He knew it was over.

"As for you, our young prince," the king whispered, "you shall be confined to one of our guest rooms until the feast is prepared—you will be the guest of honor, of course—and then, we shall have our wedding!"

The crowd let out a cheer at the mention of the wedding.

"And if I refuse?" Baelath asked.

"Then you will watch your friends die, and then, you too will forfeit your life," said the king, smiling at him. "For breaking your promise, of course."

The king gave another quick glance and a nod, and the guards who surrounded Baelath closed in on him and easily subdued him. Baelath couldn't muster the will to struggle against them. He let them drag him out of the room and down the hall but in the opposite direction from friends. *It seems the king has a different place for you, you fool*, Baelath chided himself. Up a couple of staircases and down a few halls, the guards dragged Baelath until they finally reached a door at the end of a hallway that led to a dead end. Flinging open the door, they threw Baelath inside and slammed it shut behind him. He heard a click as they locked the door, and he then heard their footsteps retreating down the hall.

Baelath was left alone in the dimly lit room—a couple of candles were placed in each corner of the windowless chamber. He stood and tried to take in his surroundings, waiting for his eyes to get used to the dim light. Against one wall was a rickety bed, its base having been gnawed on by rodents and the mattress stuffing coming out from each side. One straw pillow was on top of the bed; holes in the front and back allowed the straw to spill out. A small table was against another wall; on it was nothing but a pitcher of water and a small cup. It wobbled on uneven legs when Baelath lifted the pitcher to pour himself some water, and he almost dropped the entire pitcher on the cold floor. The floors and walls were bare stone. The small rug in the middle of the room had an intricate pattern etched across it, gold and red streaks crisscrossing back and forth until it left you in a trance if you stared at it for too long. Baelath could see rat droppings scattered on the floor, among the loose stuffing from the mattress. He strode over to the bed and sat upon it.

Not all kings are the same, he thought. Some were there to help him along his way; even his own father had helped, though he had stood against it the entire time. *Some kings, though, are only here to see someone punished, just to get a cheer.*

His thoughts drifted to his friends and the peril they are faced now, all because he hadn't thought things through. *Of course, the Dark Elves betrayed me. How could I have been so stupid?* He wondered where his friends had been taken and if anything had happened to them. He dreaded the thought and wondered if they were still alive. He pictured Max, his midnight-black hair covering his face, all alone in this world now, and that made Baelath's stomach drop. Then Grul, his mohawked dwarf friend, entered his mind, beardless and defeated, resigned to his misery. Baelath felt a lump in his throat, but the worst thought was the one that came next. He pictured Evelyn, her dark emerald eyes angry and her soft hands on her slender hips as she glared at him. Her anger turned to fear and terror, held in her eyes, and it all became too much to bear. He fell forward to the ground, with tears streaming down his face.

Baelath lay there for what seemed like forever, feeling the seconds turn to minutes and the minutes to hours, until finally the door opened, and a bright light flooded the room that made Baelath shield his eyes.

"Come, *River Elf*, it's time for the feast," spat the guard, and Baelath felt two others grab his arms and hoist him onto his feet, his knees still buckling, and drag him out of the room. He couldn't tell where he was being dragged, but eventually, he found himself in front of another door down another long hallway, but when he peered inside, he saw that this room wasn't bare. Instead, Thane was waiting for him with some type of formal gown. Baelath assumed that he was to wear it at the feast.

The guards dropped him to the ground in the doorway and then left. Baelath .slumped on the floor with his head bowed. *Is this what defeat feels like?* He raised his head to look around the room and noticed how elegant it was, compared to the hole in the wall he'd been dragged from. A golden chandelier hung from the ceiling, the candles making the entire room glow. A canopy hung above the bed, and Baelath noticed that none of the mattress stuffing was hanging out, and the bed looked well kept. Tables lined the room, topped with more candles and bowls of fruit. There was blank parchment paper but no pen or ink to be found. On the far wall, a healthy ire burned in the fireplace. A few beautiful rugs—all perfectly designed with such detail that you could get lost in them for days—were along the floor, allowing you to walk from the bed to the fireplace to the door without touching any of the cold stone.

Baelath couldn't help but feel jealous. He thought that he should have had a room like this given to him; he should have been a guest of honor, an invited prince in a foreign land. Instead, he had been treated like a common criminal or something to be pawned off or added to a collection. He felt like a lowly prisoner, while his friends actually were imprisoned—if they were still alive.

"Here, take my hand," Thane said, extending his arm toward Baelath and helping him off the floor. "I am deeply sorry for what has happened. I truly wish it had gone a different way."

Scrambling back to his feet, Baelath glared at Thane. "And which way would you like to have seen it go? The way where I don't get tricked into siring a Wood Elf child for my land's throne, or where my friends don't get dragged off and thrown in a dungeon to rot in the darkness—if they don't get executed in the middle of the night or something."

"I assure you that your friends are alive and well," Thane interrupted, his posture becoming less honorable and more embarrassed. "I had a feeling that was why the king wanted to bring you before him—to get your throne. I just never thought he would lie and betray you as he did."

"You must not know your king too well, for that seemed to be the plan all along. And everyone but you, it seems, was in on it. Or maybe you were and just calmly led me into the heart of the trap."

"It is true that I do not know the king as well as I used to, for it seems time has changed him," Thane said sadly, his eyes downcast. "But still, a part of me hoped he had not become what he so obviously has."

They stood in silence for a moment. Baelath wondered if this was part of another trap or scheme. *Can I trust him?*

Thane continued to gaze off into the distance, thinking of a time when he once admired his king. Baelath shuffled his feet on the silk rugs, and that seemed to break the trance that Thane seemed stuck in. Thane then offered the gown to Baelath, saying, "It's the custom for the male elf to wear this on the night before his wedding."

Reluctantly, Baelath took the gown from Thane. "Is anything else expected?" he asked.

"I wouldn't think so. It's mostly a gathering for the king to gloat and such," Thane said, waving away any concerns Baelath might have. "You just have to get through tonight and tomorrow, and then we can figure out what to do next."

"We?" Baelath asked suspiciously, still not trusting Thane.

"You may not believe me, but I am on your side," Thane replied, taking note of Baelath's skeptical tone. "My loyalty still lies with my king and always will. But I do not want a war between our people. Maligor does and will do whatever it takes to get his way. Maligor's actions have grown tiresome, and not just for me but for most of those who were here before his rise up the ranks. For some reason, King Nathrak adores him and encourages him. So I will help keep you and your friends alive while you're here, if you help me rid Maligor from the king's court." Thane extended his hand to Baelath. "So, what do you say?"

Baelath studied Thane and his expression for a moment, trying to see the lie behind it. Tried as he might, though, he could not find anything about the Wood Elf to dissuade him from agreeing to his help. Baelath had an uneasy feeling that he might need Thane's help not too long from now.

Thane got Baelath ready for the feast, and once they were finished, he led Baelath out into the castle's halls once again—but not before he rolled some parchment into his sleeve. He anted to take notes on the castle and any conversations he would have tonight. This time, as they began to walk, Baelath paid more attention to his surroundings and the layout of the corridors, trying to make a map of it in his head. After a few minutes, they stopped in front of the doors that opened into the great hall, where King Nathrak was holding the feast. *My feast*, Baelath thought.

"Ready?" Thane asked.

"I don't know. You're the one who did the work. Do I look like a Dark Elf?" Baelath cracked a small smile, which Thane quickly returned right before he threw open the doors. Baelath's smile quickly disappeared when he looked inside the room.

At the back of the room—behind the long tables, each covered with platters that were brimming with food, some of which Baelath had never seen before—stood the last person he wanted to see. The glowing red sword again swung on his hip, and the black cape clung to him, though no armor was worn underneath it this time. The gold batlike wings were still perched on his shoulders, and his midnight-black hair swayed just below them, as if a soft breeze was blowing right next to him. Maligor slowly turned toward him, his icy blue eyes striking Baelath from across the room. The smile etched on his face showed just how ecstatic he was to be sitting there.

Baelath felt frozen in place; fear and anger had rooted him to the spot, and the memories of Jax swirled in his head.

"Come," whispered Thane. "You sit next to the king."

Thane hooked Baelath's arm in his and dragged him down the main aisle. Baelath had been so transfixed by Maligor that he had ignored the rest of the room, but now, he refocused on his task and turned to look at the king.

Baelath smiled once he approached the table. "My king," he said, bowing slightly toward King Nathrak. "I am honored by this feast that is being held for the event of my marriage into your kingdom."

"*Ha!*" roared the king, his hand slapping the table. "I'm sure you are. After what you've been through and the lengths you've traveled, food and a roof must be the only things you care about."

"Yes, what a tumultuous journey you must have had," Maligor sniped, that sickening smile still across his face. "The difficulties you must have overcome have to be interesting, and I know I would be delighted to hear some of these tales."

"Oh yes, for sure," the king added. "I would be glad to hear of them."

"My king," Baelath responded politely as he took his seat. "I have a plethora of stories, even a few I'm sure you would be quite interested to hear." Baelath's eyes flickered toward Maligor, whose smile had evaporated and was replaced by a cruel snarl. "But alas, I do not think them suitable for this joyous occasion."

"Perhaps you're right," the king agreed. "Let us drink to the future, then, when we happily reunite our two sides as one again." The king raised his cup, giving an obviously fake smile to the crowd and to Baelath, who knew this was all a ruse. Maligor joined his cup next to the king's, his gaze locked on Baelath. Baelath was next to raise his cup with theirs, nodding his head toward the crowd, acknowledging the cheers. Thane joined with his cup, and Garrus was there too, and two others seated with them at the table joined their cups with the group's.

Finally, the room let out a loud cheer, and all banged their cups with those across or next to them. Soon, they settled down, and everyone began to eat, and chatter soon filled the room. Baelath glanced over to the king and noticed that Maligor was sitting quietly, like a stone. He went back to his food and his cup, which he hastily emptied. He got a refill and would have emptied that one as well, if Thane hadn't slowed him down. He looked back at Maligor and saw he was deep in a conversation with one of the older Dark Elves who was sitting next to him. Baelath decided this moment was his chance.

"My king," Baelath whispered, leaning in toward him. "I truly am humbled by all of this, as well as the honor of marrying your beautiful daughter. I see great things in the future for our two sides."

"I'm glad you feel that way." The king beamed while he stuffed his mouth with food. "Honestly, I thought you'd be reluctant to offer your services after I said your friends could not leave quite yet."

"Yes, at first I was quite upset," Baelath said, leaning in even closer to the king. "But then, I realized what advantages we could have—you know, provided certain things were handled in the right way."

Gulping down the last of his cup, the king leaned over to Baelath so that their heads were now almost touching. "And what would these *certain things* be?"

"Well, take this land you rule," Baelath said, motioning outward with his arm to all around him. "Your castle is the finest one I've ever seen. The village on its outskirts is lively and brimming with activity. Not to mention the extraordinary beauty that dwells down here, from the eloquence of the staircases to the awe-inspiring lightning bugs that give this land a shine that I had never seen before. But the land up top"—Baelath pointed upward—"the place we call the Dark Woods. That could be worked on. Maybe someone could build a road for everyone to use. Maybe have a friendlier welcoming party. You need to surround yourself with those who are trying to help your people, not those who look to take your place."

Baelath's eyes flickered over toward Maligor, whose ice-blue eyes were locked on him. Maligor's thin black eyebrows arched inward, and his mouth clenched in anger. The king kept talking, but Baelath couldn't hear him. For some strange reason, all other noise was blocked out of Baelath's head, and he and Maligor just locked eyes, each refusing to give up the stare. All Baelath could think about was the sword plunging through Jax's back; all he could see was the blood pouring down to the ground; all he could hear were the screams of his friends. It took a fight between two random guests from the regular tables to knock Baelath back to his senses, and that was only after one guest's neck had been snapped and the body was dragged away.

"My king," Maligor said. "Should I retrieve the bride-to-be now?"

"Ah yes, now seems like as—*hic*—good a time as any," the king replied, after one more large gulp from his cup. "Go and bring my daughter."

Before Maligor got up from the table, he shot one last look at Baelath and then broke out in the smile that Baelath had come to hate. "If you'll excuse me," he said, and with that, he strode out of the room as quickly as he could.

Better now, Baelath thought. *I can work on the king without Maligor's nagging presence. I just hope the king doesn't get too drunk to comprehend what I want.* He still had to try, though, and he didn't know how much time he had before Maligor returned with Princess Freya; then, any hope he had of convincing the king would be almost nonexistent, not with Maligor hovering over him.

"Speaking of those who seek to replace you," Baelath murmured to the king, nodding his head toward Maligor as he walked away, "I would fear for your life in these next few days, at least until you can be assured that your line will continue."

The king's eyes narrowed as he watched Maligor leave the hall and disappear around the corner. "And what makes you say that?"

"Think about it," persisted Baelath. "Your rule has never been as unstable as in these few moments. Your only child is a daughter, for whom who you have just found a suitor. If you should die before I marry your daughter, who would rule?"

"What makes you think I'm going to die?" the King grunted with a bubbling anger.

"No one, my king. I only meant to say things here are at a delicate place," Baelath said. "Here, let me show you." He unrolled the blank piece of parchment he'd grabbed from the room. Thane handed him a pen, and Baelath offered it to the king. "Write your name in the middle here, and then draw two lines going upward. Now, write down the name of your successor after your death above one line."

The king wrote his daughter's name above the line on the left.

"And if your subjects won't accept a female on the throne? Who will it be then?"

"I'm not sure," the king said, suddenly perplexed. "Who would dare say no to my daughter?"

Baelath shifted his eyes to the elf behind the king, and he let the king notice.

For the next few seconds, the king's gaze remained unchanged; he fixated on the parchment with narrowed eyes. Then suddenly, his eyes grew wide, and his mouth opened slightly. The king whipped his head around to Baelath, the anger clear on his face. "We shall rectify this immediately. Trust me," King Nathrak growled. "Make sure you get a good night's sleep tonight. You're going to have a day to remember tomorrow."

Maligor returned with the Princess Freya on his arm, and the room grew quiet. Baelath rolled up the parchment quietly and slipped it into his sleeve while Maligor and the princess made their way down the room. When they reached the table, its occupants stood. Maligor walked the princess to her seat. Her soft footsteps looked like a glide next to Maligor's hard pace. He sat her next to her father on his right, pushing Maligor and the two other older Dark Elves he didn't know farther right.

The king talked to his daughter for a few minutes, quietly enough so Baelath couldn't hear them, but from the sad smile she gave him, it seemed it wasn't what she wanted to hear.

That's OK, Baelath thought. *I'm sure she'll have a brighter smile once I talk to her.*

The king rose to his feet, and the room grew silent, with all eyes turned upon him. "Friends, we have gathered here tonight to celebrate the announcement of not only my daughter's marriage, but the future as well, for the next generation will be ruled by my grandson, a Wood Elf." A loud cheer erupted from the crowd on that note, and the king had to raise his hand to silence the room once more. "Yet I am not one to wait for things to come. I get what I seek, and I won't wait for what I've worked hard for. And so, it only makes sense that my blood would feel the same, and my daughter has pushed for this moment for too long for me to deny her any longer, just for the sake of a so-called ritual we haven't upheld in decades. So, due to her persistence, I have decided to agree to her wants and demands." The other elves sat still, most confused as to what the king was talking about, although Baelath knew exactly what he was about to say. Thane had let it slip earlier, if not the king too lost in his drink. "The wedding will be held tomorrow!"

For a tick, the room remained silent, but then, in epic fashion, a roar was unleashed and glasses clinked and clanked. Thane seemed happy, and the others were joyous in their celebration, slapping each other and hugging. But Baelath wasn't looking at them. His eyes locked once again with Maligor's, but this time, it was Baelath who wore the smile.

The king motioned for Princess Freya and Baelath to stand, and to Baelath's amazement, the cheering grew even louder. *Little do they know*, Baelath thought.

The rest of the feast went smoothly, and Maligor's sulky mood made it an even merrier occasion for Baelath. When the food ran out and the drinks stopped flowing, the king, who barely was able to keep from burying his head in his chest, finally stood on wobbly legs and motioned for the feast to end.

First, Maligor stood with the princess on his arm, and together, they walked out from the hall. Next, Thane stood, hooking Baelath's arm with his and helping him to his feet; together, they walked down the aisle and out the doors.

Such an odd custom, Baelath thought. They turned the opposite way from where Maligor and the princess had gone, and once they were out of earshot of the hall, Thane congratulated him on the turn of events and said it was a good first step in getting rid of Maligor for good. He was happy to help, but his thoughts were more focused on tomorrow and all that he had to do.

"I need to see my friends tonight," Baelath whispered to Thane as they walked down the hall.

"Impossible," he said. "Not only would someone see us and tell the king, but the guards to the dungeons won't let us through without written permission from the king."

"Don't worry about that," Baelath said, smiling as he pulled the piece of parchment from his shirt sleeve. "We have what we need right here."

He gave it to Thane so that he could write a more formal request, but the king's signature was what mattered most, and the king had given it to him freely. After they had made the parchment presentable, they quickly scurried down to the lower levels. Baelath noted the passages as they hurried through them until they finally found themselves outside the doors to the dungeons.

"You ready?" Thane asked.

"Yes," Baelath said. His friends were all that mattered. He needed to talk to them; he needed to see them. To see Evelyn.

Thane opened the door and led the way, and Baelath quickly followed, trying to not be seen. The damp air was the first thing Baelath noticed. It clung to the air like burrs sticking to clothing. He could taste it in every breath. The second thing Baelath noticed was the slimy green moss oozing out from the cracks in the wall. It half covered the floor, giving a soft bounce when Baelath walked on it.

He followed Thane down the hall through a few twists and turns until they came upon another door. On this one, an old rusted padlock dangled from the handles on the door and wall. Thane swiftly removed a key from his cloak and inserted it into the hole; with a loud clang and a vigorous tug, the lock came undone. Baelath scampered over to help pull open the door, just enough for them to slip through, and then he hastily followed Thane when he slid through the crack.

It was dark now, and they moved gingerly down the corridor. Baelath let his hands graze the slick walls to cautiously guide himself. With each step, he moved slower than with the last, and soon the pair were tiptoeing. The only sound was the repetitive dripping of water drops echoing down the halls. Baelath felt a corner, an edge, and hugged the wall even closer as he turned it. He immediately saw Thane's shadowy figure ahead. Torchlight flared from the distance, and as the two of them got closer, Baelath could see a room ahead. He had begun to scan the room when a figure suddenly leaded from the shadows, and a glimmer caught his eye. All he had time to do was slam himself against the wall. Steel flashed at him and bit red on the top of his shoulder; a searing pain jolted him, and he felt his shirt sleeve become wet. He had no time to think of it, though, and jumped back at his attacker, his hands aiming for the wrist that held the dagger.

The two figures collided, and Baelath felt his muscles strain as neither one of them moved. But Baelath had leverage, and he forced his attacker to stumble back into the light, where he saw a too-familiar face. Maligor was sneering at him with death in his eyes as he tried with all his might to wrench free his wrist and drive home the knife into Baelath's body.

Thane interrupted, tackling Maligor up against the wall and slamming his arm until he dropped the knife. Thane tried to kick it toward Baelath, but Baelath blocked with his own kick to Maligor's leg. He was just about to reach down for the knife himself when two more Dark Elves scuttled over from the other side of the room.

They were waiting for us, Baelath thought. He and Thane were outnumbered, two to three now. Baelath was positive that Maligor would end his life, given the chance. He looked at Thane and nodded toward the way they'd come. Thane spun his head around to see the new arrivals, looked back to Baelath, and nodded in agreement. They stood no chance.

In one heave, Baelath threw Maligor over Thane's outstretched leg and sent him tumbling to the ground; then Baelath pushed himself closer to the dark corridor. There was no slowly feeling his way this time. They had but a few precious moments before Maligor and his lackeys would be on their heels. He ran as hard as he could, waiting until the hallway turned back toward the creaky door.

But the turn never came. Baelath ran and ran until no light was behind him, and he listened for footsteps. He didn't hear any, not Maligor's or Thane's. Was he lost in this labyrinth dungeon below the Dark Elves' castle, which was lower than the trees and the ground? *Is this as deep in the ground as you can go?*

He couldn't stay there forever, but continuing on seemed foolish. He didn't want to die at Maligor's hands, yet being lost in darkness for all time wasn't appealing either. So he headed back the way he'd come, though slowly this time. He didn't want anyone to know he was coming back, just in case Maligor and the others were still headed this way.

His shoulder hurt, and he grabbed it instinctively. Blood still ran down his arm, and he could feel that his entire shirt sleeve soaked. He would have to take care of that first thing, once he made his way out of here—*if* he made his way out of here. With his hands on the left side of the wall this time, he crept forward. Each step sent a shock wave of pain into his shoulder. He could feel the cut moving with each step as his arms swung back and forth. He just had to push through it and find his way out. He hoped he wouldn't see Maligor again. If he did, Maligor probably would get the better of him and finish him off here in this dungeon.

Finally, though, he felt the corner edge and breathed a sigh of relief. *Almost out.*

And then his head collided with someone else's, and his feet were tangled in feet. Two figures stumbled to the floor, and Baelath did all he could to maintain the upper hand. He wrestled with the other elf, hoping it wasn't Maligor, and then he realized he was on top and in a better position.

He was going to cave in his skull, given the chance; he was going to cave in his skull for Jax.

Just as he balled his fist and raised his arm, a voice cried out. "Baelath, it's me," Thane said.

For a moment, Baelath just sat there, confused in his anger and inability to have any action. Everything in him told him to rain his arm down on his head and crack it open, but the voice made him stop, and now he didn't know what to do. Finally, he stood and rested his aching body against the cool walls. He could feel the condensation on his wound, and the relief made him relax slightly.

"I need help," Baelath said. "He got my shoulder pretty bad."

"OK, follow me. The way ahead is clear," Thane said, grabbing Baelath's good arm and pulling him out of the dungeons.

Baelath barely remembered the journey back, as his head started to spin. Once in the light, he quickly saw that his entire left side was drenched in red—shirt, arm, leg, everything. He wondered how much blood had he lost and if he could afford lose too much more.

Once they got back to the room where Baelath had gotten ready for the feast, Thane closed the wound and dressed it. He fetched some hot water to wash Baelath a little. They talked for a few moments while the candle burned down. Baelath said he was going to talk to the king about Maligor and what he had done.

"Best word it correctly, though," Thane warned. "Don't want the king to know why we were in the dungeons." He smiled and stood up and looked at the half-burned candle. "Tonight, you need your rest, for I doubt you will have any tomorrow." With that he turned and left Baelath alone in his thoughts again. Thane closed the door behind him as he left, and Baelath heard the soft clink of a lock turning into place.

So I'm supposed to trust Thane, but he won't return any? He wasn't surprised, though, as surely those orders were given prior to the feast. Tomorrow night, his door wouldn't be locked or guarded—at least, he hoped it wouldn't be. *Hard to tell with these customs.*

He readied himself for bed and blew out the lamps and lay in the darkness, thinking of the night's events and plans for tomorrow. Though he tried to think of them, his thoughts drifted to his friends, both those here and those not. And to Evelyn. His thoughts always drifted back to her when she wasn't around. He promised himself that he'd do whatever it took for his plan to work tomorrow, no matter what or who got in his way. He kept repeating it to himself in the blackness, over and over again, until soon, the thoughts overtook him, and he could feel himself drifting off.

He felt cold, as if a chill was in the air. He was standing on top of a red mountain ridge, looking down across a valley; the land was covered in white. Off in the distance, a tower rose from the land—nothing spectacular about it, but he could feel the menace within. Terror gripped him as he began to descend the mountain. He found himself at the base of the tower, looking up to all it offered, and he only felt dread, like he knew that by being there, something terrible was going to happen, but the only choice that existed was to enter. He went to the doorway and looked in. Nothing but black stared out at him, so he stepped gingerly inside. He was greeted by a high-pitched laughter, and a flash of white light filled the room. He saw the evil that resided in this place, but it was over in that instant. Baelath looked around but couldn't bring anything into focus, almost as if everything wasn't really there. He felt heavy, liked he was weighed down and barely able to move. He looked up ahead of him and saw two small figures beckoning him toward them. He felt a rush of wind beside him, and he saw something run past him, with long, glowing object in its hands.

Baelath was mesmerized by it, unable to take his eyes from it, and he could feel the lightness returning to his body, allowing him to lift his foot forward. It was when he took his first step that he heard his name being screamed from behind him. He turned around to see where it came from and at first could only see a burning white light in front of him, and he could have sworn it was reaching out to him. He wanted to reach out to it, but for some reason, he couldn't. The heaviness had returned to him, and try as he might to move, he felt rooted to the spot. He heard his name again but softer this time, like a whisper, and he strained every muscle in him to just reach out. Still, he was unable to make even the slightest twitch. Suddenly, he saw a hand reach out toward it and thought that he had willed himself forward. But that's when he noticed it wasn't his hand at all, for it emerged from the gray that surrounded his vision, and it extended out, almost skeleton-like, its ghost-pale flesh closing around the white light.

In an instant, it was gone, leaving nothing but the gray smoke that swirled around him, pulling him down to his knees and filling his lungs until he choked and gagged. He couldn't breathe anymore, and his chest felt like it was being ripped open. Six black hands reached out and grabbed him, while an evil cackle pierced his ears until he was sure his head was on the verge of exploding. The pain continued to build pressure in his head, to the point where his vision turned a bright red, and finally, he felt himself explode into a thousand pieces, bursting out into the air and shattering all that it touched. And in the end, when the dust had settled, only half of him remained.

CHAPTER 10

BAELATH AWOKE TO a cold sweat soaking his body and his room still filled with darkness. He got up and shuffled over to the lamps, still dazed from slumber. The room glowed softly after he lit them, enough for Baelath to at least see the perimeter of it. He tried to open the door but, not to his surprise, it was still locked. He lay back in bed, eyes fixated on the dancing shadows on the ceiling above him, and his thoughts meandered to his friends again—Grul, beardless and defeated, alone in a dark cell, far from the action he sought in the ruins. *Far from the action I took him from.* Max, alone now in this world, his brother's corpse rotting somewhere far from his home. *His home doesn't exist now because of me. His entire family, gone, because of me.*

He thought of Jord and everything he had taught Baelath from a young age, everything he had believed in. He thought of why he was here and what chance he had of seeing Jord again. *Does he even want me to come?*

But the worst thoughts involved Evelyn. She had so strongly believed in him and had stood by his side through every step of this journey. She had even saved him, more times than he could count, but he thought of every time now. *Can I hope to do the same?* He couldn't help but wonder if she was still alive, but the thought of her lifeless body, lying in a cold, dark cell—or even worse—was enough to almost break him, and he had to shake those thoughts that lingered in his mind.

A soft knock came upon the door, followed by the click of the lock. Thane's head popped in, looking somewhat amused. "Ready?"

"For a wedding? Always," Baelath said, returning an amused smile.

"Good." Thane pushed the door open now and stepped in. He wore an elegant black robe with a golden trim. He walked over to the lights and brightened the room, and Baelath watched the shadows on the wall disappear in a flash. "Here, put this on." Thane placed a somewhat similar robe to his down on the bed. "This is what you'll wear for the ceremony."

Baelath picked it up and looked over it, his fingers running against the silk. He had rarely seen fabric this magnificent, let alone wear anything of this caliber, yet still it felt like a betrayal. Seeing the black and gold colors draped over him was a sight he was not used to seeing and one he hoped to never see again after today.

"Also, good job last night," Thane said, interjecting his thoughts. "The king sent Maligor back to guard the boundaries early this morning, so he should be gone for at least a few days or so. Hopefully, you can gain even more of the king's ear by then."

"Hopefully," Baelath replied. He felt bad, for it seemed like Thane did have the best of intentions for him, and Maligor needed to be removed somehow. He just didn't have the time; his friends needed him more.

"But there will be time for that later. Come!" Thane exclaimed. "We have a wedding to get ready for."

Baelath followed Thane out the doors and down the hall, past the feast hall and down more corridors. They twisted and turned, going left rather than right, taking the right path rather than the winding left, and climbing staircases that seemed to appear out of nowhere to Baelath. It wasn't long before Baelath felt lost and unable to trace every movement they made, which he guessed was probably by design. He wondered how he would search for his friends or even where he would start. He didn't even know where *he* was going or how he got there. He couldn't use any landmarks to remember certain spots, for the halls were filled with nothing but empty air and the bare, black stone walls.

Minutes ticked by as the pair rounded corners and passed closed doors, until finally, Baelath could see the shine from those bugs that filled this underground cavern. They reached an archway that opened up into a courtyard, a relatively desolate one, if Baelath had ever seen one before. There were no benches, no sculptures or fountains. The grass looked unhealthy, and even the stone walls were cracking; pieces of it had fallen and gathered at the bottom. The only meaningful object was the tree that stood at the back, and even that wasn't as remarkable as it should have been; it was basically as dead as those that grew on the forest floor, yet the difference was its color. The whiteness of its trunk seemed rich and lively, and the branches swayed back and forth without a hint of wind. No leaves sprung from its tips, yet somehow, its beauty was entrancing, as if it had been frozen in time and would stay this way forever.

Glancing around, Baelath saw some familiar faces but plenty of new ones as well. Many were from the feast last night, minus Maligor, of course, but he noticed the king was missing as well. Baelath saw Garrus and the two others who had sat at the head table with the king and him last night. Servants were scurrying around, likely getting the last details worked out and tidying everything up. Baelath noticed that the stone piles had suddenly disappeared.

Thane stayed by him, conversing with him every so often, for which Baelath was thankful because time felt like it had come to a sudden halt. It seemed all eyes kept glancing toward him, and the whispers were growing louder. Sometimes a finger or a gesture would be thrown toward him. A buzz crept into the courtyard, and more lightning bugs filled the area until it glowed in yellowish-orange light. It really was a beautiful scene.

"So," Baelath said to Thane, "does the king not have a wife? I'd very much like to meet my bride's mother before I marry."

"I'm afraid she died a few years back now," Thane replied, a somber tone replacing the joyous storytelling one, "giving birth to their third child."

"How unfortunate," Baelath responded, knowing exactly the pain the princess had been dealing with. "Still, I guess meeting the siblings would be just as nice."

"Tragic again," Thane said. "A couple of years ago, one was lost in a hunting accident, and just last year, the other fell from one of the castle towers and didn't survive the fall. Some say he'd had too much to drink that night, though it felt rather odd."

"Odd, you say?" Baelath was confused by Thane's assertion.

"Well, I had seen the king's son drink on many nights, and he was known to be quite the heavy drinker. But he always seemed to handle it well and never got hurt or hurt anyone." Thane's eyes narrowed and his voice dropped when speaking of it, as if he was reliving that night all over again. "But I guess if you keep throwing the dice, the luck will run out."

"So, it's only the king and the princess in the royal family?" Baelath asked, not really to Thane but more to himself. "No wonder the king was in such a rush to have a wedding."

"So it would seem, but this is all still relatively new to me," Thane said. The somberness had left his tone, replaced by a curiousness, like he was figuring out a puzzle in his head.

"What makes you say that?" Baelath asked. He needed to get as much information as possible before it was too late.

"Well, less than a moon cycle ago, this wasn't even talked about between the king and his commanders," Thane began, "yet one day, it just seemed to be put into motion, and it was to be carried out by Maligor, which again made it all the more suspicious. I still don't see his play here, but as long as he's removed from the field, he can't make his move for the throne. And that's what I'm counting on."

"I'm afraid that tonight isn't the night for his planned move," said Baelath, who couldn't help but smile. "Now, tomorrow night is a whole different story."

"Well, either way, he's gone for at least today, out on the forest edges," Thane said, smiling and raising his glass to give a toast. "Today is yours."

Baelath raised his glass in response and downed the rest of it, and it was then that the music began. It was slow but with a swift tempo; soft, yet it vibrated inside him with a vigor; quiet, though it filled the air all around. Baelath couldn't see where it was coming from, but he didn't have time to search it out. The crowd began to file together and part down the middle, leaving a wide enough path for two to stroll down. Baelath didn't even notice, but somehow, he was in front of the white tree at the back end of the courtyard. He didn't know if that was by chance, or if Thane had steered him here without his knowing it. It didn't matter now, for suddenly, the king appeared in the doorway, opposite where Baelath and Thane stood, with the Princess Freya on his arm. Baelath couldn't help but be in awe, for beauty like this didn't come around often.

Her hair illuminated the air around her. Her smile penetrated any defenses one would have, and everyone swooned when she passed. A black-and-gold dress wrapped around her slender figure, this time wrapping around her shoulders and opening at the neck in a frilled fashion, and stretching out toward the back and encompassing the entire back of her head. A thin silver crown wrapped around the top of her head, resting on her elegant ears, which reached toward the heavens and came to perfect points. Her stride seemed to be in slow motion, and Baelath was helpless as she floated down toward him, her dimples growing larger with each step.

As she grew closer to him, Baelath became more trapped in her eyes, more lost as the seconds ticked by. They were a perfect blue, if he had ever seen it, shining at him, a slight glisten in each eye. He could have sworn that when she was born, they just took some of the sky and gave it to her for her eyes. And though he knew she was the most gorgeous thing he had seen in his days, he knew it wasn't her beauty that would entice him.

The king, who paled in comparison to his radiant daughter, still stood majestically in his finest robe, a lush gold with a black trim that broadened his figure somewhat slightly. A long sword hung from his hip, almost scraping the floor behind him and sometimes knocking into those who stood behind him when he turned to wave and acknowledge the ones who cheered and applauded. Together, they made their way down the yard, somewhat slowly, the king taking it all in.

Baelath glanced over to Thane, who returned a friendly smile. Baelath's plan was working, and that became even clearer to him, once the king reached them at the white tree, for the princess stood next to him while the king gave a warm embrace to Thane. The king seemed genuinely happy; at least, it was a different vibe from last night. After his hug with Thane and a handshake with Garrus and with the others who stood up with them, the king took his place behind his daughter, and the music stopped.

A low hum began from the crowd, and it brought back memories from that night when Maligor had them tied to the pole and was about to kill Grul. The sound was similar, though different, in a less threatening way. Still, it rather upset Baelath, and he had to concentrate on controlling the anger that rapidly rose inside him. He thought of his friends and what he had to do tonight, and he thought of Evelyn and that it wouldn't be long until, hopefully, they were free and back together.

The humming stopped, and from behind the tree emerged a figure in a hooded robe, which was all black and looked old and worn, like a flag that had become tattered in the wind. A few tears were at the bottom, and off-color black patches littered the shoulders and sides. Still, Baelath couldn't help but feel perturbed by this hooded figure and wondered what the meaning of it was. He soon found out as the figure took his spot in between the princess and Baelath and held one of their hands in each of his. He began muttering under his breath, his head still bowed toward the ground. Without warning, he threw both their hands violently toward the ground, while tossing his high into the air. Blue and gold smoke rose from his palms and twisted above them, entwining the newlyweds before melting away into the air.

Baelath was amazed. The crowd cheered behind him, and others clapped his back. He lowered his gaze toward Freya—his wife now, apparently—and saw her beautiful smile beaming at him, filling him with warmth and comfort. He stepped closer to her; she stepped closer as well and fell into his embrace. She lay her head upon his chest, their hands still interwoven. She raised her hands out to the crowd to a large cheer and applause; then, stepping back, she smiled at Baelath again, then turned and hugged her father, while Thane and Garrus lined up to shake Baelath's hand.

So I'm married now, thought Baelath.

The next few hours went in a whirl, between meeting random friends of the king's, the conversations with Thane, and the small dinner that was more of a drinking gathering than an actual dinner. Soon, it was nighttime, when the newlyweds would head off to bed. All Baelath could do was pass the time until they could leave, but in the meantime, he made sure everyone was happy, especially the king, eating and drinking themselves into a slumber. He couldn't have any wanderers late at night; he wanted everything to go unnoticed until it was far too late.

Finally, enough guests had either wandered off to sleep or had passed out in the courtyard that Freya whispered something to her father, who was barely able to keep his head up.

The king stood, and the room grew silent, though it was already very quiet to begin with. "To a happy marriage and the joining of our kingdoms," he sputtered, barely forming the words. The king raised his cup toward Baelath, nodded, and downed the rest of the cup. He slumped back into his chair, his head bobbing up and down.

The princess grabbed Baelath's arm and pulled him out into the castle corridors, twisting and turning, climbing up and down. After a few minutes, they began climbing a large staircase, and Baelath thought it would never end, but he eventually found his feet on flat ground, looking at a large golden door. The Princess Freya opened it and stepped into the doorway. She turned, smiling still, and beckoned Baelath to come inside. Nervously, he strolled inside, and she softly closed the door behind them.

He turned to face her and saw that her smile had been replaced by a frown. She burst into tears and collapsed onto the floor in a heap. Baelath was confused, but instinct took over, and he went to comfort her.

"What's wrong?" He reached down and helped her to her feet.

"I'm scared," she said in between sniffles.

"What are you scared of?" He had no idea what could have changed her mood so drastically. She had been so happy, moments ago.

"I don't know if I can do this," she finally muttered after she wiped away the last of the tears. "I told Father I didn't want to do it."

"You don't want to be married?" Baelath asked, now beginning to put the puzzle together. "Your father forced you into this, didn't he?"

She nodded. "You seem nice, and I want to make Father happy, but ..."

"It doesn't make *you* happy," Baelath said, finishing her sentence.

"It's not just that. I'm afraid my heart belongs to another." She lowered her head in an almost shameful way, yet it was all music to Baelath's ears.

"Well, I have a secret that I think you'll be very happy to hear," Baelath whispered to her.

She looked up at him, slightly confused, no longer sad. Her mood changes astonished Baelath. "What is it?"

"I plan to be gone by morning, for my heart too belongs to another," Baelath said, smiling.

"I don't understand." An even more confused look came across her face. "Where are you planning to go?"

He couldn't keep it to himself anymore. He had to tell someone. He had to trust someone. "I'll tell you, but you have to promise to keep it to yourself," Baelath said. "You can never reveal what I say, for many lives depend on your silence."

"I promise," she swore, a small smile slightly showing underneath her sadness.

"I planned to search the castle tonight for my friends and escape with them," Baelath began, lowering his voice to below a whisper. A strange feeling that someone was listening who shouldn't be gripped his insides. "I set out from my home to rescue my friend, who I heard was being held here by your father, the king. It was just a friend and me in the beginning, but along the way, I met a few others, whom I proudly call friends now. We fought, ate, and slept at each other's sides, keeping those who stood next to us alive, but that all changed when we stepped foot inside these woods." Baelath hung his head in sadness for a moment before he raised it up again to look at Freya. "I lost a friend here, and I'll never forget that moment. I hope that one day, justice can be paid. But I'm not here for that. I'm here for my friends, who are imprisoned now. Even if it costs me my life, or I'm trapped here for life, they don't deserve that. I need to get them out of here, and I hope to join them."

She smiled wide. "Not only do I promise not to tell anyone, husband"— she laughed even harder at that word—"but I'll even help you free your friends. I know where they're being held, and I'll lead you right to them."

"You'll help?" he asked, stunned. "Why?" *Is it another trap?*

"Like you said, you're going to try to free your friends, no matter the consequence," she said, skipping over to her dresser on the side of her room. "And it would be better for me if you weren't caught but instead disappeared, as if you never existed. Besides, like I said before, my heart belongs to another. This way gives me a chance at happiness with him."

"Your father wouldn't approve of this other one?" Baelath wondered, eyeing her wondrous room. It was filled with bright tapestries and shiny objects resting on polished wooden furniture.

She turned back to him and smiled sadly. "No," she replied. "He would not."

"Well, that's a shame," said Baelath, shaking his head. "Love isn't something you can sell; love isn't designed. Love is something you'll never know until you do, and then it's never forgotten."

"You talk as if you know love," Freya said slyly, her smile exposing her tiny dimples. For a moment Baelath stood in shock, and the princess chuckled at him. "Come." She gestured to him. "The night isn't getting any younger."

They darkened the lights inside the room and creaked the door open. Peering out, the princess motioned for Baelath to follow, and together, they set off down the staircase and past the feast hall and into the darkened corridors.

Finally, I'm going to free my friends. Going to free Jord. And Evelyn too.

The pair twisted throughout the castle, jumping from corridor to corridor. Each passing one grew darker and damper; the soft drip of water echoed down the black halls. They flew down staircases and hid behind closed doors when unsuspecting late-night wanderers passed by, sometimes huddled almost on top of each other in a small broom closet. He almost coughed at the amount of dirt and dust that coated the room but held it in long enough until the traveler passed.

Baelath definitely noticed a difference this time of traveling in the castle. They seemed to be in a constant descent, rather than the upward path he'd taken with Thane. Soon, the princess and Baelath were in the corridors that held no torches to light their way, and every step splashed into a shallow puddle of what Baelath hoped was just water.

Following Freya at every turn, Baelath saw a glow up ahead and a murmur of voices after they turned up one hallway. The princess stopped and turned to Baelath, pressing close to him to whisper in his ear. "I'll distract the guards, and you can sneak past. Once you do, head down the stairs and go left. Not right. Your friends should be at the end of the hall, through the last door. Ready?"

"Where do we go after I get them free?" Baelath whispered, completely lost on how they got down here.

Baelath could see her smile, even in the darkness. She turned back from him and headed toward the end of the hall without giving a reply, and Baelath had no choice but to creep slowly behind her, letting distance grow between them, waiting for his chance to sneak by unnoticed.

Baelath could hear the princess begin to talk to the guards, and he approached the area where the three of them stood, carefully remaining in the shadows. He could see some generic-looking guards dressed in the black armor he had seen most Dark Elves wear, their backs turned to him. He slowly stepped from the blackness and into the light, hoping they wouldn't spot him, like an unsuspecting fawn crossing your path on a hunt. Freya kept them distracted; her beauty could entrance the most strong-willed.

Quietly, he made his way past the guards and found himself standing at the top of the staircase. Glancing back once last time, he looked over to the princess and saw her looking back at him, her light-blue eyes gleaming with some sort of happiness, like someone finally getting something they desired, and Baelath couldn't help but smile back at her. Perhaps in another life, he would have just stayed in the room, but they both knew where this life would lead them.

And like that, he turned back around and headed down the stairs, his smile slowly fading until it was gone by the time he reached the bottom. One way went left; a long hallway stretched out, with doors lining it along the way. Another went right, but just one door stood up against the back of the shallow hall. *Left, she said.* So Baelath turned left and ran down the hall until he reached the last door. Grabbing the handle, he heaved it open with all the strength he could muster and stepped inside, panting.

There, in the dimly lit room, with the few torches about to burn out, his friends stood behind thick, rusty bars. Grul stood up against the bars, his small, thick hands wrapped around them, peering out at Baelath with a wide-eyed grin. Max was slumped against the side wall, head lowered at first, but he scampered to his feet when he realized who stood at the door. But it was Evelyn, rushing from the back of the cell, who called his name and finally eased the worries that had coursed through his mind.

"Baelath," she whispered, her arms wrapping around the bars and pulling herself against them, as if she was trying to squeeze through. "You came?"

"Did you think I wouldn't?" he asked, coming closer to inspect the lock.

"I wasn't sure," she said. "We didn't know if you would have time to leave your new wife."

"Well," Baelath responded with a half-smile, "I'm here. The real question is, how do I get you out?"

"The guards have the keys," said a familiar voice from the back of the cell, and from the shadows, an old man appeared, wearing the same old tattered brown cloak that he had always worn. A pair of dusty black boots shuffled into the firelight. His gray hair was matted on the top of his head, and his wrinkles seemed thicker than the last time Baelath had seen him. His face was a deep shade of purple and blue, his nose hung in an odd place, and his one eye was half shut. Dried blood stained his lips and chin, but no matter the damage done, Baelath would always recognize the voice of Jord.

"The guards?" Baelath wondered out loud, a hint of confusion in his voice.

"Where did you think the keys were? Sitting on a table just out of our reach? Har!" boomed Grul, his belly shaking.

"She just said to …" Baelath began, his eyes widening when he realized what had happened. *No!* he screamed in his head. *Betrayed again? I'll kill her. I'll kill them all.* The blood already began to boil inside him.

"Who's she?" asked Grul, but Baelath had already turned and was running out of the room, hoping he wouldn't find a squadron of guards waiting to wrap him in chains.

He raced back down the empty hall and ran up the steps, hoping to find two guards and Freya still locked in conversation, but his stomach dropped when he reached the top. The room was empty; the three had gone. *Did they figure out what she was up to? If they did, why didn't they come down for me? Did they know and are just waiting for me to come up from the dungeons? Did Freya lure the guards away and leave me here on my own to help my friends escape? Was she lying to me the entire time?*

He had no time to figure out any of the dozens of questions that raced through his head, for at any minute, it could end, and guards could swarm him. He had to free his friends in this unexplained chance he had. He flew back down the steps, jumping the last ten or so, and turned left again and ran to the last door. Bursting through, panting once again, he looked at the others, his hope slowly draining from his eyes as he saw them locked behind bars.

"I don't know how to get you all out of here," he finally said, his shoulders slumping. "We all came this far, and now I get to exactly where I wanted to be, and a wall of bars blocks me from my path. I fear this will be nothing but a failure, and our lives will surely end, once the guards pour in."

"It wasn't a failure," Jord said, making his way to the front of the cage and extending his hand for Baelath to grab. "You made it here, and that's all I could have asked for. The rest, I always knew would be up to us and not you."

"Argh, I've tried bending the bars, laddie," grunted Grul, who again gave it one last effort before giving up in an exhausted heap. "But they won't budge."

Silence overtook the group as the seconds dwindled away. The whooshing of a dying fire from the last ends of the torches was the only sound that filled the room. Baelath watched as the light retreated to its source.

"To get where you want to be," Evelyn began, her quiet whisper calming the room. She suddenly jumped to her feet. "The key! The key will get us out!" she exclaimed.

"And the guards have them. I cannot get them without being seen," Baelath said, looking curiously at her. *I thought I made that painfully obvious.*

"Not that key. The key from the king of Nox! To get to where you want to go!" Evelyn repeated, brimming with excitement.

"What are you talking about?" Baelath asked, still confused, but Evelyn paid no mind to him or to anyone else. She began fumbling around her neck below her cloak until she removed an old, brittle black key and held it in her hands.

"This is the key that King Rodrigo gave to me before we left the first time," Evelyn said with a smile beaming across her face. Baelath did not remember it; he just remembered the map he was given, but he could not have been happier than he was at this moment. *She saved us all—again.*

"I thought this key would be useful in trying to get us *into* a locked place. I never thought it would be used to get us *out* of somewhere," Evelyn admitted as her hands fumbled with the key, trying to slip it into the lock from the other side of the bars. It seemed to be harder than it looked to Baelath, but soon enough, it caught, and with a hard turn, the lock clicked, and the door swung open.

Evelyn dropped the crumbling key and came running out the door and into his arms, her force almost knocking him down. "Never leave again," she said to him, tears welling in her eyes.

Grul followed her and slapped Baelath on his back. "Ah, laddie, I knew you'd never leave us." The dwarf smiled up at him. "Not with the promise of a dwarfen feast still left unfulfilled."

Max came next and nodded at Baelath. "Let's go kill us a Dark Elf," he said, a look of anger still dwelling in his eyes. He walked to the door and peered out into the hall. "Still clear."

Jord came last. He hobbled over to Baelath, and at first, the two just stared at each other. "I can never thank you enough, my friend," he said, a look of pride beamed toward Baelath, who couldn't help but feel some sort of satisfaction, knowing he had accomplished what his own father had said couldn't be done.

"How do we escape the castle?" Baelath asked, once Jord made his way behind Max in the doorway.

"You mean you don't have a plan?" Evelyn asked, slightly surprised. "What did you expect to do once you got to us?"

"The princess was supposed to be here and guide us back," Baelath said, shrugging his shoulders. "But she's gone now, and so are the guards."

"I know the castle," Jord said from the hallway. "Follow me."

"How do you know the castle?" Grul asked, his face scrunching up, unable to believe this old man knew his way through the castle.

"I helped build it," Jord quickly answered. Without waiting for a reply, he set off down the hall, with Max following.

Grul turned back to Baelath, a look of complete confusion across his stubbled face. "How old is he?"

Baelath laughed. "I have no idea, my friend," and he followed them down the hall.

They reached the staircase, and Baelath had begun to climb it when Jord cleared his throat at him.

"I need my staff," Jord explained, standing in the tiny hall that stood to the right of the staircase. "And I'm sure you all want your weapons."

"I assumed they were gone," Baelath said, making his way over to the door.

"They're not that smart," Jord said with a smile, pushing open the door.

Baelath saw stacks and stacks of weapons, mostly rusted and blunted, but on the table at the back of the room, he could see their weapons.

Grul's ax was on top, and the dwarf waddled over and quickly grabbed it, twirling it in his hands. Max picked up his bow and began to scavenge the room for arrows. Evelyn grabbed their swords, throwing one to Baelath and sheathing the other. Last, found against the wall, Jord wrapped his withered hands around his staff and whirled it around. A light-green cloud emerged from its tip, so light that Baelath was certain that he was the only one to have seen it, and that was only because of the many times he had seen Jord do it, as well as the one time he had Baelath try it. Baelath knew it somehow revitalized the holder, gaining energy and healing scrapes. And indeed, Jord looked a little better, though still worse for wear and needing proper caring.

But Baelath was still missing something, and his eyes searched wildly. "Where's the map?" he asked.

"You lost the map?" Jord's full attention now was focused on Baelath. "When did you lose it?"

"When Maligor captured us. He took everything," Baelath explained as he began to search the rest of the room.

"Come," Jord barked, trying to spur the rest of them out of the room. "We need to leave this place as fast as possible. They may already know we're out."

"How would they know?" Baelath asked, confused. It was just a map of the land, not a personal tracker. Yet he never could explain how it had showed him where Jord was.

"The map shows you what you're searching for," Jord answered, still trying to get Max out of the room—he still was busily searching for his full quiver of arrows. "If someone else has it, and they're searching for us, they'll know exactly where we are."

Baelath's jaw dropped. That's why Rodrigo had given the map to him—to help him throughout his entire journey, not just to get to Jord. *How stupid can I be*, he thought, *and how unlucky!* The map had landed directly into the hands of the one person who had been out to get him since they first set eyes on each other. Now, there was literally no time to waste. They had to escape the castle and the Dark Woods entirely. "Let's go. Forget the arrows."

The five of them raced out of the room, up the stairs, and back into the dark corridors of the dungeons, with Jord leading the way and Baelath right on his heels. Grul's heavy footsteps echoed right behind Baelath, and Evelyn ran along beside him, helping push him onward. Max crept along behind them, making sure they weren't being followed, his bow nocked with an arrow, ready to drop whoever stepped out in front of them.

Jord held true to his word and guided them through the maze that the elves called a castle. Soon, torches became more frequent, and the group climbed staircase after staircase. Baelath had no clue when they'd reach the main floor or which floor they were actually on. They could still be below the ground or climbing up one of the towers. Baelath was all but lost in this place, and he could not wait to leave it behind him.

Left, then right. Right, then left. They picked up their pace, and soon passed the feast hall, and then they traveled down the main corridor. They passed the creepy statues of the Shadow Walker and the beast from the ruins. The giant spider and wolf. The bat-like men who looked ready to swoop down on them and swallow them whole.

Just as they were about to reach the tall red doors, two random guards stumbled into view, still somewhat dazed from their adventure together. The group came to a sudden halt, and the two guards almost continued past them, but they spotted them standing in the middle of the hall. Baelath saw that it was the two guards who were supposed to be guarding the dungeons. Before anyone could speak or do anything, an arrow whizzed by and struck one guard in the neck. He collapsed instantly, and a pool of blood formed around his head. The other one stood in shock and turned to run from them, but an ax caught him in the back, and he dropped to the ground with a grunt.

No one moved for a few seconds; the only sounds came from the first guard, still gurgling in his own blood, gasping for air. Grul ran over and put his large ax into his chest, ending the noise, hopefully before anyone heard it. He ripped out his throwing ax from the guard's back, and the guard couldn't help but make a noise as it was pulled from his flesh. Shocked momentarily, Grul whacked him again quickly, blood splattering all over the front of him.

"Let's leave before any more unwelcome passersby come along," Jord calmly said, stepping around the dead bodies. "I'm sure they weren't the only ones wandering around the castle."

Grul pulled opened the doors, and the heavy creaking made them cringe in despair.

Trying to leave this place is like trying to sneak past Father when I was a kid, Baelath thought. *Everything made a sound ten times louder than it ever had before.* Baelath was sure someone heard that sound but nobody came running. They flew past the doors, once they were cracked open enough to slip through, and the five of them ran along the pathway that led back up to the ridgetop. The lightning bugs overhead began to swirl around as they ran past them, lifting off into the air and illuminating the area around them.

"We need to get away from these things," Baelath said to Jord, running up alongside him. "They're giving off exactly where we are."

Jord stopped and looked around, giving enough time to let the bugs around them settle once again. "There," he said, pointing off to the side at one of the staircases that led to the forest floor. "We'll take that one up and make our way in the woods. We should be able to leave them altogether, depending where that leads."

Together, they set off to the left, making a straight shot for the staircase, moving slowly so as to not disturb the lightning bugs around them. It went relatively smoothly, as not too many flew into the air, and they were able to keep a low profile. Once Baelath put his foot on the first step, though, they heard some sort of alarm being raised from the castle. Baelath wondered what had set it off. *The dead bodies or the princess.*

"No going back now," Baelath said, smiling while looking back toward the castle. Its black towers rose up like fingers reaching upward.

Evelyn looked at Baelath and shrugged her way past him. "Thinking about going back to your *wife?*" she asked, and her tone sounded resentful. Without waiting for his answer, she started to race up the stairs.

Slightly annoyed, Baelath looked at Grul, who just shrugged at him. Baelath raced after her, not bothering to listen to what Grul was complaining about. She continued to pull away from him, racing faster and faster up the stairs. Baelath could see the others were following him. Max, the closest to him, ran easily up the stairs, while Grul seemed to be having trouble making his way up quickly. He was still faster than Jord, though, who had decided to walk calmly up the stairs while the castle alarm rang in the background.

Even with them all running, minutes had passed before Baelath climbed out of the tree upon the forest floor. He was immediately greeted with the sight of a heavy fog and decaying trees. That heavy wood smell filled the air, and for a moment, Baelath lost sight of Evelyn but then spotted her waiting up ahead. He walked up behind her, placing his hand on her shoulder. She turned around, tears on her cheeks. They said nothing to each other but spoke with their eyes. She lowered her head onto his chest and sobbed, one arm wrapped around his back, her other braced upon his chest.

Max strolled from the trunk opening and made his way up to them, peering out into the fog ahead of them. Grul came out next, panting and muttering something about dwarfen staircases not being as hard to climb. He took a few steps forward but then had to stop and double over to catch his breath. Baelath couldn't help but laugh, and Evelyn joined in. Max even broke a tiny smile.

But a cold familiar laugh also joined in with them, and Baelath's blood froze at the sound of it. From behind the tree from which they had emerged, Baelath could see the winged armor appear in the fog and could hear the clanking sound of the skulls, signifying each step he drew closer. The red glow from the sword burned at them, and sprouting the angriest of smiles, Maligor made his way in front of the tree, blocking the stairs from them.

"Got what you came for, River Elf?" Maligor spat at Baelath, his hands inching toward his sword hilt. "Figured you take more than a night, at least."

Max raised his bow and let loose an arrow, but Maligor easily blocked it. Grul lifted his ax and was about to charge, but Baelath held his arm out.

"We do not wish to fight. We only want to leave," Baelath said, hoping to avoid any confrontation. "But we will fight, and seeing that there are five of us, I don't think your chances are good."

"Ha! Of course you don't wish to fight me, for then you'd wish for death," boasted Maligor, pulling his sword half out of its scabbard and stepping toward them. "And five of you? I only see four pathetic people. The dwarf only counts as—"

A small *thwack* echoed through the forest, and Baelath saw a staff whip through the fog. Even from a distance, Baelath saw Maligor's eyes roll backward. Jord stepped out from the trunk of the tree, grabbed Maligor's cape, and whipped him down into the dark, where he tumbled down the stairs.

"There's no time to talk," Jord said, once the four of them rushed over to see what had happened. "We must keep moving."

Baelath took one last look down into the black abyss into which Maligor had just been sent tumbling. He wondered if he would see him again, if justice could finally be served, and if Max could have his revenge.

"Come, let us get moving," Baelath finally said, "before we are noticed."

"Where do we go?" said Max, looking off into the distance. "And which way do we choose?"

Baelath looked around as well. Nothing but a fog and dead trees surrounded them. A mountain range stood off in the distance, and the sun began to rise in the east. Baelath could hear the cawing of crows to the west, and there was nothing but clear skies to the south. Once again, he had no idea on where they were to go, and he felt completely lost. He lowered his gaze back to the group and saw all eyes upon him, each willing to follow wherever he said. He just didn't know what to say.

"Well," Grul said, stroking his chin, a wide smile across his face. "I have been promising you a dwarf feast since the day we met. Now is as good a time as any. Har!"

Baelath looked down at the dwarf and smiled at him. "I suppose you're right, Grul the Berserker. I am feeling rather famished."

"Well, let's get moving, then," Grul said, puffing his chest out. "It's only a few days' journey, and I'm about sick of trees."

Baelath laughed, turned to the rest of his friends, and smiled. "I'm almost inclined to agree with you, my friend—almost. Come, let us see your kingdom."

And all together, they set off into the woods toward the welcoming mountains.

Epilogue

Maligor threw open the large red wooden doors, just enough so the metal wings on his armor could pass through. His black boots stomped forcefully on the ground, making the skulls bang against each other viciously. His sword bounced along his hip, the red glow warming his leg from underneath its sheath. He passed a dried pool of blood, which looked to be a few hours old; a few servants were scrubbing vigorously at the stain.

The castle was still in a frenzy. No one was sure of what had happened, though most knew who caused the alarm. Whispers of guards being killed didn't bother Maligor, but the talk of the princess being beaten and tied up boiled his blood. As if he didn't have reason enough to kill the River Elf, now he could wring his neck and all of his friends.

He swept down the main corridor, pushing past those who got in his way. He wrapped around the corridors and up the staircases. He knew the way by heart, having taken it many nights. He climbed the giant staircase and pushed open the golden doors. There she sat, brushing her hair, ever so gingerly. She didn't turn when he entered, but he could tell she was smiling. Her shoulders were always slightly raised when she was smiling.

"Did he hurt you?" Maligor growled, his anger still bubbling on the surface.

Finally, she turned to him, smiling, just like he knew she was. Putting the brush down, she stood up and strolled over to him. She reached up with one hand and pushed his raven hair from his face. "Now, why would he hurt me?"

"Then how did he escape?" Maligor wondered, letting her hand soothe him.

"I helped him," the princess chirped, walking over to her desk.

His blood began to boil again. "You helped him? Why would you do that?"

"So he could be gone." She giggled, stroking the brush through her hair.

"But the king wanted him here. That was the whole reason you said I should be the one to capture him—to gain more favor," Maligor said.

She quickly hushed him. "Father wanted the elf prince—" Freya started.

"Don't call him that," Maligor spat.

She glared at him before continuing. "Wanted *my husband* here because the sorceress ordered my father to have him here, along with the old man. Now, what happens when she gets here, and they're not here?"

"I'm guessing the sorceress will be angry, but why did you have me do all those things if you were just going to set him free?" Maligor asked, beginning to pace the room.

Freya sighed, annoyed. "Do all of what?"

"Well," Maligor began, still pacing, "why did you have me kill your brothers?"

"So I could become next in line to the throne," she said, seeming pestered by the question.

"Then why set him free after the night when you had the throne secured?" Maligor asked, still confused by the events. He wished he'd been here instead of stalking the forest, waiting, but that's where the princess wanted him, so that's where he waited.

"I told you—so the sorceress would be angry at Father. And if Father fails, but then someone brings back this elf prince to her, who then will look like the hero and be allowed to marry the king's daughter?"

Maligor, beginning to see the big picture, turned and smiled at his love. She was perfect, and he would do anything for her. *It'll feel good to kill the fool who left this beauty after one night*, he thought. If he had been in the other's shoes, he would never have left—the rest be damned.

"You better hurry," she said, turning back to her mirror and brushing her hair. "The sorceress arrived a few hours ago and is about to meet Father in the throne room. I'm sure you wouldn't want to miss that." She turned and smiled at him, and he walked over to her and leaned down to kiss her.

He almost forgot the feeling every time—her lips soft against his, her nose pressed into his cheek. "I'll be back tonight," he whispered before sweeping around, striding out her doors, and back down the staircase.

His body still ached from the fall, and his head throbbed from the knock from behind he had received. Thoughts of how he was going to kill those fools racked his brain, but remembering their screams from watching him kill their friend brought joy to his face. He couldn't wait until he did it again, killing them all and dragging that pathetic elf on his knees and throwing him in front of the king—and seeing the princess smile at him.

Soon, Maligor was standing outside the throne room. Straightening his cape and armor, he strolled in and saw the King, nervously shifting on his throne. Thane stood to his right, and Garrus was at the bottom of the stairs. Thane looked rather pleased with himself, but if Maligor had his way, he'd wipe that smirk off his face, right when he'd throw the lumped body of the elf at the king's feet. Maligor whipped down the hall, passing the black marble pillars with the torches lining the entire wall. He took his place next to the king, on the left side of the throne, and threw a quick glare at Thane, who was still smiling smugly at him. Maligor couldn't wait to kill him now too.

"Did you get him?" the king asked, looking up at him.

Maligor shook his head.

"She won't like that at all. She won't like it," the king muttered.

Maligor almost felt bad for him, but then he noticed the elegance of the throne—the black and gold melting together on the marble, a small white tree growing up through the back of it, the branches extending out to be the arms of the throne. Maligor could just picture himself seated upon it, with the princess sitting beside him, together, ruling the kingdom.

He was getting lost in his dreams when a cold rush of wind whipped through the room, rapidly damping all the torches for a few seconds—and then she appeared. She wasn't any kind of elf but wasn't human either—at least from what Maligor could tell. She was taller than Maligor, and her black off-the-shoulder dress glided effortlessly behind her. When she approached the throne, Maligor noticed her blue lips and violet eyes when she glanced his way, giving no indication of acknowledging his presence there. The lace on her arms was worn and tattered, yet it looked so new. A silver necklace hung on her chest, just above her exposed cleavage.

The king scurried to his feet before she reached him, and he bowed to her while motioning the others to do the same. Maligor slightly bent forward, his head still raised and his eyes peeled on the sorceress—from fear or pure beauty, he did not know.

"You're here early, Sorceress," King Nathrak said, fear shaking his voice.

"Apparently not early enough," the sorceress exclaimed, looking around the room. "I've heard my new prisoners escaped."

"He tricked me! He told me he wanted to marry my daughter. I figured ..." The king's voice trailed off; his eyes locked onto the floor.

"You figured you could give me what I wanted while getting what *you* wanted, not trusting that I could give you everything you wanted—and more," the sorceress proclaimed, her eyes burning into the king. "If only you had listened to me—such a shame. So much of your father is in you."

"I have a plan to get them," the king began, his head snapping up to look at her. "Maligor is my best hunter. He's going to capture them and bring them back. The old man too."

The sorceress's expression immediately changed when the king mentioned the old man. "You let Jord escape with them?" she growled, her fists clenching. "Does he have his staff?"

"He does," Maligor said. "He hit me with it when I was trying to capture the rest. I wasn't aware there was a fifth. I'm sorry."

"It isn't your fault," the sorceress began. "But it is someone's fault, and that can't be left unnoticed." Her body relaxed, fists unclenching and fingers stretching open.

"Well, wait, no, I can get them back here," the king stammered, taking steps backward.

"How?" the sorceress asked, stepping closer to the king.

"Maligor will get them," the king insisted, shrinking into his throne.

"And I'm sure he will. Isn't that right, Maligor?" she asked, motioning to where he stood, frozen in his spot.

"I can get them," he replied, not sure of what he should be saying.

"See? He's going to get them—of that, I have no worries." She smiled at the king. "My worries are how are we going to keep them here once they're brought back. You couldn't even keep them for a day!"

"I kept the old man the entire time—since you brought him here," whispered the king, his face growing more fearful than ever.

The sorceress laughed and leaned over to face the king, who was cowering on his throne. "That you did, and I thank you for that. But like you said, Maligor will bring them back. And I'm here now for when they do come back, so I don't really have a use for you, do I?"

"No, wait. I can—" the king began.

The sorceress reached up and placed her hand on his cheek. A small flash of light radiated from her fingers, and Maligor watched as King Nathrak, sitting on his throne, turned to dust.

"Tragic," the sorceress said when nothing but a pile of ash was left. "I oddly enjoyed him." She plucked the crown from atop the ash, stood up, and turned to tower over Maligor. "Here," she said, throwing the crown at him. "You're the new king." Then she turned and began to stroll out of the room. "Bring me back my prisoners or face the same consequences as your predecessor."

In a moment, she was gone from sight. Just Maligor and Thane were left looking at each other, both in shock, with a pile of ash on a throne in between them.

Walking calmly over to the throne, Maligor wiped away the ashes. He slowly sat down, his arms caressing the wooden arms of the throne. He rested his back against the cold gold-and-black marble and turned his head to look at Thane. "Run," he whispered.

Thane stared at him, at first confused; then a look of terror spread across his face. He quickly ran out of the hall, with Garrus at his heels.

I'll deal with them another time, Maligor thought. There were other pressing matters that needed his attention. He rose from his throne, crown placed upon his head. His hand reached into his cloak and pulled out a piece of parchment. Unrolling it, Maligor stared at a map of Arcane, with a tiny dot labeled elf just to the north of him.

"It's time to hunt some River Elves," Maligor said, a wicked smile spreading across his face. His right hand gripped his sword hilt, and the red tint glowed just below his line of sight.

Printed in the United States
by Baker & Taylor Publisher Services